# GREEN
# RISING

## LAUREN JAMES

WALKER
BOOKS

*For everyone who is angry, and everyone
who is scared. Hope isn't lost.*

First published in Great Britain 2021 by Walker Books Ltd
87 Vauxhall Walk, London SE11 5HJ

2 4 6 8 10 9 7 5 3 1

Text © 2021 Lauren James
Cover design © 2021 Walker Books Ltd
Cover design by Beci Kelly
Industrial landscape © Nataliia Darmoroz / Alamy Stock Vector

This book has been typeset in Fairfield, Arial, Ubuntu, Verdana

Printed and bound by CPI Group (UK) Ltd, Croydon CR0 4YY

British Library Cataloguing in Publication Data:
a catalogue record for this book is available from the British Library

ISBN 978-1-4063-8467-3

www.walker.co.uk

*I incite this meeting to rebellion.*

Emmeline Pankhurst

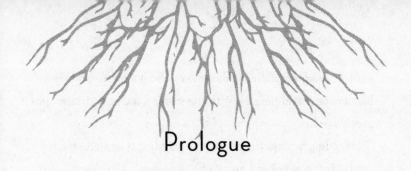

# Prologue

There weren't many of them at first. Just a few students standing outside the conference centre. Gabrielle lingered on the outskirts, trying not to give off the aura of someone skipping school. A girl in a pageant ribbon embossed with THERE IS NO PLANET B was painting green and blue splodges on people's cheeks.

The protest had seemed like a good idea when Gabrielle had read about it online. A climate forum thread had suggested people protest the annual Fuel Summit taking place inside the exhibition hall.

The people who were contributing most to climate change were there, as the biggest energy companies in the world made deals to drill for more oil and open more power plants. But the crowd was just lingering around the car park, so none of the executives inside could even see them. It seemed such a waste, after coming all this way.

Gabrielle had to do something. She slipped away as a boy shouted into a megaphone, "Hello, Climate Rebellion! Let me hear you repeat after me: *Climate change is not a lie, do not let our planet die!"* He'd draped a sheet over his shoulders like a cape, hand-painted with the words SAVE OUR FUTURE in messy strokes.

Heading around the rear of the building, Gabrielle hid her cardboard sign behind an overflowing waste bin. She tucked her school tie into her pocket, so that her uniform looked vaguely like a business suit.

She lingered around the staff entrance, pretending to send a text. Faint shouts of, *"No more coal, no more oil! Keep our carbon in the soil!"* drifted over from the car park.

When a harried-looking employee unlocked the door with their key card, she slipped in after them. Head down, she moved along the corridor, adrenaline surging up her spine. As soon as she was alone in the network of corridors, she smashed a fire alarm with her elbow.

A piercing alarm echoed down the empty hall. She followed the stream of staff out of the conference centre, where they joined up with the river of conference attendees.

Hiding a grin, Gabrielle retrieved her sign from behind the bins and joined the group of protestors.

*"This world is not for sale, your pipeline plans will fail!"* she chanted at the annoyed crowd of evacuated oil executives.

Even though this protest was only small, they had to make their voices heard whenever they could. The climate emergency was huge – an impossible crisis almost beyond solving. But if enough people, in enough cities, in enough countries, spoke up, then maybe someone would listen. Their voices were all they had right now. Most of the students here were too young to vote or make any real political difference.

*"We will choose, we will decide, we will fight to turn the tide!"* she shouted, adjusting her grip on her sign. Pins and needles tickled her fingertips.

Gabrielle had been six when she'd found out that the carbon emissions from burning fossil fuels were raising global temperatures. She'd assumed that the grown-ups were dealing with it, back then. But even when wildfires burned up entire continents and hurricanes tore up coastlines, no one seemed to be doing *anything*. Her planet needed Gabrielle's voice, because even though it was crying out for help, nobody was listening.

*"There is no Planet A,"* she mumbled, too late to correct herself. Her fingers were really aching from holding up the sign now. She kept losing track of the words. It was supposed to be "Planet B".

She swapped the hand holding the banner, rubbing her palm flat against her trousers. There was a throbbing pain as blood rushed back into her lowered arm. Her fingernails were pulsing, fire-hot blood beating below the skin in time with her racing heart.

*"Stop denying that the Earth is dying."*

There was something underneath her nail. Something green, twisting like it was trying to get free. Her fingernail felt like it was going to come loose.

The chant changed to, *"Say it loud, say it clear, polar bears are dying here!"* as the green thing – insect? parasite? – writhed beneath her nail. It curled upwards, like it was searching for the light.

Gabrielle's panic was replaced by fascination as the tendril thickened into a flat surface. A leaf.

*"When the air we breathe is under attack, what do we do? FIGHT BACK! What do we do? FIGHT BACK!"*

The stem moved faster, growing more leaves over her palm. Another strand burst from her thumbnail, and another, until vines covered her arm in a green, seething mass of vegetation.

It didn't hurt, not physically. She should be terrified, but somehow it felt – good, like a release of pent-up tension. The vines grew stronger, stems thickening and sprouting strong, glossy leaves. They engulfed her banner, reaching up towards the sky.

There were exclamations of alarm as the vines wove through her hair. Someone started filming her, as if the plant was some kind of art piece that Gabrielle had created especially for the protest.

This was true and right and inevitable. This was what her hands were meant for. How had she not noticed that she could do this before? She was absolutely certain this was a good thing, not a danger at all. A gift.

The other protestors circled her, shouting questions she couldn't answer. Even the fuel executives drifted closer to stare at her.

Gabrielle swayed in the centre of the pulsating layer of green leaves, peacefully lost in a glowing haze of endorphins. Her sign remained valiantly upright under the weight of the plants. Its carefully painted message was still visible: IT'S TIME FOR A CHANGE. WHAT YOU SEE IS WHAT YOU GET — AND YOU AIN'T SEEN NOTHING YET.

She was calm. She was ready. The temperature was rising, but so were they.

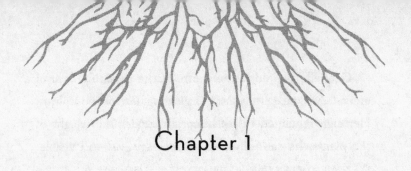

# Chapter 1

Theo was lugging a crate of iced haddock across the boat's deck when a deafening alarm cut through the wind. He stumbled, fish flying everywhere as he sprinted towards the bridge.

This was exactly why he hated helping his dad out on the weekends. Not the crashing waves, rocking boat or getting up at sparrow's fart in the morning, but the constant threat of the ocean.

Theo swallowed back dizziness as the deck rolled beneath him. He fixed his gaze on the oil rig looming on the horizon, its metal crane crouched over the water like an unnatural, ghastly insect.

Theo's family had been fishing for generations – his dad, his grandad, and *his* dad, all the way back as far as they knew – but there wasn't much money in it these days. Good hauls were rare everywhere now, but since Dalex Energy had arrived, it had got much worse.

The energy company had built a new oil drilling rig right in the middle of the North Sea where Theo's dad normally fished. The hulking orange platform dumped bilge water into the ocean as they processed oil, covering the sea bed in chemicals and dirty sediment. The shoals were moving to different waters.

"What's going on?" Theo yelled at Dad, just as the deck shook with a dull scraping sound. He fell to his knees, chin banging on the sharp edge of the desk.

A second alarm was sounding now, harsh and discordant on top of the first. Theo's heart tripped over itself. This wasn't a minor issue. This was real.

Scanning readouts, Dad said, "We've hit something! Bloody Dalex must not have marked a wellhead platform."

Theo wiped slick blood from his mouth as the boat shook around them. Dalex were supposed to put buoy markers in the water and send the coastguards the coordinates of their underwater structures. If they'd missed one, the boat's early warning radar would have only picked up on the structure seconds before the collision.

On the screen, a bright-red warning was flashing: BILGE FLOOD DETECTED.

"We're taking on water!" Dad yelled. "Lifejackets, everyone! Get the pumps!"

The deckhands rushed into action. They uncoiled the tubes of the bilge pumps, trying to slow the flood of water pouring into the boat through the damaged hull.

As Dad steered the boat away from the underwater structure, Theo's emergency training finally kicked into action. He radioed the coastguard and gave their coordinates over the roar of the pumps' engines.

"Good lad," Dad called, turning on the emergency radio beacon. "Inflate the life raft? It's going to be close."

Theo nodded. A calmness had washed over him. This was unreal. He'd been having nightmares about Dad's boat sinking since he was a child. But he hadn't imagined being on board when it happened.

The floodwater was pouring over the concrete ballast lining the fish hold now. Their pumps weren't going to be enough.

Two deckhands were already using the power block to lift the life raft down from the wheelhouse roof to the poop deck. Theo helped them to inflate it, his eyes going blurry. How could he be *sweating*? It was freezing out here.

Most of the time, Theo felt like the useless skipper's son who mistook plaice for haddock, only worked on the weekends and couldn't handle the early starts. But Dad didn't have to pay another deckhand when Theo helped out. That was something, at least.

"Time to leave," Dad said grimly as the boat tilted steeply, heeling in the swell. "It's no good."

Theo desperately wanted to call his mum. But even if he could get a signal, what good would it do to tell her what was happening now? They were too far away. She would just panic.

Instead he helped Dad climb onto the raft. The boat was almost too small for all the men in their bulky lifejackets.

Dad perched on the edge, holding tight to the roping as they untethered the raft from the sinking ship.

Theo tried to make himself smaller, feeling young and useless and lost as the men guided the raft away from the boat. They were ten metres away when it finally sank below the waves.

"We didn't lose anyone, lads," Dad said, a resigned note in his voice. "That's all that matters. And this is what insurance is for."

Theo could hear the tremble hidden inside those words. He shivered, wriggling on the narrow wooden bench. The wind was scorching cold.

He glared at the looming Dalex rig. Why couldn't they mark their structures properly? They were already destroying the sea, and now they'd taken Dad's boat, too.

The coastguards radioed with an update, saying they were fifteen minutes away. The crew sat in silence, teeth chattering audibly, until one of the deckhands turned the radio on.

"Are you hoping they'll mention us, Reg? The coastguards aren't even here yet."

"Eh, you never know."

Theo could barely focus on the words through his white-hot panic. Dad tapped Theo's boot with his toes reassuringly.

On the radio, the news presenter was saying, *"Warren Space unveiled their latest plans for Mars in a conference this morning. The company is opening up advance orders for purchase of real estate in the settlement, though residencies won't be built for several more decades."*

The red light of the sunken boat flickered into darkness below the water. What did this all mean for Dad? They barely had enough money to pay the bills normally. Even if the insurance covered the cost of the boat, they'd still lost a day's haul.

Theo was probably too young to be worried about mortgages, but he thought about bills constantly. If his parents could only hold on for another year, then Theo could lend them his student loan payment when he went to uni. He'd been planning it for ages. But this was too soon. He couldn't help them yet.

The deckhands were chatting about the news now, voices forcefully bright and cheerful. "Would you go, though? Just give up your whole life on Earth?"

Theo tried to think of a pun about Mars as Dad said, "As if any of us would ever get the chance to go there! It'll be pure billionaires for the first hundred-odd years."

"They'll need manual workers, though, Jeff. Someone's got to build all these fancy new houses in the colony."

"Yeah, the maths lads won't be faffing about digging foundations, will they?"

The waves were getting bigger now, smashing over them as the sky split with a booming crack of thunder.

"I'd rather buy one of those new-fangled yacht-bungalows that move with the rising sea levels," someone said dreamily.

"You probably need a *Mars*-ters degree to even apply," Theo blurted out.

They all stared at him.

"To go to Mars," he explained.

There was a pause, and then another huge wave rolled over the raft. Theo swallowed a mouthful of salt water, white froth splashing his eyes. Dad was shouting something into the wind, scrambling for purchase on the edge of the life raft.

Knife-sharp fear tore into Theo's chest. He flung himself forward, reaching for Dad's outstretched arm. Another wave flooded the raft. When the water drained away, Dad was gone.

A scream rose up Theo's throat. He searched the dark ocean for any sign of movement. "DAD!"

A pale hand briefly cupped the crest of a wave, then disappeared again.

Theo threw himself towards the edge of the raft, not knowing what he was going to do but needing to stop this. There was a feeling like pins and needles under his skin. Something shot from his palm – a slippery dark-green tendril that coiled into a tangled cord. The frilled rope sank into the water after Dad.

The tendril curling from his palm looked like ... seaweed? Was that possible? He'd seen that girl on the news who'd grown plants at a climate protest, but he'd dismissed it as a scam. Some kind of trick to try and go viral. But this was really happening.

An enormous pressure pulled against the strands of seaweed. Theo heaved it in, barely able to hope.

Dad broke the surface of the water, coughing as he fought to breathe. The seaweed was twisted around his chest, holding him tight. The deckhands tugged him onto the life raft as he choked on sea water.

"Dad?" Theo cried, desperately peeling away the strands of seaweed suctioned onto his father's chest. "Are you all right?"

"Theodore? How did you do that?"

This couldn't be real. The girl from the viral video had been *pretending*. She'd hidden vines up her sleeves. Hadn't she?

Something was writhing under his jumper. Theo shivered, ice-cold to the bone. Slick strands of kelp trailed down his chest. The plants were still growing.

An RAF helicopter circled, a bright search beam passing overhead. But Theo just stared and stared. It was real. It was actually real.

# PUBLIC SAFETY NOTICE

All parents and guardians must report any new cases of plant growth to the government by filling out this form. Latest reports indicate that 3% of all young people aged 12–20 are displaying some degree of ability to grow flora. The oldest case is a 20 year old in Cambodia, and the youngest is a Russian nine year old.

All young people with the condition need to be monitored extremely closely for their own protection. The following protocol has been developed in response to several cases of suffocation due to a large mass of vegetation collecting in small rooms.

While it is important not to panic, all parents must be aware of the potential for danger.

- Do not close inward-opening doors, such as in bedrooms or bathrooms
- Keep a hammer or heavy object near to windows in case an emergency exit is needed
- Avoid car journeys on motorways without regular laybys

Investigation has found that the plants themselves are not dangerous and can be cut from the skin without damage to the young person. Do not be alarmed if the plants continue to grow after removal. Standard health and safety measures should be undertaken when handling unknown plant species.

**Caroline Price** my daughter has **#greenfingers**, and the way she's been treated by her school is despicable. Segregation & suspension like she's got a contagious illness! The government should be ashamed of themselves.

**Edgar Warren** ✓ disagree that the **#greenfingers** lunacy is a matter of public security. can't see why senators are wasting the president's time on safety briefings when warren space are still waiting for three separate bills to be put through congress

**Kate Finchley** BREAKING NEWS: Teenager Found Dead, Encased Inside Tree Trunk in Bedroom **#greenfingers**

**CrossfitKing** Are **#greenfingers** the new millennials? Join the discussion over at r/greenfingers.

**Lola kpop updates** A new study has found that eating beetroot makes **#greenfingers** stronger! More info at **mirrored.co.uk**

**Ellie Hammond** sick of these **#greenfingers** taking resources from underfunded schools. They should be pulled out of class for antisocial behaviour, not given more funding. The government needs to get off their arses instead of arguing whether it's the responsibility of the Department for Environmental Affairs or Health and Social Care. They're gonna waste another month opening up a dedicated Organization for the Management of Youth Magic before anything gets done.

**Shen Zhang** love that I can follow the trail of a **#greenfingers** through the city as they grow their fave plant. it's like growing cow parsley or dock leaves or whatever has become a personal graffiti tag.

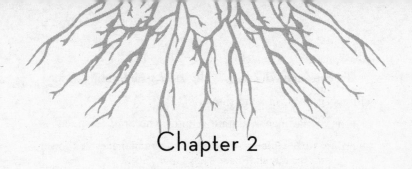

# Chapter 2

Hester tried desperately to swallow down the algae that was threatening to bubble up in her throat. Somehow, the plants always seemed to grow at the worst possible moments, at her most upset or excited. She absolutely could not bloom while the President of Iran was standing only a few steps away from her.

Hester was tagging along on Dad's latest "little look-around", as he called his carefully crafted tours of their deep-sea platforms. The only thing "little" about the look-around was the guest list.

"It's something we're very proud of," Dad was saying, reciting a speech designed to oil up potential investors and government representatives. "Our bedrock boring drill is one of the largest in the world, actually. A new oilfield in Iran would allow for even greater expansion. We anticipate receiving approval for the permits from the public commissioners within the month. Now, if you'll come this way…" He gestured to a narrow steel stairway that led towards the hulking separators, which processed the crude oil being pumped up from the sea bed.

"Be careful on the steps, y'all," Hester said, trying to show willing. "It does get a tad slippery!"

One of the men – a state senator who bred toy poodles, according to her preparatory notes – touched Hester's lower back as he passed by. She smiled forcedly at him. It was funny how they never did that to each other, these men in suits. It was only the teenage girl who apparently needed physical contact for assistance.

The iron taste of algae pressed against her tonsils. Holding her hand to her mouth, Hester discreetly spat a mouthful of green slime into the drain. She had to stop getting annoyed – it just made it worse.

She had been aware of the so-called Greenfingers for weeks before her own plants started appearing. They had been an irritating meme at first: a reaction gif of a girl looking disgusted as a flower shrivelled up on her shoulder; dance choreography using a vine as a skipping rope; reels of hyper-speed baking guides where people tipped raspberries from their fingers into fresh cream.

Her shock and awe at the whole *magic* thing had soon evaporated. Hester was bored of the constant think-pieces analysing whether the Greenfingers were a result of kids spending too much time on their phones, or pollution, or even just plain old aliens.

Then it had happened to her. It had been the week before her period was due, so she'd been irritated by life in general anyway. She'd spilled chia seeds all over the marble countertop, and then she couldn't find her tablet charger, and then her tutor had berated her for misinterpreting the gross profit on an economics problem. It was too much, all at once.

Slime had exploded around her, covering the terrace – and her tutor – in green silt. At first, she'd thought a bomb had gone off. That had happened once when she was little. She'd been colouring in with crayons in Dad's office when a group of protestors had burst in wearing tiger costumes, shouting about the climate emergency and throwing grenades filled with red paint.

Hester had been crouched, braced for impact, when microscopic algae had dripped down her neck. The damp slime was nothing like the pretty orchids people made online. It was absolutely *not* ideal.

Hester had immediately made her tutor swear that he wouldn't tell her father about her new powers, at risk of losing his Christmas bonus. Only their housekeeper had noticed the sudden appearance of bowls of fresh fruit and vases of flowers around the house.

Dad wouldn't have asked her to come along to the meeting today if he knew what she could do. He hated anything unsanitary or disordered. Her wild plants didn't fit into his world.

"Princess?" Dad said now.

Hester tried to look attentive, pushing her sunglasses up into her hair.

"Don't you agree?" he prompted. His expression was unreadable.

"Absolutely," she said, risking a guess. She should know better than to get distracted in the biggest meeting they'd had all year. Hester had to pay attention – she was going to succeed Dad as CEO of Dalex Energy when he retired.

"I just don't see it," a senator said. "Oil is a dead industry, isn't it? We should be focusing our investments on solar and wind."

Dad raised his eyebrow at Hester expectantly, gesturing subtly for her to answer.

Right. It was time for her to give her speech. The one she'd been memorizing for months. It was the whole reason she hadn't been able to miss this meeting, even though algae was dripping down the back of her silk blouse right at that very moment.

Hester prepared to modify her Texan accent into something slightly more middle-American, just like her voice coach had trained her. From her outfit to her breathing pattern, every part of Hester's appearance had been adjusted until she received the best possible responses from their test audiences.

"Simply put, gentlemen, there's no reason to be wary of oil," she said. "Our market predictions have never looked more optimistic."

That was a lie, of course. Everyone hated Dalex. Fossil fuels caused climate change, and they were the ones who *produced* fossil fuels. Eventually that was going to impact their profits.

She continued speaking on autopilot – she'd practised this speech so often it was almost muscle memory. "We definitely need more renewable energy, but our oil will help build wind turbines and solar panels. We're investing in our future here. Our increased profits will reflect that over the next few decades."

She didn't add: *as long as you give us this approval for Iran, because our current oilfields are nearly empty and the supply will run out soon if you don't, you morons.*

Dad nodded at her approvingly, but the politician still looked wary.

"It just makes us look bad," he said. "My constituents are pressuring me for immediate action on the climate emergency."

Dad murmured, *"Developing nations."*

"I totally understand that, Senator Williams," Hester said, and squeezed his arm in contrived reassurance. "Investing in oil seems backwards, but think of it this way – most developing nations have never had access to energy like us. Some places still don't have running water or electricity. For them, a supply of power can be the difference between life and death.

"Those starving children in Africa will never get the chances that America has had, to build a great nation. It's simply not possible to construct urban cities using wind and solar energy alone.

"Dalex needs to keep drilling for oil to provide the infrastructure for a good life to everyone on Earth. Of course, we are working hard to fight the climate crisis. But our first priority will always be *helping humanity*."

Senator Williams looked pleasingly convinced. A Texas Railroad Commissioner was making notes on a tablet, nodding along with her.

This was why Dad had wanted Hester here. He was always saying how broad her public appeal was: biracial, young and passionate, charismatic, and good on social media. Dad wanted her to be the public face of Dalex, using her age and influence to improve their image.

Climate change was one of the big areas where Hester could really bring in new support from investors. At eighteen, she was part of the generation who were skipping school to protest. But if *Hester* supported Dalex Energy's oil fracking, then the rest of the world would follow.

"Next time your constituents ask you why you're still supporting oil," Hester added, gearing up for the home run, "remind them that fossil fuels power their hospitals, homes and schools. Night and day, on demand. There are no wind turbines ready to fill that gap yet."

Adrenaline sped through her blood, thick like tar. She had them all eating out of the palm of her hand. Every single one was convinced; it was written all over their faces. The truth seemed so obvious to Hester that it was hard to believe anyone needed this stuff explaining to them.

"If the oil runs out, the electricity runs out," Hester said, calm and deadly serious. "This new oil bed in Iran will meet the energy demands of our great nation. We need to grow renewable energy sources, yes. But never forget what's most important – *keeping your families safe*."

Hester finished her speech triumphantly. She felt like she'd just run a mile. A team of specialists had rewritten her lines over and over, searching for the best way to explain how important their work was. Hester had even been allowed to add that part about "keeping your families safe".

The dozen drafts had been worth the effort. The men were all gazing at her in awe. Or – there was a look of confusion on Dad's face, slowly turning into horror.

Sweat ran down her cheek. It was so hot today. It hadn't been like this when she was little, but in the last few years Texas had become a burning wave of heat from dawn to dusk. She tried to avoid the unbearable summer heat as much as possible, moving from house to car to office in a perfectly cool haze of air-conditioning. There were even tunnels connecting the city high-rises, so she could go shopping without sweating through her clothes, or coming into contact with the year-round spate of mosquitos.

She wiped away the sweat dripping thickly down her forehead, then took in the horrified looks of the men. They were staring at her like – like—

It wasn't sweat at all. It was green and living. She'd been so focused on her speech that she'd forgotten the plants. She could feel them building inside her, feeding on her excitement until—

Algae exploded from her palms, covering the men in a giant mass of seething, pulsating froth. They jumped back, shouting in horror.

Hester blanched. Dad's face turned thunderous. She fumbled for a handkerchief, trying to fix the damage. But the sheer quantity of algae made that impossible.

"Sorry about the mess!" Hester said feebly, tucking her thick dark hair neatly behind her ears and smoothing down her skirt.

What could she possibly say to fix this? She'd proven herself to be an out-of-control teenager, just as bad as the hooligans causing trouble on the news. Nothing like the sensible entrepreneur she tried to emanate.

"Do you have plans for the Greenfingers powers?" a younger man in his mid-thirties asked, examining the algae that coated his suit jacket.

Hester rifled through her mental profiles, trying to identify him. Edgar Warren, the founder of Warren Space. Dad had invited him on the tour because Dalex was trying to win a contract with Warren Space to provide power for the Mars colony.

The settlement's expansion was still several years away – and it would be decades before it was ready for anyone except scientists to really live there – but Dad thought it was important to get in early, to prove that they were the world's number-one energy supplier.

Hester stared at Edgar, confused. What did he mean, use the Greenfingers? But the others had stopped panicking about the algae to listen to her response.

She tentatively said, "Oh, yes, the Greenfingers. Th-that brings me neatly on to renewable energy. For example … *biofuels!*"

She dipped down to the floor, pressing her palm flat to the deck. Drawing it upwards, she carefully grew a bulrush. The long narrow stem crept up as she stood. That was better: careful, controlled, delicate. Not a messy, disgusting explosion.

"We have high hopes that the new plant-growth phenomenon can be used to generate vast amounts of biomatter, which could be used as consistent, reliable fuel. As you can see, I'm investigating this personally."

She gestured towards the algae puddling around her heels. There was a chuckle. This was working.

"It's an infinite, unlimited resource, gentlemen. We can't go wrong. This magic could be the gift that will help us solve the climate crisis. But we need your support – here, and in Iran. Let's make a difference today, shall we?"

She dipped her head, taking a minute to recover. There were murmured noises of approval. Edgar Warren had even cornered Dad to ask him some follow-up questions.

There was a restrained, maniacal grin hiding behind Dad's expression that Hester recognized – one that she saw when the stock market did interesting things, or when they got government approval to start fracking at a new oil reserve.

Her brain was running cartwheels. She couldn't believe she'd improvised a speech, without their PR team approving every single clause and verb choice. It went against all of her training, but it seemed to have worked.

The algae dripping steadily from her nose felt like victory now, showing them what Dalex could do. *We have so much energy that it's leaking from our pores. We're trustworthy. We're reliable.*

When the group had boarded the helicopter to take them back across the Gulf of Mexico to Houston, Dad said, "You should have told me you'd developed this … Greenfingers thing. You risked our whole presentation today, Hester."

He stepped gingerly around the mess of algae.

Hester's face flushed. "I'm so sorry, Dad. I thought I had the plants under control. It's a good idea, though, don't you think? The biofuels?"

Her father nodded grudgingly. "You did well to think that up. Edgar Warren seems intrigued. Hopefully it'll sway him to consider our bid proposal."

Dad was obsessed with Mars. They'd been to visit the settlement on vacation last year, and he never stopped hyping it up. It was gorgeous, of course, but the commercial shuttles were only allowed to orbit the planet. None of the tourist trips could land yet, so they'd spent a few days looking down at the barren red landscape, while a tour guide – who clearly thought he was hilarious – told them stupid, made-up anecdotes about the names of the valleys and hills.

The most exciting part had been when the shuttle passed over the base on the ground. There was a cluster of white habitation domes, each one owned by a different company – NASA and the ESA, of course, but also private space companies like Warren Space, who sold commercial trips. The astronauts on the ground hadn't even looked up at the tourist shuttle. They must see them fly overhead every day.

Dad was already talking about going back to Mars for another visit, but Hester couldn't see the point. In fifty years the settlement might have developed enough to be fun. Right now it was only a cluster of tents. It was probably fascinating to the scientists, but for normal people it was just an interesting investment opportunity.

"Hopefully we get the contract," she said. "Maybe the biofuels idea is something we can investigate further too, though? I've been reading this really interesting article about—"

"Why don't you take the lead on this one?" he said briskly.

Hester gaped at him. "Really?"

"Sure, give it a try. It will be good for you to have your own project to practise on."

Hester didn't even try to quell her joy. She let a sunflower bloom from her wrist. *He trusted her.* She could finally do some of the things she was always giving speeches about. "I won't let you down, Dad."

"Go ahead and set up a team. Hire whoever you need –

I'll allocate the resources. Just ... get this under control."
He gestured warily towards the sunflower.

Hester resisted the urge to start making a to-do list. Her *own department*. She'd begin by recruiting people with the plant-growth abilities. Then she'd need a research group, and perhaps a new test site, with some fields and a lab for practice, and – *oh*, Hester was going to have so much fun. This could be a whole new strand of the firm. One that she and Dad could build together.

They were going to make a fortune. Well. Another one, anyway.

## @firstwithmagic ✓

Hello, world! I'm Gabrielle, the first teenager to grow plants. I'm seventeen, studying for my A levels, and I've got a pet chinchilla. It's nice to meet all million+ of you (wow). Somehow I've morphed from a nobody to someone with a PR manager, a blue tick and DMs full of paid spon con offers.

It's strange that anyone cares about me since so many other teenagers have now followed me into this new normal. I'm not an anomaly any more, just part of a whole generation with powers.

But while the world's attention is (inexplicably) directed towards me, I'm going to make myself heard. Our plants might be eminently gif-able, but, pals, this is our best chance to make a difference.

**We need action, desperately. The climate emergency is real, and dangerous. It's going to get much worse if we don't make changes to the way we create energy. Right now.**

Join me, will you? Let's use these miraculous, ridiculous plants to help the planet.

Here's the plan, in four (4) easy steps:

1) **Hone those powers.** Train your Greenfingers to the max, full Olympic-gold standard. You've been given a gift. Build it up. Expand your repertoire by growing veg for your local food bank in your jungle haven backyard or scrubland park. Make bamboo canes & willow furniture. Train up, soldier, 'til it's as natural as breathing.

2) **Find your people.** If you can't grow plants, then get someone else on board: write a chalk message on the pavement, DM your schoolmates, talk to your parents (especially if they're deniers – only you can change their minds. Make this issue personal: tell them they are failing to care for your welfare if they don't engage with the climate crisis).

3) **Join the @ClimateRebellion network.** We're partnering Greenfingers with manufacturers to create sustainable materials: eco-friendly straws, paper and fabrics, all with a local, low-carbon footprint. You'll be paid to produce reusable shopping bags and coffee cups.

4) **Save the world.**

It's a small start, I know. But before I got involved in activism, I really struggled with my mental health. It's so hard to find a point to living when the world is burning. But we do have a future, I promise.

We aren't helpless. Our efforts are important. Don't be a spectator to history. Let's fight the climate battle the only way we can – together.

–gabrielle

#plantsfortheplanet

P.S. does anyone know any good accounts about capoeira? I've just started the sport and I'd love to follow some fitness insp!

## COMMENTS

**Skillmop** show us where you donated money to climate change or shut your mouth

**Elito09** your last pic has a plastic straw in it you dummy. Get real your a poser

**Lucifr** woooow uninterested

**Mrbriggs** if I was your father I would ground you. Focus on your homework, kid. You need to learn the value of hard work before you start lecturing others about their failings.

**Flipoff** global warming is a hoax, you're brainwashed. Look up Qanon, china 5g network, pizzagate etc and open your eyes. I'll DM you to explain darling

**Aesethics** Virtue signalling? More likely than you'd think.

**fitterg** go back to school and learn something useful little girl. We're only here for plant vids. Want to see you grow stuff bb

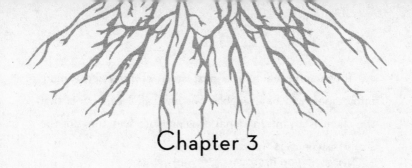

# Chapter 3

"Take a seat, Mr Carthew," the interviewer said, when Theo entered the uncomfortably fancy office. "Thank you for coming in."

Theo sat down gingerly. There was a young woman on the conference screen behind them.

"No problem. Can I ask, er – what company do you work for?"

He'd been looking up ways to grow pot when a Greenfingers job ad popped up. After an informative twenty minutes reading badly encoded forum posts, he'd decided that growing cannabis was beyond his skill level just yet. The job had seemed easier. All he'd needed to do was fill out a survey about his power, and he'd been called to an interview the next day.

He had to get this job. It had been two months since the shipwreck. Their bills were being paid with savings, plus anything Mum could earn by selling homemade food at the local car boot sale. But some lemon drizzle cakes and samosas from her *amma*'s old family recipe were nowhere near enough to cover the bills.

"If you proceed to the next stage of interviews, more information will be available. For now, all I can say is that the client is an international conglomerate searching for the sharpest teenagers we can find."

"Well, that's me! Sharp as a scalpel."

There was a brief silence. Theo didn't know why he even bothered trying to make jokes. He was absolutely useless at it. He wished he'd dragged Mum in with him.

"To start with, how many types of plant can you grow?" the man asked. There was a coffee machine behind him that looked brand new. Theo would probably have been able to flog it for seventy pounds at the village car boot sale.

Theo shrugged nonchalantly. "Around twenty so far."

He wanted it to be true. He wished he could fill their sunburned garden with sweet peas and clematis and holly hocks and daffodils and irises, but he could still only grow boring seaweed. If he said that, though, they would definitely give the job to someone more talented. He would catch up with that skill level soon, anyway.

The man looked pleased.

Theo had only had an interview once before, for an after-school job unloading container ships at the docks. But that had been a chat in the shipyard; nothing like this. The job wasn't very well paid, though sometimes the boxes were damaged. Theo could slip items out, which was an absolute goldmine of leather phone cases, headphones and Bluetooth speakers.

Sometimes, his sneaky grabs were the only thing keeping them all afloat. Literally – Theo's car boot sale earnings had been used to buy fuel for the boat last year.

"Could you demonstrate your power for us? You can grow anything you'd like."

"How…" Theo swallowed around the dryness in his mouth. "How much shall I make?"

The interviewer's expression was blank. "As much as you can, please."

Theo looked around the room. It wasn't very big. "Are you … sure?"

"Absolutely. Don't be shy. It's OK if you're too nervous."

Theo was certain that wasn't going to be a problem. Quite the opposite, since whenever he used his power he ended up spraying seaweed in all directions. He'd outgrown wet dreams, but now he was waking up in pools of goo all over again.

Their compost heap had filled up after three days. In the end, Mum had started taking wheelbarrows full of the stuff to the farm down the lane. The farmer mixed it into the cattle food, cheerfully thrilled by his good luck.

"Just keep going?" he checked again, holding out his palm. This man must know what he was doing, right? He'd interviewed three people just while Theo sat in the waiting room.

When the interviewer nodded, Theo let go. For the first time, he didn't try to stop the plants from growing. He focused on the buzz in the base of his neck, encouraging it until seaweed exploded out of all his pores. It hit the ceiling and sprayed over the conference call projection.

The man jumped back in surprise. "Oh, stop!"

It was too late. The floodgates were open. By the time it was over, the man had climbed onto the table to escape the rising tide of seaweed. The woman – *girl?* – on the conference screen began to laugh. "Hire him!"

Incandescent happiness filled Theo. "Really?"

The interviewer shook his hand, despite the seaweed stuck to his palm. "Welcome to the team, Theodore. If you can do that on demand, you've got a job for life. The other candidates only made a few leaves."

"What's the job, then?" This all seemed too easy.

"We're recruiting Greenfingers for an energy corporation that wants to produce ethanol and biofuel. There's potential for huge rewards if the powers can be manipulated successfully." He retrieved a plastic folder from the seaweed-covered tabletop. "There's some more information in here, so you can discuss it with your parents."

Theo flipped through the folder, but the letters jumped around on the page. He tried to focus past the way his dyslexia scrambled the words. The salary on the first page made him gape. He'd be making more money than his parents had made in the last two years combined.

The company must be very confident that the Greenfingers powers were going to stick around for good if they were willing to invest that much. Or they were trying to make the most of the situation while it was here.

"Wow," Theo said. "That's ... I'm interested." He shifted in his seat, trying to play down his excitement. He wasn't used to getting this lucky.

"I should mention that the firm is based in America. They'll pay for flights, food and board, but you'll have to commit to a six-week probationary period."

That seemed to be a bonus rather than a downside. A free trip to America? Theo had never even been on a plane!

He would have to miss some school, but all Greenfingers were allowed to retake the term if they couldn't control their powers yet. His parents needed this money. It wasn't even a question – he had to do this.

"There are details in the folder about who you'll need to contact at Dalex if you decide to accept the offer."

He froze. "Dalex?"

"Dalex Energy, yes."

His blood ran cold. He should have known it was too good to be true. No amount of money was worth working for those scumbags.

"I'll think on it," he said, actually meaning *no, thanks*.

He found Mum outside, talking on the phone.

"Waste of time. Let's be getting on," he said.

She held up a finger, finishing the call. When she hung up, her eyes flooded with tears. "Theo. Dad's heard back from the insurance company. They think the collision was his fault, because the radar warned him that the boat was approaching a hazard before the crash. About *thirty seconds* before, but apparently that's sufficient warning. They're not giving us the payout."

Theo's knees crumpled under him. "None of it?"

Mum huffed, wiping her eyes. "Not a jot. And Dalex are kicking their heels about paying for the damages too. Apparently they 'can't take any responsibility' because they'd marked up the hazard, but the update hadn't rolled out on the mapping system for private fishing boats yet." Mum sighed. "Bloody Dalex."

Theo grimaced. Why were Dalex so profoundly terrible, in every way? "What are you going to do? Will Dad get a new boat?"

"He's done with fishing. These days it's not worth the investment in equipment, even if we had that kind of money."

Theo swallowed. "Can he get a job in a factory or warehouse or something?"

"Love, you know it's all automated machinery now. The AIs don't need human help. Even the morning post comes by drone." She quickly brightened her voice. "Sorry, *jaan*, how did the interview go?"

Theo hesitated. He couldn't turn the job down now. He'd get the money for their boat out of Dalex one way or another.

Carefully pushing the information pack under his arm to hide the company logo, he said, "It was great! I think I'm going to accept."

"Thank goodness you got this power, eh?" she said, wiping her eyes.

Theo frowned. "Do you think it's just random chance that I got it? It feels like I'm supposed to do something useful with it. It feels important."

He'd been picked to have this power for a reason, hadn't he? Out of everyone in the world, it had chosen him. Now he had to use it to help his family.

# WHICH BILLIONAIRE PLAYBOY ARE YOU?

**What are you most likely to be cancelled for?**

- ◯ Crashing my own share prices via sick memes
- ◯ Dropping acid with my synth-pop band
- ◯ Transitioning to a full meal-replacement shake diet
- ◯ Online spat with radicalized trolls
- ☑ All of the above

**Where's your bunker for when society inevitably collapses?**

- ◯ New Zealand (five storeys underground + pool, baby)
- ◯ Alaska (with a robotic patrolling security system!)
- ☑ Mars (with a supercomputer ready to port back to my robot body on Earth, duh)
- ◯ I've got one on each continent

**Quick! What's your most embarrassing pre-start-up fashion look?**

- ☑ e-boy platinum dye job + anime tee
- ◯ Mullet and five-inch-thick specs
- ◯ Don't remind me of my misbegotten corporate youth
- ◯ My lawyers have stringently removed every single trace of my past from the internet, thx

**Congratulations, you're Edgar Warren!**

This tech baron made his big bucks in his teens through cryptocurrency. In the last decade, he's expanded his empire from Silicon Valley unicorns to infinity and beyond by reinvesting his self-made billions into space exploration. But at least he's stopped dressing like an internet goth.

**Related News**

Hundreds of Elephants Die from Algae Blooms in Watering Holes, Caused by Rising Temperatures

South American Teenagers Protect Tornado-Struck Village Using Conifer Tree Barrier

Greenfingers Powers: Do they come from microplastics in drinking water, food additives or vaccinations?

Gabrielle Ventura owns En-corp in the comments: "Efficient lightbulbs? I'll reduce my emissions when you stop destroying the planet"

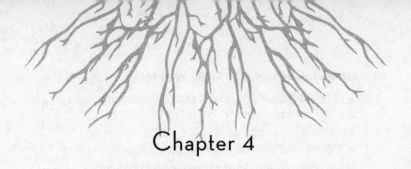

# Chapter 4

Hester requisitioned a plate of mini cheesecakes, looking around the milling crowd. This was it, at last: the launch of her biofuels project. The Greenfingers teenagers they'd recruited were arriving tonight from all over the world, so Dalex was throwing a welcoming party in her new training centre.

Hester had spent the last few months renovating an old farm on the outskirts of Houston. The site had been an oilfield back in the fifties. There was still a broken-down, rusted pumpjack on the brow of the hill, abandoned when the reserves had run out. There was plenty of space for the Greenfingers to practise in the glorious glass greenhouses, and the building was now a modern, welcoming space, decorated in the company colours.

Dad always leaped at the chance for a party, because it was the perfect way to woo investment clients. Just in this room alone there was a senator who'd voted on a committee that had approved a new pipeline being laid in Canada and a middleman who'd helped set up meetings with the

President of Kazakhstan to discuss a new contract. Even Edgar Warren had shown up. He was wearing a silver suit with a graphic T-shirt, his arms slung over the shoulders of two blonde models.

Hester watched him work the room. There was an hour before she was due to give her welcoming speech to the trainees with Dad. Since he was still trying to land Dalex the energy contract on Mars, maybe Hester could just ... go and talk to Edgar right now?

He'd been really interested in learning more about the Greenfingers powers after her embarrassing algae explosion. She could suggest that her Greenfingers grow plants for biofuels right there on Mars. It would save Warren Space from needing to lift endless supplies out of Earth's atmosphere in rockets. Instead, they'd only need to send up a few teenagers.

It was a whole new angle. Biofuels made from Greenfingers' plants in space. She was willing to bet that no other energy companies had thought of it. If she could get Edgar on board, Dad would see that she was more than just an appealing public speaker.

Across the room, Edgar Warren puffed on a menthol-flavoured vape pen and hollered at a joke.

Hester adjusted the hem of her pinstriped pencil skirt. She knew exactly what to do here. All of her PR training was designed to appeal to the egos of businessmen like him.

"Good evening, Mr Warren," she said, putting some mustard on her accent until she had a hint of the high society drawl used by her Southern debutante grandma. It was perfect for charming investors: harmless, nostalgic and reassuring.

Hester held out a hand for him to shake, ignoring the way that rosebuds on a nearby bouquet of flowers opened up. Dad had given her a firm warning about avoiding any more botanical accidents, so she'd grown a whole trash can of plants before the guests arrived. It clearly hadn't been enough.

"Mr Warren – Hester Daleport," she said. "I toured Mars last summer. Great vibes. I convinced my dad there would be a river under the Einstein-Rosen bridge."

He stopped telling a long story to his two lady friends and laughed, making his gold earring flash in the light. "Call me Edgar. You're the Greenfingers girl, aren't you?"

"I am. I was hoping to talk to you about that, actually. Can I – " she paused, flicking her eyes towards his throuple – "get you a drink?"

She held her breath, waiting for Edgar to shoo her away. Hester was used to being the little kid who was ignored so that the grown-ups could talk. But, magically, Edgar took the hint and told the women, "I'll catch you both later."

Dad caught her eye from across the room, raising his eyebrows in surprise. When he stepped towards them, she held up her fingers to ward him off. She didn't need a pre-written speech for everything.

"I have a question about Mars," she said, choosing her words carefully. She had to guide Edgar in a particular direction, but she needed to keep it subtle. This had to feel like a natural epiphany they were having together, rather than a heavy-handed advertisement. "How is it all going to work when people start living there? Will you use the surface rock for construction material?"

Edgar took two whiskey shots from a waiter, passing one to Hester. "One day the rock will be used, sure. But right now, we're 3-D printing building materials from bioplastics."

Jackpot. "Made from cellulose? What about food – does everyone eat vacuum-packed meals?" She wrinkled her nose in mock disgust, toying with her necklace – a pendant made from a real dinosaur tooth that Dad had found in a fragment of rock when drilling for samples in a new oilfield.

Edgar licked a drop of whiskey off his wrist. "Well, no. It's too expensive to ship food all the way from Earth, so it all has to be grown on the planet itself. The main food source is algae, actually. No one likes it much, but it's fast growing and high in protein. I've started to prefer the efficiency of a liquid meal."

Hester grinned. This was going even better than she'd imagined. She took Edgar's hand, growing a spiral of glimmering algae in his palm.

"You know, I think my Greenfingers could produce all the products you've described – corn for bioplastics, vegetables for food and oxygenators for living spaces. My group is only just starting up, but potentially Dalex can offer you something beyond electricity. We could turn an empty habitation dome into a thriving farm in weeks."

She grew a small pea vine out of the algae and snapped off a fresh mangetout. "Imagine eating that on Mars."

His eyes widened. It felt like a significant gesture to feed him something grown from her own fingers. To show him what they could offer – but also to share something personal. Dad would probably say that she was flaunting her powers, but then, he'd never hesitated before showing off his new cars or art acquisitions to investors.

"Better than algae," Edgar commented.

"You're telling me. Edgar, this could change everything for Warren Space. Dalex would like to help you power your colony from the ground up. Literally."

While she was talking, her power shot a frond across the floor. She nudged the goldenrod away from Edgar's toes, trying to pretend it was intentional.

Edgar smiled. "You've got my attention. What about numbers?"

Hester met Dad's eye. He immediately started walking over.

"We're going to begin training our specially recruited Greenfingers tomorrow," she said. "We do have other parties interested in hiring them, but we're willing to secure you exclusive rights on their services if you're able to make an offer tonight."

It took Dad barely a second's pause to catch up to what was happening. He shook Edgar's hand. "Mr Warren, I see my daughter has beaten me to the punch."

"She has indeed. And I think she's just secured you a contract with my company."

Hester was ecstatic. While Dad saw Edgar out, she started typing out a to-do list. For this to work, she would need to learn more about Mars. Could they make biodegradable plant-based alternatives to the building materials being used? Would they need to commission lightweight, compact versions of the processing equipment? There weren't enough hours in the day for everything she wanted to do.

"Good work, princess," Dad said, clapping her on the back. "You do take after your old man, don't you?"

She grinned. "I didn't want to miss our shot."

"I'm really proud of you. You're going to make a fine CEO one day."

Happiness rang through her. She leaned against his shoulder, drawing in a deep breath. He was always so solid.

One of the perks of working on a bigger project like this was that she got to see Dad all day. Usually she ate dinner alone in their empty house while he worked long hours. Today they'd had takeout salads together over a conference call.

Her parents were divorced, and Mom split her time between New York and her hometown of Rio de Janeiro for her work as a hedge fund manager. Hester only saw her when she was in town for meetings with her investment clients, but it did mean that Hester could catch a lift in her private jet whenever she wanted to go and see a Broadway show. And it wasn't like home was totally empty when Dad was away. Her tutor and housekeeper were usually around too.

Dad picked a leaf off her collar and dropped it into the bin as if it were radioactive, rubbing hand sanitizer into his palms. "I really didn't like the idea of you having these powers at first. It's so … vulgar. But it does seem to be opening up some big opportunities for the firm. Just get it under control, OK? You managed to get rid of that old stutter. Why is this any different?"

"Sorry," she said, mortified. "I've been working on it, but it's tough."

"Ah, it looks like the recruits have arrived," Dad said, nodding to a group of teenagers gathered in the reception. "All set for your welcome speech?"

She lost her smile. High on the buzz of a successful deal negotiation, Hester had almost forgotten to be nervous. Why did the trainees have to be her own age? She could talk to a delegation of businessmen without breaking a sweat, but a group of *teenagers*? There was no training course she could take to prepare for that.

She'd always been taught alone at home by a tutor, who tailored her education to the business skills she needed at Dalex. How should she even talk to the trainees? *Hello, fellow teens? Greetings, ladies and gentleman?* It was like trying to find a way to communicate with an alien species. They wouldn't be afraid to laugh at her if she messed up. She had to make them respect her from the beginning, or this whole project was hopeless. At least Edgar Warren had already left, so if she messed up too tragically, he wouldn't be here to witness it.

"This is your demographic, remember – it's the perfect opportunity to showcase your public engagement training." Dad tapped his whiskey glass with a fork. The room went silent.

"Welcome!" Dad spoke in the confident, commanding voice that she could never quite manage to impersonate. "As chairman, it's a pleasure to be here to establish the latest branch of Dalex Energy. I'm excited to see where this innovative project takes us – maybe even to the *stars*, as it were."

There was a polite chuckle from the investors. She was willing to bet that Dad was already drafting a letter to the shareholders to share the good news about the Warren deal.

When Hester's hand drifted up to fiddle with her necklace, she forced it down. It was a nervous gesture that her PR advisors always highlighted when they watched back the footage of her press conferences, just like the occasional remnants of her childhood stutter.

One of the Greenfingers recruits had fat catkins growing from her curls, scattering pollen across her shoulders like dandruff. A boy was yawning into the sleeve of a damp-looking Fair Isle sweater that had a hole in the shoulder. They didn't look that scary. Mainly dishevelled and tired.

"I'd like to hand you over to our executive, who will be leading your training programme over the next six weeks. Hester?"

She took a deep breath. It was time to begin.

# Transcript of UPSIDE DOWNSIDE podcast

**Ronald:** Hello and welcome to another episode highlighting the newest trends online.

Today I have a big treat for you guys. It's Gabrielle Ventura, the lady of the moment. This girl is no one-hit wonder. She's really blossomed – pun unintended, ha – over the last few months.

I had such a great time chatting to her, so I'm going to dive straight into her interview. But first, I'm sure many of you savvy listeners have a passion project that you'd like to grow into a business. Well, have you heard of Sharespace? This amazing company lets users connect with new-build development companies using crowdfunded investments to buy auctioned lots of land on Mars.

With a few simple clicks, you can contribute on a sliding scale towards a shared ownership mortgage scheme that gives you a chance at future fun, planet-side. Whatever your budget, with the low variable interest rates available, your future grandchildren will have their dream vacation spot ready to go when it's habitable.

Sharespace let me play around with their app and let me tell you guys, this is incredible stuff. Use offer code RONALD10, that's RONALD10, to get a discount on your first order. Don't miss out, this is a great deal.

All right, let's get this show on the road. Over to the interview.

**Ronald:** Hi, Gabrielle, how are you doing today?

**Gabrielle:** Not too bad, Ronald. How about you?

**Ronald:** Can't complain, can't complain at all. Now, let's start off with a softball one for ya. How have your Greenfingers changed your life?

**Gabrielle:** It's given me a valuable tool in a world that's determined to make me feel worthless. I joined Climate Rebellion when it was a group of a few teenagers in my area, and now there are thousands of us all over the UK. I don't think we'd have got that kind of growth without the exposure from my Greenfingers. It's given us real, quantifiable power.

**Ronald:** Wow. Well put. Now I know you've got something to ask our listeners. Would you like to go ahead?

**Gabrielle:** Yes, actually. There's, um, a petition to parliament asking for the national power supply to transition to full green energy. The science has been clear for years on this. We need to stop using fossil fuels immediately if the planet is going to recover. So I'm asking listeners to sign the petition and join me in putting pressure on the government.

**Ronald:** Well, you've convinced me. I'm honestly shocked that this isn't already a thing, you know?

**Gabrielle:** Every time the government debates this issue, the science is always ignored in favour of propping up the oil industry. I've been fighting this battle since I was ten, attending marches and writing to my local MPs.

**Ronald:** Wow. That's wild. Ten, really? I was still eating dirt then.

**Gabrielle:** Yeah, I wrote a letter to the prime minister with an idea to recycle foil waste. It's something I've always felt really passionate about, but it's like screaming into a vacuum sometimes. No one listens.

**Ronald:** That must be tough.

**Gabrielle:** Right?! This is supposed to be a democracy, but our voices aren't being heard. Now, with all these Greenfingers, maybe we can get some drastic changes. Not in a year, or a decade – today.

**Ronald:** How are you planning to make that happen?

**Gabrielle:** Let's just say that I'm kicking things up a notch. Plans are in the works...

**Ronald:** How intriguing. Well, Gabrielle, it's been great to have you on the show. Next up, we have Storm West here to give us the lowdown on their new booty booster injectables. Get the filter look I-R-L. But that's after a word from our sponsors.

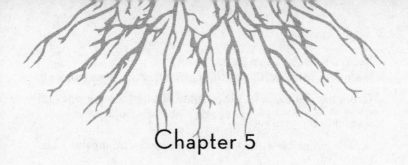

# Chapter 5

Theo hadn't slept in twenty-two hours, through two connecting flights on his way to Texas, then a drive to some middle-of-nowhere dodgy estate with a group of other Greenfingers teens.

They hadn't even had a chance to drop their luggage in their rooms before being ushered straight into a welcoming party full of suits. Theo was very aware of his own personal smell in the artificial cleanliness.

His eyes kept slipping closed as a stocky man with an expensive suit and Bluetooth earpiece droned on and on about their recruitment.

"…it's an exciting opportunity to expand into a previously unimagined market. As soon as I heard about the Greenfingers phenomenon, I knew there was an opportunity there for profit. Dalex Energy has branches all across the world, and the potential for expansion is…" The man adjusted his gold-rimmed glasses.

Theo stifled a yawn. He needed a Dalex propaganda speech like he needed a hole in the head. He'd spent the last few weeks working his way through endless study assignments on botany and biofuels. Why couldn't Dalex have put this dull speech in the paperwork?

The other Greenfingers were all distinctly organic. The boy next to him had skin covered in thick stems of ivy, and a girl was idly growing a new branch from her thumb. The twig stretched upwards, expanding by generations, a ring a second. It sprouted leaves, fluttering as its trunk thickened.

They were all intimidatingly powerful. He'd kill to be able to make plants like that.

"…it may seem daunting at first, but you'll be amply rewarded for your efforts. Dalex is rated one of the best in America for employee care, and had the honour of receiving an award from…"

Theo picked green gunk out from under his nails, trying not to let his irritation show. How could the guy claim that Dalex cared about people, after they refused to help Dad with his boat? It was all lies.

There was a girl in a very fancy suit standing behind the stocky man. She was listening attentively to everything he said, nodding along and occasionally making notes on a tablet.

"…who will be leading your training programme over the next six weeks. Hester?"

She stepped forward, smiling at them.

"Good evening, folks," Hester said, voice cracking. "I know that y'all've had very big journeys, so I won't keep you listening long."

She toyed with a gold necklace that had some sort of fossil pendant (a full thirty quid at the car boot, Theo estimated). "If you have any problems at all during your training, I will be your first point of contact. This is obviously going to be a learning curve for all of us, so I hope you'll tell me if there's anything you think we could improve on."

A little daisy flowered from her collarbone as she spoke. Theo was curious. If she had Greenfingers powers then she must be around his age. She definitely didn't look any older than seventeen or eighteen. How had she got a management job at such a big company? He remembered seeing her on the conference screen during his interview too.

"I'm very much looking forward to seeing everyone's skills develop over the next few weeks. I think that together we'll be able to make something really incredible here."

The man nodded reassuringly at her. There was something similar in their noses and eyebrows, although her skin was darker and his hair was dishwater blond. Was she his daughter? That would explain why she was wearing such an expensive suit and jewellery. She must have come to work with her dad, like Theo had done.

Except that instead of gutting fish in a rocking boat, she got to wear designer suits and boss around employees. Some people had all the luck.

"Dalex is committed to finding long-term, sustainable energy sources to meet the growing global demand. This project is just the first step we're taking on that journey together." There was something grating about her voice: stiff and formal, like she was reciting a memorized speech. It was robotic.

A girl who kept sneezing rose petals raised her hand. "Does this mean that you'll stop drilling for oil?"

Hester paused for a moment, looking surprised. "Absolutely not. There'll always be demand for oil, even if this biofuels project is successful. Our global infrastructure depends on it."

"But don't we need to stop emissions to fight climate change?" the girl asked.

Theo nodded. Didn't Hester know even the most basic climate science? Fossil fuels released carbon dioxide, which was heating up the atmosphere. But Dalex were planning on burning it *for ever*?

Hester shook her head. Something dark green flew out of her ear. "Dalex isn't qualified to address the climate emergency. That's best left to the scientists and environmentalists, not energy producers. We'd get in the way."

Theo's blood ran hot. How could she say that? Dalex made billions of dollars each year, more than enough to hire scientists of their own.

"We're focused on producing power to keep society running. Once the science is ready, we'll be able to support climate efforts." Her curly black hair was growing flecks of moss.

Theo snorted. This rich girl was spouting such rubbish. She was clearly trying very hard to convince people that there was plenty of time to work on the problem. As if the whole planet wasn't already in crisis.

His laughter was unintentionally loud. Everyone in the room turned to look at him.

Hester swallowed, making a clicking noise in her throat. Leaves were budding between her fingers now, curling over her thumbnail. "Is something wrong?"

He raised his eyebrows. "Sorry, but there are new hurricanes forming every week, and constant wildfires in Australia. And you must have seen the state the oceans are in."

Dad's brother's farm was perched on top of a cliff-face that had been eroding for years as the sea levels rose. Every winter they expected it to crumble off the edge into the sea, though it kept clinging on. But Dalex obviously didn't care about him any more than they cared about the fishing industry.

"But, sure, wait until the science is *absolutely right* before doing anything," he said sarcastically. "Maybe climate change will magically reverse on its own and you'll get to keep burning oil."

Hester's hand jumped up to twist around her necklace again. The plant growing from her hand now curled up her arm, digging livid red thorns into her skin.

The man whispered something to her. Was Daddy going to jump in and answer?

"W-we're working hard to make our business practices sustainable, as new science about the world's complex climate comes to l-light." She was clearly reciting it from memory. Her accent was thicker now: a hint of a Texas twang creeping in between the words.

The audience was listening with genuine rapt attention for the first time. Theo was exhausted and jet-lagged, and he didn't want to carry on heckling her. But he couldn't let her get away with this nonsense.

"Everyone has known about the climate emergency since before I was even born. You've had decades to act, but you've just been faffing around, hoping that someone else will clean up your mess. It shouldn't take some convenient free magical powers for you to decide it's worth investigating ways to stop polluting the planet."

The branch tightened around Hester's arm, oil-slick blood beading on her wrist. She didn't react to the pain.

Theo couldn't look at her blank expression for a moment longer. He stormed outside. Immediately, seaweed exploded from him, spraying the ground in green sludge.

Why had he ever come here? This was never going to work. These people were pure evil. Using the Greenfingers' plants to make biofuels was a good idea, if it was done properly. But energy companies were all the same. They were only interested in profit. They didn't actually care about the planet at all.

He was probably going to get a bollocking for shouting at Hester like that. In the middle of the welcoming party. What if they sent him home? His fury morphed into sheer panic. His parents needed him to keep this job. And he'd just screamed at the people who'd hired him.

What had he done?

Theo waited the whole night for someone to chuck him out. He was so worried that he hadn't even been able to enjoy the amazing king-sized bed, free room service, complimentary iPad and en suite with claw-footed bathtub. Though he'd managed to give the Xbox a test run, when he wasn't brooding over Hester Daleport's social media.

Annoyingly, her account had popped up as soon as he put an "h" into the search bar. She was Anthony Daleport's daughter, like he'd suspected. She had one of those blue ticks by her name, and a frankly ridiculous number of followers. All her photos were cool blues and whites – sea views, marble floors, swimming pools, sparkling diamonds. It was very irritating.

If she didn't fire him over breakfast, he would have to apologize profusely for his jet-lagged stupidity and make this right, somehow.

"That was wild last night," a boy said, as they queued for the breakfast buffet. "I can't believe you went off on her like that."

"Me neither," Theo muttered.

"I'm Jason, by the way." He had an Australian accent, and ivy curled in his hair. "I, um, I use they/them pronouns."

Theo poured a glass of orange juice, offering one to Jason. "Got it. I'm Theo. Did you get here last night too?"

"Yeah. I've only had my powers a few weeks. It's all gone pretty fast," they said.

"Wow, that's quick. I've had a few months to get used to

mine, and it still feels weird. Do you know what that is?" Theo pointed to a bowl of some white, lumpy sauce next to a plate of scones.

Jason shook their head. "Some Southern thing, I guess?"

Theo tried to look it up on his phone. When Jason peered over his shoulder, he tilted his screen away. He was always self-conscious about the display settings. He used a special font for his dyslexia, which put a colour gradient on the lines of text so that they slowly changed from blue to black, then back again. That – plus an extension that made the page backgrounds cream instead of white – made it a lot easier to read. But the lads at school pestered him about his "dumbo" settings whenever they saw his phone.

"Biscuits and gravy, apparently." Theo steered clear of it, as Hester Daleport entered the dining hall. "I can probably live without that at seven in the morning, actually."

"Morning, everyone!" Daleport said, clapping her hands together. Theo was too embarrassed to look directly at her. She represented everything he hated, about himself and her company. "After you've finished eating, Daisy here is going to take you over to the greenhouses for your first training session. You might recognize her – she's made a name for herself online with her impressive mastery of her powers. I thought we could start off the training by having her bring y'all up to speed on some of the tricks she's discovered."

"Daisy. Appropriate name," Theo said to Jason in an undertone. They just looked at him in confusion. Somehow his jokes weren't as funny when he had to explain them. It was probably a sign of how rubbish he was at humour that he had to do it so often.

Daisy waved at them. She looked incredibly nervous, and couldn't be any older than fifteen. To Theo's relief, Daleport left without looking in his direction.

Fifteen minutes later, he was staring down at an empty seed tray in the humid greenhouse and trying not to panic.

"You should be able to feel it as a buzz or a niggle at the back of your mind," Daisy said.

Theo had seen Greenfingers online projecting their powers into a seedling, but he'd never managed to make one grow. Daisy made it look easy, though.

He still couldn't grow anything except seaweed. He'd practised every day before his flight to Texas. He'd tried just picturing a different type of seaweed – the kind that grew on the harbour, coating the surface of the iron posts sunk into the sea bed.

Even when he'd imagined it down to the smallest detail – the texture of it underwater, the crisp crackle as it dried out, the pop when he stood on its pods – he hadn't been able to grow it. On one occasion, when he'd pushed himself until a vein throbbed in his temple, a small tendril had appeared in his palm. But then blackness had washed over him, and he'd fainted.

"Tap into the vibrating energy in your mind and try to focus it on the plants on your bench," Daisy said. "It doesn't have to come from your skin. If you project it into the seeds, they'll grow with that same wriggling feeling that comes when you use your power."

The tiny seed on the soil didn't seem very alive. When Theo grew seaweed, there was an electric tingle at the base of his skull before the stems bloomed from his skin. It was almost like magic, the way it glided from the surface of his body.

Now, Theo tried to recreate that feeling, attempting to make the seedling bend or flex or do *something*. Everyone else could control this – why not him?

"I can feel it!" said the girl at the bench in front of Theo. "It's hibernating."

Daisy said, "That's right, Beatriz! Focus on the potential inside it. And kind of – push at it, I guess? Until it starts to wriggle."

Daisy guided Beatriz's hand to touch the seed. Immediately, it exploded in half, shooting a stem upwards. Leaves burst free until the tiny sapling towered above them.

Beatriz gasped. "Your power! It made mine suddenly jump forward."

"I felt it," Daisy said, awed. "Let's see if we can grow something else?"

Daisy and Beatriz pointed at a monstera, still touching. It tripled in size.

"I think it's stronger if we team up!" Daisy called out. "Everyone, try growing something in a pair next."

Sinking further into despair, Theo prodded his seed.

The others were already moving on to their next party trick, and Theo hadn't even taken his coat off.

"You nearly had it then!" Daisy said, watching Theo's feeble attempt to do anything at all. "Keep trying?"

Theo buried his fingers in the rich, dark soil. There was nothing. The seed didn't vibrate at him, or grow leaves, or whatever else it was supposed to do. He could feel the focused powers of everyone around him, as leggy, tender shoots grew into supple branches.

"Oh, wonderful!" Daisy clapped her hands together as Jason made a celery stalk shoot upwards. Beatriz's tree had blossomed with delicate pale-pink flowers. She picked a full-sized ripe apple and took a bite, seemingly blasé.

Theo pushed harder with his power, until a wave of dizziness rolled over him. Maybe he could slip away to look around the Edwardian greenhouses instead. He breathed in the rich mulch smell that was just like his nani's garden shed. If only Dalex hadn't spoiled the greenhouse by putting their stupid logo everywhere: a cartoon yellow sun with the slogan *Beyond Oil*. Theo couldn't believe that people actually fell for that stupid marketing campaign. It was just a scam to trick people into thinking they used renewable energy, like the solar panels and windmills on the roofs of their petrol stations.

At the bench in front, Beatriz wobbled slightly.

"Are you OK?" Theo called. Her face had gone pale, the whites of her eyes showing as she gasped for breath through blue lips.

"I-I—" Her eyes rolled back in their sockets.

He leaped over his bench, grabbing her just before she stumbled and fell.

"Someone call a fire eng— I mean, ambulance! Call an ambulance!" he yelled, trying to remember absolutely any basic first aid. She was unconscious, hanging limp in his arms.

She must have exhausted herself growing the apple tree. He rolled her onto her side, checking that her airway was clear. When something poked his arm, he flinched back. There was a bulge under her T-shirt. It flexed, jabbing his finger. There were plants inside Beatriz. *In her stomach.*

Theo yelled again, "Did someone call for help?"

"It's coming," Daisy called. She sounded very flustered.

Should he do something? What *could* he do? As Theo watched, the plant under Beatriz's skin enlarged, pushing outwards. Why was it still growing? She'd passed out, so she wasn't using her power any more. It should have stopped by now.

He looked around the room. The plants were still jumping up in height on the benches. Beatriz wasn't doing this to herself. Everyone in this room was using their powers right now. They were doing this as a group, somehow.

"Everyone, stop using your powers! Now!" he shouted.

Theo pressed his hand against Beatriz's stomach, concentrating on the living plant inside her. He recalled the way he sometimes stopped his seaweed, when it threatened to burst from his skin at an inopportune moment.

For the first time, he understood what Daisy had meant about a vibration. The bright, white glow of life nudged back against his power, testing his strength. It was an apple tree, desperate to grow.

Beatriz had eaten one of the apples she'd made. A seed must have grown inside her stomach, encouraged by a whole room of Greenfingers sending out commands to any seed in range.

Theo pictured his power as a shield, repelling everyone else's power. Blood dripped out of Beatriz's mouth, but the branch seemed to have stopped growing.

"The ambulance will be here in five minutes," Daisy said. "What – what are you doing?"

Theo ignored her. It was there. He could feel it. If he just—

Something clicked into place, and the bulge in her stomach collapsed. He felt the life retreat inside the tiny apple pip. This actually felt easier than trying to force a plant to grow. There wasn't that strange blockage he usually experienced.

Beatriz moaned, blinking her eyes open. He'd done it.

Theo swayed, feeling woozy and sick. The next thing he knew, he was being pulled away by paramedics and Daisy was helping him up. "You saved her life. You did it."

Theo blinked at her, drowning in exhaustion. "She's OK?"

Daisy nodded. "She will be. How did you do that?"

"It was a lot easier than growing those seedlings," he admitted. "I just reversed that vibrating energy you were telling us about."

"Your powers are so strong. I could never have done that."

She guided Theo towards the door. Jason gave him a thumbs up, looking stricken. "You should sleep. I've cancelled training for the rest of the day, and you look like you need it. Thank you, Theodore. Really."

Theo stumbled up to bed, feeling like a massive fraud. He might have saved Beatriz, but he hadn't even been able to grow a simple seedling. His power was a lie. However strong they thought he was, soon they'd realize the truth.

On the bright side, at least Dalex wouldn't fire him now, especially if Daisy told the bosses that he was really powerful. Every day he managed to keep this job was another bill paid for Mum and Dad.

# I was the first person to get Greenfingers. Ask Me Anything.

Submitted by firstwithmagic

Hi, guys. I'm Gabrielle, the first person to grow plants. Happy to talk about my powers (or my work as a climate activist!)

Top 200 Comments

Sorted by: **BEST**

[-] lowriembw 456 points

Do you wish you'd never got powers?

[-] **firstwithmagic** 1232 points

Would not change a thing! I feel like I was always meant to have this power, it comes so naturally. Plus, I don't have to feel guilty about eating imported fruit out of season any more. Catch me chomping alllll the mangoes.

It's changed everything tho. I'm still revising for my A levels but all of my weekends are booked up with press events for basically the rest of my life.

[-] mattgalloway 4517 points

Which A levels are you taking?

[-] **firstwithmagic** 1232 points

Law, economics & English. I think I want to study politics at uni? Would love to overhaul our broken government system from the inside out. #dreambig

[-] cascodeddeangirl 345 points

What do your parents/bf/gf think of all this?

[-] **firstwithmagic** 1232 points

My parents think the powers are going to disappear after a while, so they're encouraging me to do as much as I can while I still have them. They think it'll be good experience for my cv lmao.

They were actually more confused by the activism stuff lol, but now that climate rebellion has opened groups in the US and ANZ and become a proper Thing they've started to realize how big it could grow. now they're fully on board.

(and I'm AroAce – no partner!)

[-] kasperj 456 points

Can you grow cannabis or coca? Not suggesting you're personally making cocaine, just wondering about the legal implications of drug production?

[-] **firstwithmagic** 1232 points

There is some kind of drugs boom happening right now, based on the emails I'm getting from people looking to hire me lol. But I've only ever done [redacted], so it's not really my area.

[-] stopbeefing 456 points

what's the best thing we can do to help the planet?

[-] **firstwithmagic** 1232 points

Vote. That's the only thing that will make a difference. Vote with your money too: make sure you & your fam's bank accounts/pensions/savings aren't going to companies making fossil fuel investments. Otherwise they're literally using your cash to kill earth.

Truth be told, no personal lifestyle changes can make a big difference to the planet. Everyone says that things like car-pooling and low-energy light bulbs help, but huge companies are pumping out endless pollutants each day. The "sustainability" movement is just a distraction from fixing the real problem in industry.

Not to sound bitter or anything. I'm super glad I started a conversation about using Greenfingers powers for sustainable packaging and bamboo clothing. But that zero-waste shit isn't going to change the laws that let companies pump out giga-tonnes of plastic and pollutants, is it?

[-] **rimahamid** 171 points
Clearly you need to become a space tycoon if you want to see progress, gabby. You'll get all the laws changed that you want then. See edgar warren's latest post:

> **Edgar Warren ✓ said:** had a lovely round of golf with **@POTUS** today! rad to see movement on space legislation. finally some common sense in congress, hurrah! 💯

[-] **silentsteph** 456 points
Hi gabby! i've been loving your posts about Climate Rebellion. do you think the GFs are going to affect the battle for climate action?

[-] **firstwithmagic** 1232 points
It could change everything. It's the best weapon we've received in the battle to fix the planet.

[-] **romysilversisalive** 456 points
"weapon"? "battle"? thanks for your service, soldier, but maybe tone down the fightin' talk? Not everything has to be about violence

[-] **firstwithmagic** 1232 points
I don't know about you, but I personally think the future happiness of every human on the planet is worth fighting for. Ymmv, whatever. But this is the biggest war humanity have ever faced.

I've tried doing things the legal way: protests, petitions, letters to government representatives, social media speeches, GETTING FAMOUS. None of it works. We need to be more disruptive to get real change, like the suffragettes, slavery abolitionists, anti-apartheid campaigners, feminists – these incredible people only made big changes by fighting for what they believed in.

1% of people are causing the most pollution on Earth. The other 99% of humanity needs to stop them, whatever it takes. Eat the rich.

[-] derpderpderp 456 points
Damn firstwithmagic didn't come here to play

> [-] **firstwithmagic** 1232 points
> Absolutely not. As soon as I understood
> the science, I started feeling guilty about
> everything. Should I be drinking from
> a bottle of water? Eating quinoa? Driving
> in a car? Buying a cheap dress? Using air-
> con? It feels like I'm bleeding Earth dry.
> But the truth is that if we really want to
> save the planet, we have to change the
> system from the ground up.

**Related threads**

▲ UPDATE: My (17M) GF boyfriend (16M) keeps giving me
▼ roses – how do I tell him I have allergies?

▲ My (40F) son (20M) walked into the forest and never came
back. His skin was mottled green and growing bark. He
was always lonely. I think he turned himself into a tree.
▼ Can I visit or should I give him space?

▲ Did I get scammed? I bought a human-grown wooden
bracelet from a Greenfingers artist that's supposed to
▼ cure arthritis but it hasn't made any difference

# Chapter 6

Hester decided to join the trainees for breakfast on the day after Beatriz's accident. It had been an absolute health and safety nightmare, but at least Beatriz was safe.

She loaded up a plate with sausage, biscuits and cream gravy from the breakfast buffet, adding a healthy spoonful of spinach and kale. She'd told the chef to include iron-rich foods with every meal. The trainees would probably need it after making plants by the gallon.

She hesitated over the drinks. Recently, she hadn't been able to stand drinking anything except spring water. She could taste the chemicals in everything else. Her power was repulsed by it.

She looked around at the scattered early risers, hoping that someone might make eye contact and invite her to join them. A group of the trainees were amusing themselves by growing helicopter seeds and seeing how long they could keep them in the air. Theodore Carthew was sitting alone in the corner, staring sullenly at a plate of maple fried chicken and waffles.

She still felt scorched with humiliation whenever she

remembered how he'd taken over her welcoming speech. She'd planned it so carefully, only for some British kid to ruin her big moment with some misguided argument. Nothing he'd said made a lick of sense.

How dare he challenge her, anyway? This Theodore was nothing – just a kid from England. She'd been taught everything there was to know about climate change for her speeches, and no one had ever accused her of getting anything wrong. She highly doubted he'd been taught as much as she had, at whatever public school he went to.

The cheek of him, implying that Dalex didn't care about the environment. Hester did her part – she used paper straws now, like everyone else! Dad's town cars were all electric! She had a reusable coffee cup! Carthew – "Theodore" didn't feel right, somehow – was even eating his breakfast with their recycled plastic cutlery.

She'd memorized all the recruitment reports for the trainees. Carthew was seventeen years old, of Bangladeshi British and Caucasian mixed ethnicity and from a small coastal town in England. He was an only child, and his power had a ten-out-of-ten strength rating. She vaguely remembered watching his interview on a conference call – he'd filled the entire room with seaweed, though his application said that he could create more than twenty types of plant.

His social media (@theocarth, "out here causing haddock", 32 followers/53 following) was filled with pictures of boats and stormy oceans. There was a shot of a stand full of cakes at a market, early in the morning or late at night. Another of him in a knitted hat and waxed jacket, thick eyebrows scrunched up against the wind on a clifftop, standing with a man who could be his dad. One with a small puppy in his lap, his head tipped back as he laughed. Annoying tousled brown hair.

The report hadn't said anything about his strong anti-oil views. Hester had made a note to check candidates for that during the next round of tests.

"You should go and sit with him," a voice said. Hester startled. She hadn't realized she'd been staring across the dining room like an idiot.

"Who?" she asked, pretending to choose a condiment.

Daisy smirked. "He's one of our strongest Greenfingers, even if he did yell at you. He seems quite quiet, actually. I think he was just a bit tired on that first day."

"I suppose he did save Beatriz," Hester said grudgingly. She would have to swallow her feelings and apologize. Dad would say that taking the higher ground was the sign of a good manager, or something.

Hester approached Carthew's table, taking a plate of freshly fried beignets as a conciliatory gesture.

"Is this seat taken?"

"Er." He blinked up at her.

That seemed to be all he was planning to say, so she sat down and pushed the sugared doughnuts towards him. "Thank you for saving Beatriz's life yesterday, Mr Carthew."

"Oh. How is she doing?"

"She's healing well." Beatriz had mainly seemed annoyed about failing out of the very first training activity.

"That's good," he said, looking wary.

She added, "I think we got off on the wrong foot, didn't we? Your thoughts in our first meeting were very valuable – you've certainly given me a lot to think about."

All of a sudden, he relaxed. Bingo.

"Well. Good!" He was actually smiling a bit now. It had been worth coming over here.

She wished she'd been able to see him using his powers on the security footage, but he'd been hidden from view of the cameras. Today she would have to make sure she got a look at his skills in person, to see what he did that was so impressive.

"I wanted to clarify that Dalex does have plans in place to fight climate change." Hester rubbed her wrists. Her skin was starting to crack with eczema from the constant plant growth. "But we don't need to stop using oil to control the crisis. We can simply capture carbon dioxide from the air and store it out of harm's way in underground rock."

"Right. Well, are you doing that, then?" Carthew asked.

She paused. "We need to wait until an efficient method has been developed by scientists."

"So you're *going* to fight the climate emergency … just not yet?" he asked slowly, chewing on a beignet. "What's the hold up?"

Dad always said that they had to wait until there was a technique that really worked. Apparently, before Hester was born he'd invested a lot of money in a climate intervention that had completely failed. It had been a waste of millions of dollars, and he'd been overly cautious ever since.

"It's a matter of risk management," Hester said, trying to find a way to articulate herself clearly. "We can't spend all our resources on something that might not work. We have to help the real people who are struggling right now, not hypothetical people who may suffer decades in the future."

She could live with a temperature increase. She *couldn't* live with knowing that hospitals might lose their power because Dalex stopped providing energy.

"Why do you talk like that?" Carthew asked suddenly.

Her cheeks went hot. "Like what?"

"I dunno. Like you're a business robot or something."

"What? No, I don't." Everything she'd said was perfectly sensible. Most of it was memorized from press documents!

Was he goading her? This was exactly what she'd been so scared of. That these – these *kids* – wouldn't understand her. Anyway, Carthew talked like he'd been dragged out of a backwater swamp.

"OK." He leaned back in his chair, folding his arms over his chest. "I get where you're coming from, but you know you're totally wrong, right? About all of that."

Hester snorted, but his expression was utterly serious. Aconite began wiggling around her ankles.

Carthew said, "We don't have time to waste planning what to do in the future. There's, like, two years max before everything suddenly gets real bad, real fast."

"That isn't right," she said uncertainly. The temperature increase was happening slowly. There was no reason to panic and destroy the civilization humanity had worked so hard to build. "You're trying to freak me out."

"I'm not trying to be a doomsayer, but you need to see how desperate the situation is. If you don't panic, then nothing is ever going to get done." Carthew sighed. "Climate disasters are happening all over the world *at this very second*. Ask any of the trainees! Alisha – that girl who keeps sneezing rose petals – lives in a small farming village in the Himalayan mountains. Their crops have failed for the last few years. It's too hot in summer now, so the lakes all dry up and they can't water the plants. Then in the rainy season, the monsoons wash away the crops because the trees have been cut down."

Hester gaped at him. There was something spiky working its way to the surface of her arm. A cactus; sharp and tender.

Carthew was still talking. "She thinks her power is a gift from the gods, because she filled the mountainside with new trees, and grew enough crops to feed her family for the rest of the year. And that's literally just one example! Ivy-hair Jason grew a currant bush barrier to stop a wildfire from destroying their house in Australia. Everyone here has been affected already."

Hester's brain was filled with hot white noise.

"There's no reason to think any of that is connected to

emissions," she said. Something had suckered to her stomach, tendrils tickling her ribs. "Wildfires and storms have always happened. At least Dalex can provide fuel to people trying to repair the damage."

Carthew traced a line over the table with his thumb. He seemed to be wrestling with himself about something. "My dad is a fisherman. So was my grandad, and my great-grandad. But the oceans are trashed. Our family boat actually got wrecked in a collision with one of your rigs. My dad only survived because I managed to save him using my power. A storm might not have the Dalex logo on, but that bulkhead definitely did."

Was that true? Surely he wouldn't be bold enough to make something like that up. No wonder he'd been so angry in their first meeting.

On auto-pilot, she recited part of her standard speech. "Dalex Energy has always worked hard to ensure our oil drilling rigs comply with the environmental safety levels required by government policies." Something feathery was gathering around her neck. She pulled up her blazer to hide it.

"I don't care about your safety policies, honestly. You've clearly sunk a lot of time and money into getting the laws changed however you like. I'm just saying, the world is already out of balance. Trying to fix things won't make it worse, even if it takes a bit of trial and error. You've got to give it a go."

Every retort she had seemed to evaporate into smoke. She'd started the conversation knowing that she was in the right. But somehow that had gone south fast.

Carthew looked *sorry* for her, of all the ridiculous things. "Dalex needs to put their money where their mouth is. Now, before it's too late. Every corporation and government on Earth is saying, *'It's not our responsibility! We don't have the expertise!'* But someone has to step up and actually do something."

Dad would have found a way to explain the truth, calmly and concisely. But all Hester managed to do was stare. Her anger seemed to have trickled away, leaving behind a dull kind of panic. How was she supposed to know how to respond to any of this? It wasn't like she'd researched this herself. She was just given the results to use.

She stood up, kicking a stray petunia under the table. She should have joined a debate team just to prepare for Theodore Carthew. "I have an appointment to get to, Carthew."

"You haven't eaten your breakfast."

None of this should feel as terrifying as it did, but somehow she couldn't stop a shivery fear from quaking through her. "I'm not hungry."

He was staring at her neck. She touched her collar, where liverwort curled against her skin. Yet again, she'd let her emotions run away with her. "Do you know how to stop it? It never goes away."

She'd never seen Carthew grow anything at all, even when he was really angry with her.

He frowned. "You're not doing that on purpose? I thought you were flexing to show off."

"No. It keeps going all the time, even when I'm asleep."

Carthew shook his head. "That's messed up."

Leaves curled against her tonsils. Mortified, she tried to swallow them down. A forgotten memory pulled itself out of her subconscious: sitting on the President's lap as a toddler at some fancy event. She'd thrown up her dessert all over her shirt. Dad had been mortified. He'd always hated mess.

"Can you help me?" she choked out, coughing up a shard of branch. Carthew's eyes were fixed on her throat, where the skin was swelling. She clasped a hand over it, holding her breath.

"Um…"

"Never mind." Trying to hold back tears of mortification, Hester fled the curious eyes of the trainees.

In the entrance hall, she clawed at her throat until she could breathe again. She felt more alone than ever, utterly deflated and lost.

It was strangely dark in the hallway, even though it was nearly seven a.m. The doorway was still dark – absolutely pitch-black. There was something wrong with the front door.

Glass crunched under her feet as she approached it. Tendrils of ivy were creeping underneath the door, sharp branches protruding through a smashed window.

She tried to remember when she'd last gone outside. There hadn't been anything unusual about the training centre when she'd arrived at work the day before. Overnight, something had changed.

# 33 EPIC THINGS GREENFINGERS DO WITH THEIR POWERS

**33** This girl who grew a rose for a promposal to her girl-friend during math class.

**32** The trio in Virginia who grew a 45m-tall oak tree around a controversial confederate statute that the state refused to remove. The trunk encases the statue completely.

**31** This Dublin borough's compost bins were turned into mini gardens on rubbish collection day, as the vegetable scraps blossomed into life along pavements throughout the city.

**30** Gabrielle "firstwithmagic" Ventura's bamboo grove stunt outside a TV news studio to protest climate erasure in the media. Ventura told journalists: "We do not have a free press in this country. The owners of our news sources have vested interests in the fossil fuel industry. They are actively concealing the danger of the climate emergency by not reporting on it. The government is allowing these individuals to lie to us in order to protect their investments. We demand change." You go, gal!

## Comments

**JeffwithaJ** Anyone else worried about the Greenfingers? Where is all this energy coming from? What if they're slowly killing themselves by using their own bodies to make plants? This kind of output can't last for ever.

**Harrietstoker** You're really going to glamourize the green-fingers without even mentioning the young girls in third world countries whose hands are being cut off to stop them growing plants? This isn't a fun gift for everyone. People are getting disowned and attacked in the streets. It's a curse for a lot of teenagers, and you should be reporting on that instead.

**Related News**

[Birdwatchers' Alliance Climate Fundraising Efforts Raise £10m After Disappearance of Local Migrating Birds for the First Spring on Record](#)

[Edgar Warren Escalates Alt-Right Online Feud; Dividing Platform, Alienating Supporters](#)

[Greenfingers Boy Uses Plant Vine to Crack Open ATM, Steals £50,000](#)

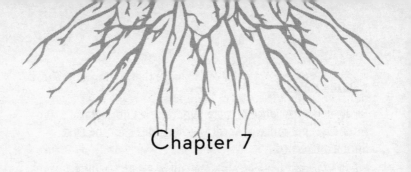

# Chapter 7

Late one night, Theo had come across something called Hanahaki Disease while trawling the depths of the internet in a bored stupor. It was a fake illness that made people cough up flower petals if they suffered from unrequited love. He'd been strangely captivated by the sketches of spurned lovers literally suffocating on rose petals. Their visible inner turmoil was always so delicate and beautiful.

That was how he felt about Hester Daleport. Her emotions were displayed so clearly through her powers. Plants frothed out of her skin constantly, in a dead giveaway of how upset she was. Her accent had got stronger too, with that southern American twang he'd only ever heard on TV.

He sighed. However obnoxious she was, he should probably check that she wasn't choking on plants.

He followed the trail of nettles she'd left on the carpet until he tracked Daleport to the front entrance.

"I can't get the door open," she said. There were dark, exhausted circles under her eyes. "There's something growing in the way."

"Is that a *tree*? How did you manage that, Daleport?" She'd only been out here for a few minutes.

"It wasn't me, I don't think."

Theo sighed. "Wait here then."

He moved down the corridor, but all the windows were blocked by an onslaught of leaves pressed against the glass. Three meeting rooms down, the floor was covered in smashed glass from a determined branch.

Theo knocked away the remaining shards and climbed onto the window ledge. He hit the ground in a painful semi-controlled fall, hissing as thorns caught on his clothes.

The first thing he noticed was the lack of heat. Every time he'd stepped outside in Texas, the humidity had wrapped itself around him like a stifling, sodden blanket. But now a cool, botanical freshness filled his lungs with green.

He was in a forest. A real, actual forest, where there had only been lawn and scrubland. The building had been swallowed by climbing plants that had crept up the brickwork and over the roof. The Edwardian greenhouses had exploded outwards, as tiny seedlings had grown into trees and forced their way through the glass.

Daleport couldn't have made this. An entire ecosystem had appeared overnight, with a canopy of oaks, elms and orange trees stretched above lush undergrowth. The group must have done it yesterday, when they'd all focused their powers in one area. It must have somehow created *this*. It looked like they had awoken everything lying dormant in the ground – every acorn and root and seed – as well as every plant in the greenhouses.

Theo hacked his way through the forest, breaking fresh ground through the thicket until he reached the front entrance. He knocked away some branches, then hung his weight off the thickest bough until it flexed. Daleport wedged open the door enough to squeeze through the gap.

"My lovely new training centre!" she cried, distraught. She trailed her fingers over the chaotic jumble of leaves swallowing the walls, dark and glimmering like oil droplets. "I don't understand. None of this was here earlier."

"I think it grew overnight," Theo said. "After the training session yesterday."

He touched the pale, papery flowers of a hellebore, shot through with the barest hint of pink. He could feel the life in it now. When he'd protected Beatriz from the other trainees' powers, something had unlocked for him. Saving her life had been the first time he'd felt really, truly grateful for his power. It was like he'd needed to accept it as a real part of him, something that he wouldn't want to get rid of even if he could, before it had come to life. Relaxing into the process had made all the difference in the world.

"Y'all did this? Together?" Daleport was subdued now – nothing like the argumentative, bossy girl from breakfast. The forest seemed to have cast a spell over her. *"How?"*

They walked through the metal arch of a collapsed greenhouse doorway. Theo jumped over a pair of shears shining beneath unfurled fan palms and wild ginger.

"I guess when we all use our powers at the same time, it makes them go further? Here, let me try something."

Theo focused on his power.

Now, he could visualize the form of it stretching into the natural world around him. He let that shimmery reach spread through the forest. The plants responded to him immediately. This was theirs, after all.

Theo projected his power as far as he could into the undergrowth. A trail of seaweed grew from his feet, stretching away for several metres until it stopped by the bright yellow flowers of a celandine. After that, he couldn't feel anything. He'd reached the limit of his expansion.

He held out a casual hand to Daleport. There was a tickle across his palm when their skin touched.

"Oh!" She jerked her hand away in surprise, then looked embarrassed. "Sorry. That startled me, is all. I can feel your power." She took his hand again.

"Daisy and Beatriz were playing around with this yesterday. I think they just –" Theo gestured vaguely at the seaweed, nestled next to the shining flowers – "used their powers at the same time?"

Daleport squinted. "Does it have to be seaweed?"

Heat shot up the back of his neck. "Yeah, I think that will make it easier to compare the distances."

To his relief, she shrugged and focused her power. She didn't have to coax it into responding, like he did. It jumped, ready and eager, from her fingertips.

There was a faint ripple of vibrations, as if she were thrumming the strings of a violin to find the right note. She was making adjustments so that her seaweed matched his. She did it naturally, as if was an extension of her body, or some innate skill she'd been born with.

Theo was so distracted that he forgot to grow anything himself. When he did, his power jumped far beyond the celandine. Seaweed burst out of an oak tree, dangling from its branches.

Daleport giggled. "What was *that*?"

"What do you mean?"

"Your power. You just opened the floodgates and let it flow. Like a full-throttle plant avalanche."

Theo swallowed. His power was a blunt hammer compared to her delicate violin. "Sorry. I guess I'm not as good at technique as you are."

"At least yours doesn't go wild when you're het up." She sighed.

Even now, he could tell that her power was trying to squeeze free. It was searching for any cracks in her composure. It must take so much focus trying to keep it all inside.

"Try pulling it back inside your body," he said, nudging against the edges of her power with his own. She flinched in surprise. "There – did you feel that? Mine isn't on the surface like that all the time. You need to rein it in until you need it."

Her eyes glazed as she seemed to wrestle with something

hidden inside herself. Theo felt her power weaken, retreating from the places where their skin touched. Daleport's forehead wrinkled, then her power rolled back out in a sudden wave. It tingled against his skin like a static shock.

"Dropped it," she explained, out of breath.

"Imagine there's, like, a jug in your chest," he suggested. "Pull it into the jug and close the lid."

After a few more tries, Daleport was pink with exertion, but her power seemed slightly less desperate to escape.

"I'll practise," she promised. "Thanks. I would never have come up with that on my own."

"That's the fun of us all working together, right? We can steal each other's tricks. Even if we do accidentally make forests."

Daleport nodded. "And the more we practise, the easier it will get. It already feels like I can understand it better. There's more nuance behind this whole thing than I realized at first." She eyed the seaweed they'd grown. "We'll have to try that again with three people and see if we can get even further."

"We might be able to do it without touching eventually," he said, then belatedly realized that they were still holding hands. He slipped his fingers free. "There's something about being around other Greenfingers. It's making my power stronger. I can feel all the little plants around me now."

Daleport's eyes widened. "Me too! It's way more intense than I was expecting it to be. If it keeps growing as we practise, that would be – wow. We could do so much with this."

"Yeah." He sighed. They could travel the world, turning wasteland into forests wherever they went. The ruined, sunburned fields of his uncle's farm; the ravaged quarries and mines in the hills; the concrete wasteland of the abandoned superstore in the next town. The thought of transforming it all into woodland was so delicious it made his mouth water.

Even though he'd ripped into Daleport about climate change, the secret truth was that he'd never actually done anything about it himself. He'd never even gone to a protest march like that famous girl, Gabrielle Ventura.

Normal life, with its money worries, schoolwork and part-time jobs, was exhausting enough without trying to personally fight the climate crisis too. That felt hypocritical now, after his self-righteous, judgemental speech to Daleport. Instead of wasting energy calling her out, he should be doing something to help the planet himself. This power was the most precious thing he'd ever been given.

"I should call a press conference," Daleport said sharply, out of nowhere.

"Wait – what?"

She huffed, as if the reason should be totally obvious to him. "Someone will notice this new forest by the end of the day. I need to make sure the news doesn't break as a scandal when they work out that Dalex is responsible." Daleport stroked the palest ivory blossoms of a trailing branch of jasmine. "This has to be intentional, rather than an error of judgement. We have to announce."

"Announce what?" he asked, baffled.

She ignored him, busy calling someone. "Get the *New York Times* here within an hour. And I want the best photographer you can find." She let out a gleeful little laugh. "We need pictures. Lots and lots of pictures!"

Daleport ducked between the trees, hurrying back to the driveway. She paced out the set-up. "The press can go here. I'll speak with the forest and training centre in the background."

She turned to Theo, a glint in her eye. "And you can give a demo of your powers to show them how the forest was grown." She wiggled her fingers, growing a dandelion from her thumb. "Do something impressive. Catch their attention."

*No.* No, no, no. He couldn't, not in front of an audience.

"Absolutely, Miss Daleport!" he said brightly, then gestured vaguely towards the forest and escaped. He tried not to have a panic attack.

What was he going to *do*? He couldn't just grow seaweed. That wouldn't impress any of them.

He weaved between silver-trunked rowan trees and verbena. Perhaps he could wrap a vine around his arm and pull it out of his sleeve like a magic trick? But that seemed too obvious.

Theo did what he always did when he was stressed and called his mum.

*"Jaan!"* she said. "How goes the adventuring in foreign parts? Is the training up to snuff?"

Theo paused, trying to work out how to fully encapsulate

the drama of the last two days – the full-volume Q&A during the welcoming speech; Beatriz's health and safety demo in lesson one; the overnight surprise refurbishment of their training centre; the non-consensual press conference. "It's fine."

She huffed out a laugh. "Informative as ever. What company are you working for? They were so secretive during the interview."

He paused. He couldn't tell her it was Dalex. She'd be furious. "Oh, it's just some small local company that builds wind turbines out here. You wouldn't have heard of them... Has Dad had any luck with interviews?"

He could hear the cat meowing in the background. She was probably sprawled out belly-up on the hearth of the kitchen fire. When Theo was little, he used to lie next to her in the mornings before school, eating his toast and feeding her butter.

Mum sighed. "Companies are only interested in hiring engineers to fix their automated equipment when it breaks down. Dad's not qualified for anything like that. Even though he's been fixing all the broken equipment on his boat alone for decades."

"He'll find something soon," Theo said firmly. "He's amazing. And I'll transfer my first pay cheque as soon as it lands in my account. I've got your back, OK?"

She was silent. "Thank you, Theo. I'm sorry to put all this on your shoulders."

By the time the driveway was filled with news vans, the forest was full of seaweed and the sun had come out in full force. Theo's stomach wrung itself into a tight knot. He suddenly felt self-conscious of his worn jeans and scuffed-up work boots.

"Welcome, everyone," Daleport said, clasping her hands in a stance that reminded Theo of a polished politician. It was hard to believe that she was the same age as him. There was barely any teenager left in her. She didn't even seem nervous.

"I've brought you here today to announce a new joint venture we're collaborating on with Warren Space."

Theo blinked. That wasn't what he'd expected her to say.

Pushing away an actual grin, Daleport said, "This woodland was grown by our new team of Greenfingers specialists, who are fine-tuning their skills to adjust certain plant characteristics to extract more ethanol and heat for biofuels on Mars. This exciting project heralds a new era in the space race."

She rubbed her necklace, pausing until the crowd's excitement went quiet.

Theo was stunned. *Mars?* No wonder Daleport was too busy to think about the climate crisis. She was working on a whole other planet. Was there a chance he might get to go to space?

"...Mr Carthew?"

Theo blinked. A sea of journalists and camera lenses had turned in his direction.

Oh, god. *He had to do a demo.*

In a panic, he stuck out his hand and grew a burst of seaweed. The reliable stream of green frills shot out like fireworks, spraying the gravel driveway.

The journalists looked at it in bemusement. He couldn't blame them. Daleport curled her hands up in a "keep going" gesture. He was sure he'd had a nightmare exactly like this – though he'd been naked then.

Flustered beyond intelligible thought, Theo copied the techniques he'd felt Daleport using. Plucking an imaginary violin, he pushed everything he had into trying to grow something new. Warm liquid dripped over his lips as a frond of purple seaweed appeared.

Theo wiped the blood from his nose, staring down at his pathetic offerings. A single, unimpressed photographer lifted his camera to take a photo. Daleport was glaring at him so hard that she might actually have an aneurysm.

"Water!" he burst out, then paused. "I mean – aquatic plants. We're growing them too. Alongside the land plants and biofuels, we're going to fill the water … on Mars … with life."

Daleport pressed her hand to his elbow. Her power tickled its way across his skin, and glorious, multicoloured plants burst from Theo's hands. He slumped, letting her take over. The journalists were snapping photos and asking questions now.

That had been an absolute disaster. But he'd survived.

# firstwithmagic vlog transcript

[Gabrielle stands in the rain, squinting at the camera.]

**Gabrielle:** Hi, guys! Last week I told you all about removing carbon from the atmosphere by burning plants and burying the biochar in the soil. That locks the carbon underground and enriches the soil. Today, we're going to look at another natural way of drawing down carbon from the air – a peat bog!

[Gabrielle walks towards a wide brown river surrounded by banks of rushes and grasses. A flock of pale birds flies away into a bank of ash trees.]

**Gabrielle:** Peat is made when plants grow on top of compressed layers of vegetation. Oxygen can't reach these compressed layers, so they don't rot. It's an amazing way to naturally pull carbon out of the atmosphere and keep it out, permanently. It usually takes decades, but Greenfingers can speed up the process in their local area.

[Gabrielle hops between tussocks of grass until she reaches a concrete trench, which cuts through a floodplain. A meandering stream drains down the gulley into the river.]

**Gabrielle:** This used to be a marsh, but the farmers dried out the land so that sheep could graze here. It destroyed the peatland, but we can bring it back.

[Gabrielle kneels down, growing a thick mass of plants inside the trench. The plants force the water to bubble up over the concrete and flood the ground. Native bushes spring up around her – huckleberries, cottonwood, wax myrtle and cattails.]

**Gabrielle:** You can do this yourself anywhere acidic and swampy near a river. You can even grow tea tree and orange trees on top of the peat afterwards.

[The plants keep growing, until there's a spongy layer of vegetation spreading across the newly flooded ground.]

**Gabrielle:** If you want to help save the planet through guerrilla gardening like this, go to the Climate Rebellion website today. We've got some big things in the works, and you <u>really</u> want to be involved. I promise.

**Offscreen voice:** HEY! What do you think you're doing?!

[Gabrielle winks, then blows a kiss to the camera. She pushes her way through a hole cut in a wire fence, picking up a pair of bolt cutters as she runs away.]

# Chapter 8

Edgar Warren called Hester the second the press conference ended. She tried to force down her rage at Carthew before she answered. Honestly, had he been *trying* to turn her into a laughing stock, or was it just natural talent? Her whole pitch had been based around how strong and powerful her Greenfingers team was, and he'd barely grown a single plant before he started *bleeding* everywhere!

"Mr Warren! Hello." She walked away into the forest, pulling a handful of stress-induced rosebay willowherb from her armpits.

She'd only rushed to hold the press conference out of some misplaced desire to prove that she could think for herself. Ever since Carthew had confronted her about climate change, she'd been plagued by doubt. What if she was good for nothing but trotting out memorized party lines?

This had been supposed to prove herself – to Carthew as much as to her father. But somehow, it had just made her feel more self-conscious.

"Ms Daleport. I saw you on CNN."

A zing went through Hester. It had been broadcast live! Now everyone would know that Dalex was ahead of the curve, with more intel on the Greenfingers than anyone else on the planet.

"It would have been nice for you to wait a bit longer before announcing the deal, though I guess you do have a bit of a flair for dramatics," Edgar said, voice dry and humourless.

She swallowed, dampening her throat. "Right. Apologies... But what better opportunity were we going to get to make an announcement? Photos of this forest will be the first things that come up when you search for Warren Space. People will think you're fixing to terraform Mars like that. You can't pay for that kind of publicity."

Mars had carbon dioxide and water in its atmosphere, but the carbon dioxide was locked away in permafrost. There was a theory that if the gas could be released by melting the ice, then plants could be grown outside. The plants would turn the carbon dioxide into oxygen, starting the process of giving Mars a breathable atmosphere.

It would take hundreds of years, but implying that Warren Space could do it with the Greenfingers would be a huge publicity boost. Everyone would rush to buy land.

Edgar clearly understood what she meant. He breathed heavily into the phone, then yielded. "That's true. But I suppose I'm a bit confused. As interesting as developing Mars will be, there are more immediate things that you could do on Earth. Up north, if you know what I mean?"

Hester paused. Up *north*? Was he talking about the pipeline they were trying to lay in Canada?

"Your father mentioned the new project to me," he continued, smooth as tar.

"Y-yes," she said, voice breaking on the words. "I know exactly what you mean."

Her mind was whirring. *What was he talking about?* How could Dalex use the Greenfingers there?

"It would have a high profit yield – more than we could get on Mars. Is there a way we can combine our efforts on both projects? Some of my atmospheric simulation software would be invaluable in mapping the global temperature variations."

Temperature! This must be something Dad was doing about the climate.

"We've very p-passionate about climate change," she agreed, trying desperately to speak clearly. Her childhood stutter always came back when she was stressed. "I'm sure that we could all work on this together."

Edgar hummed, sounding bemused. "Right. Hmm. I'd better talk to your father about this," he said, in an unflappably genial tone.

"Of course!" She needed time to get up to date on whatever was going on. This was why she wanted more involvement. It was no good for Dad to just give her some speeches and data to memorize for events. As soon as she had to actually work with someone else, the gaps in her knowledge became obvious immediately.

"In the meantime, have you grown anything in saltwater conditions yet?"

"Not yet," Hester said reluctantly. "Though I've grown algae and seaweed on land before."

"I'd be very interested to see if it's possible to create a water-based forest like you've done at your little training centre. Since, ah, there are oceans on Mars. It could be useful. Can you get a preliminary report to me by the end of next week?"

"Of course," she said, through a clenched jaw. "We can use my family yacht."

"I want daily updates," Edgar said, voice firm. "Do *not* speak to the press again without me, or we will have some serious issues." He hung up.

Hester wanted to scream. This was supposed to be *her* project, not Edgar's. His orders were jarring after she'd had a taste of calling the shots. How much of her life had been made up of people telling her where to go, what to do and say? She'd never even noticed until now. Yet Carthew had somehow called her on it within minutes of meeting her.

**Hester:** just got off the phone with edgar warren. He seems to think there's a use for greenfingers in the north – apparently his temperature atmospheric software from Mars could be used for something you discussed with him? Not sure what he's referring to, but I played along

**Dad:** I know exactly what he wants – I'll deal with it. Will update you when we next meet in person; it's confidential

**Hester:** right. Great. Is it OK if I take the trainees out for a session on the yacht next week?

**Dad:** should be fine.

**Hester:** Did you see my press conference?

**Dad:** brilliant work as usual – you were born to be on screen, princess.

**Hester:** I wrote the speech too!

**Dad:** it was fine. V comprehensive.

**Hester:** thanks.

**Hester:** also, did a fishing boat hit one of our rigs in the North Sea?

**Dad:** oh, that. our lawyers squared everything away. Blamed it on the skipper. G2G – my nutritionist is giving me a vitamin injection.

Ignoring the spiralling trails of red columbine she'd left on the forest floor, Hester went to find Carthew. If anyone was going to run a session on aquatic plants, it might as well be Mr Seaweed.

Practising using her powers with him had felt like catching lightning in a bottle. It had been uncomfortably invasive at first, feeling his energy touch hers. But the discomfort had quickly turned into a grounding calm. Her worries and concerns had seemed irrelevant compared to the slow, steady march of nature.

She wanted to try that again, and again, and again, until peace flooded every corner of her brain. In the long term, none of her work emails or forms or meetings actually mattered. Not when this little grove of plants was flourishing. It was an undeniable sign that she could do something good – that she didn't destroy everything she touched. Here, she could do things right.

Carthew was hacking away the plants blocking the entrance to the training centre.

Feeling oddly nervous, she asked, "Mr Carthew, considering the strength of your power and your expertise in growing aquatic plants, I'd be delighted if you could run a training session for us."

"Are you ... sure?" he asked doubtfully. "Because your words and your voice aren't matching up right now."

"You were right, at breakfast," she admitted. "Dalex isn't doing enough for the climate. I want to see if there's anything we can do to improve the ecosystem at sea by using my family yacht."

It felt good to form her own opinion instead of quoting back some memorized line. She'd always thought of herself as a "business" person, not a "science" one. That stuff bored her, especially since everything moved so fast at Dalex. Dad was always taking her to new places and giving her exciting things to do – things that would actually shape the future of the company. Learning about molecules and weather patterns had seemed like a waste of time in comparison.

It wasn't like she needed to reinvent the atom. Dad had already defined their official stance on the climate years ago.

But perhaps there were some things she could do that would help to work towards their goals.

Carthew's expression opened up, pleasure blossoming from surprise. "Oh. All right." He sounded nervous. "Do I, er, get a raise for teaching?"

"Five per cent."

"Thirty-five," he countered, clearly expecting to be knocked back immediately.

Just to see if she could catch him off-guard, she said, "Done."

It wasn't like Dalex was short of money – and the trainees were already a steal. They paid their *interns* more.

Carthew was gratifyingly surprised. "Then … yes."

They shook hands, both a little unwillingly. Were they actually in a truce? If she'd known all it would take was a salary increase, she'd have done that at breakfast and saved them both a lot of hassle.

"By the way, you don't actually talk like a robot," he added, looking ashamed. "I shouldn't have said that."

She paused. "It's all right. I probably do sound a bit corporate. Actually—" Taking a deep breath, she said, "I don't really know many people our age. I spend most of my time in meetings."

Now they weren't fighting, she didn't even know what to say to him. She should talk about video games or skateboarding or something. Those were things that normal teenagers liked, right? Her main hobby was trading on the stock exchange.

When she'd turned eighteen, Mom had given her a million dollars to invest in futures. She'd taught Hester all her tricks for handling investments.

Carthew probably didn't have a trading account on the stock market. And if he did, it would be the London Stock Exchange anyway, so they wouldn't even be able to share tips. Maybe she could ask about how he'd invested his, um, pocket money? That could be fun...

"You're always working, then?" he asked.

Hester was perplexed. "What else would I be doing?"

There was a long pause. The words reverberated around her, unbelievably lame and depressing. She was about to invent some extraordinary fake hobby like *scuba diving* out of sheer humiliation when he replied, "I could never do your job. It blows my mind a bit. You're, like, a CEO. At eighteen."

"Just an executive, actually." She wished she felt like one right now, instead of a speech-giving automaton. "You get used to it. Anyway, I'll try to get our yacht for a session early next week, then. Thank you, Mr Carthew."

"Call me Theo," he said, smiling.

"Oh. I'm Hester."

She could get used to working with Theo like this. They made a good team. Maybe this would work after all.

Daisy had kept the trainees occupied during the press conference with a quiz on lignin growth in plants. When they realized that they'd grown an entire forest overnight, chaos ensued. Hester couldn't have wrangled them into order even if she'd wanted to.

"Oh my god!" Daisy yelled, diving into the broken skeleton of a greenhouse. "This is awesome!"

"I'm getting my drone," Binh said, already running back inside. "This is going to make such a good urban exploration video."

"Hester! Do you know if there are any power tools around?" Theo asked, cheeks pink with excitement. "Jason wants to make a treehouse! He – I mean, they – think that we can get it right up in the treetops!"

Hester grinned. "I think we can scrounge something up."

"Are you sure you won't have another nosebleed?" Icaro teased Theo, holding up a still from the press conference recording, which was already trending online.

Theo rolled his eyes. "Laugh it up."

"I've never had a nosebleed," Zen said dreamily. "I've always wanted one. It looks so cool."

Hester wondered if teenagers were always like this, or if she'd somehow managed to hire a group of oddballs.

Alisha shrieked from somewhere deep in the forest. *"Look, I made a vine swing!"*

Forget health and safety, or training plans, or answering the growing mountain of messages in her inbox. She could afford to spend some time making friends. This was something she'd long since given up on ever having. Her powers had finally given her something in common with people her own age. Whatever Dad thought of the plants, she was proud to have Greenfingers. The powers had chosen her, for whatever reason. She couldn't waste time being ungrateful for such a wonderful gift, not when it was already making her life undeniably better.

**#greenfingers**

**Top**   Latest   People   Photos   Videos

**Clove Sutcliffe** Check out my band page! My music
is made entirely with **#greenfingers** grown plants.
Bamboo flute + gourd drum + reed violin strings. Epic.

**The Parody Times** Why You Should Forget Men and
Grow Your Own Gourd Boyfriend **#greenfingers**

**Hesterdaleport** ✓ salty breezes & green seas.
having a fun day with the new **@dalex #greenfingers**
group practising our skills on the yacht today!

**Daily** ♌ **Leo Horoscope** No negative vibes
this week, as **#greenfingers** will see botanical
success in the romance department. Don't
hesitate to give your fave floral offering to anyone
who flashes you a smile. Roses are a sign of
tenderness; be wary of the challenge of lilies.

# Chapter 9

Theo dived off the platform at the back of the yacht, shooting deep through the azure-blue water. They were anchored off the coast in a shallow bay where the water was sheltered from the wind. The sea was just on the right side of refreshingly cold.

It had been a week since they'd grown the forest through their training centre, and the group were starting to really get to grips with their powers. They'd been practising Daisy's activities in a field in the middle of nowhere instead, so their explosions of nature didn't get them into trouble. They'd managed to grow a whole field of bamboo in only a few minutes, which the Dalex accountants had been very excited about. The news that they might get to go into space had made them all even more determined to work hard.

Theo had made a few friends too. Jason was a gamer, so they'd hauled a generator out to their treehouse so they could play together in the evenings. From high in the treetops, the trainees competed to see who could grow the brightest flowers, until poppies and sunlight-yellow dandelions were scattered like pastel fripperies through the undergrowth.

Hester seemed to spend most of her time in meetings, but she checked in on the training at least once a day. She sometimes even joined in with their antics in the evenings, though she had yet to try the vine swing.

So far, Theo had managed to hide the inadequacies of his own power, if only just. It was a tiresome, familiar feeling, to be slower than everyone else in his class. Like his dyslexia, his power was another thing to feel self-conscious about and try to hide. Hopefully today he'd be able to talk everyone through the exercise without having to demonstrate anything himself.

When Jason did a somersault dive, Theo hollered and called, "Good one!"

On deck, Hester said, "Form an orderly line! If you don't want to dive in, you can climb down the ladder onto the raft."

Theo couldn't help sizing up the yacht. The fittings were solid walnut, and even the curtains were woven silk. He still couldn't wrap his head around the fact that Hester's resources were, almost literally, infinite. Whatever she wanted – whatever they needed – she could get it.

"Eyyy, mate!" Theo catcalled as Daisy did an handstand off the edge of the board.

Meanwhile, Hester tried to stop Icaro diving in wearing sunglasses and a baseball cap.

"Can we do that again?" Binh asked eagerly, as Hester dived neatly into the water, wearing a dark-red halterneck swimming costume. They were all clinging onto a raft as the waves swelled around them. Theo was trying very hard not to think about the last time he'd been out at sea.

"Yeah, go wild!" Theo said, and then caught Hester's eye. She shook her head at him minutely. Damp curls of hair were stuck to her neck.

"Actually, better not," he corrected. "All right. Hi. I'm going to be taking the lead for our session today. As you've probably guessed, we're going to do some marine stuff. You could say it's going to be … *jaw*some!"

There was a long silence.

Theo laughed awkwardly. He should probably stop making jokes anyway. Even if they were kind of friends now, he couldn't mess around with the group when he was supposed to be leading the session. Daisy and Hester always behaved professionally.

He cleared his throat. "Um – hands up if you can grow water plants."

Hester raised her hand, along with two other trainees.

Icaro said, "I can grow water lilies."

"I made a mangrove tree once," Zen said.

"Wow, nice." Theo flicked away a floating plastic bottle, which had drifted against his shoulder. The water had looked so clean from the boat, but there was a murky film of rubbish on the surface. "That's perfect. So, we're going to start by expanding our powers in the area around us, like we've been practising. You've all been doing really well at projecting on land, and the ocean is full of plants. Apparently kelp is great for making biofuels. If we can find a way to grow a low-lignin version without fertilizers, it'll be massive. So to start with, let's see what we can find. There are tiny plants in the water around us – try and connect with them."

Their powers had come a long way over the last few weeks. At first, he'd only been able to grow seaweed from his skin. Now, his power was like an invisible bubble around him, which he could stretch out to envelop the nearby plant life. If they kept developing their skills together, what would they be able to do after a few months?

Theo extended his senses, searching for the familiar quivering response that came from nearby seaweed. To his relief, it worked. Sometimes, it felt like the more anxious he felt, the more his power misbehaved. If he freaked out, he stopped being able to grow anything at all, even seaweed, as if he needed to embrace and welcome it before the plants would come.

He fell into a hazy relaxed state as the power sang through his body. Connecting with the plants in a bubble around him had felt invasive at first, but now it was nice to be part of something greater than himself. He'd never felt so connected to Earth, or aware of the other things living around him.

Ever since their forest had grown, Theo had been daydreaming about the wonderful wildlife havens the Greenfingers could make if they worked together. Mum had messaged him in excitement a few days ago, saying that Dalex had changed their mind and were paying the damages for the boat. It was a huge relief. For the first time in a long time, he had a chance to plan further ahead than the bills due at the end of the month. He could think about doing something to help the environment.

He'd been listening to a podcast from an account called *firstwithmagic*, which was full of tips on how Greenfingers could use their powers to help fight the climate crisis. There were loads of people already trying to make a difference.

It was a lot easier to listen to someone discussing their ideas than trying to read a news article about climate change. He always found those kinds of websites too intimidating, with big chunks of text that jumped out of order however much he adjusted the display. But he wanted to learn more about the Greenfingers protestors.

Theo turned his attention back to the group. "Now, I'm going to grow seaweed as far away from my body as I can. Then Hester will take my hand and do the same. We're going to keep adding people to the chain, and see how far we can project our powers."

Theo extended his senses, tapping into the life in the water around him again. Focusing hard, he managed to grow a stream of seaweed in front of him. Then he hit the wall where everything dropped away into blackness and he couldn't feel the plant life any more.

He felt Hester's fingertips touch his. Just like that, the wall disappeared. He could sense the yacht now. It was a sharp blank edge where the helm cut into his circle of awareness.

When Daisy took his other hand, his awareness ballooned again. Each time someone joined the chain, their senses extended further and further. Everyone's power felt slightly different, but somehow they all wove together, linking up their unique vibrations into some kind of strange hive mind.

Joy filled Theo's chest. He was so lucky to be here, with Hester and the others. He'd never felt like part of a team before. It calmed an anxious, insecure part of his brain that he hadn't even realized existed. He wasn't an outsider here, like he'd always been when he was working on Dad's boat. He was part of this.

By the time all of the trainees were holding hands, Theo's sensory awareness had stretched so far that he could feel the cold silt of the ocean floor. Fewer than twenty people, and they could reach all that way.

"I can feel the land over here," Binh said.

There was a tug at their web of powers, as he directed their attention to the sharp rock of the cliff-face along the coastline. The plant life was richer there, with masses of thick seaweed clinging to the rocks. Theo trickled his senses along the shoreline.

"Who's that?" Theo asked, alert, just as Daisy yelled, "There's a whale!"

She pointed out a dark void moving through the outskirts of their bubble. Theo was so attuned to the vibrations of the plants that he could actually feel the soft throb of its song as it dived down to the depths.

"Guys, that's not one of you, right? That – twiddly kind of power?" Theo copied Binh's move, nudging their collective attention back towards the shoreline. There was something there. It was interested in them, somehow.

"It's someone on the land, Theo!" Hester said, following the line of his power. "Another Greenfingers. They must be able to feel our bubble."

"There's no way we can reach that far," Theo said in disbelief.

"Let's try communicating with them," Hester suggested.

"What! No!"

She rolled her eyes at him, taking control. She increased and decreased the intensity of their powers until it was almost like she was waving at the person on the shoreline. When she stopped, there was a moment's pause, and then the pattern came throbbing back towards them.

"How is that possible?" Theo gasped.

"I need to get more recruits if it makes this much of a difference to our strength," Hester said, awed. "We should be doing this with hundreds of you!"

"Are we going to have to share rooms?" Jason sounded dismayed.

They lost control of the bubble then. It broke apart as everyone laughed, leaving Theo with nothing but his own power. It was oddly cold and lonely. There was something addictive about the electrical cloud of energy they created together.

Rubbing his arms for warmth, he tried to remember what he'd planned with Daisy. She'd helped him come up with a training plan to stretch their powers in new ways. So far, everything had gone as they'd anticipated. It was a lot less scary than he'd thought it would be, to lead the activity. Though maybe that was just because he was friends with them all.

"Great work," he said. "Next up, I want you to each choose a plant. See if you can focus your attention on that one species. Isolate its frequency from the others. This is the important bit. I reckon this is what went so wrong when we made the forest. We were all trying so hard to grow our seedlings that we made all the plants around us grow too. The main goal today is to try and avoid that."

"They all kind of blend together," Jason said, frowning down at a bristling mermaid's fan. "I can't tell them apart."

Theo stalled for time, utterly stumped. He couldn't tell them apart either, except the seaweed. How was he supposed to teach the group something that he couldn't do himself? Even when he'd sensed Hester fine-tuning her seaweed in the forest, he hadn't been able to feel any difference between the plants.

Hester squinted at him.

Before Theo could answer, Alisha said, "Picture the plant in your mind, and try to … project an image of it. It'll kind of respond to you when it recognizes itself."

Binh said, "I think of it like music scales. When you play an instrument, you can sing in harmony with the music, right? That's what you need to do. Find the note the plant responds to, and then harmonize with it."

Theo cleared his throat, pretending that explanation had made total sense, instead of propelling him deeper into an existential crisis. "Exactly. That's, er, just what I was going to say. There are lots of different ways to start growing other plants. Try and find the method that works for you."

Hester's eyes were fixed on him. "Why don't you demonstrate for us, Theo? Grow something. Not seaweed – something else."

Panicked, he tilted his head towards the deck. "I will do, but guiding that bubble wiped me out a bit, actually. I'm going to nip to the loo and grab an energy drink. I'll be right back."

He lunged towards the ladder, but Hester swam after him. She planted herself staunchly in his path, immovable as asphalt. "Come on, let's see you make us something. It's what I'm paying you for, after all."

The trainees were silent, straining to listen in over the swell of the waves.

Theo wiped sweat off his forehead. "It's not that – " he stumbled over his words – "there just needs to be – maybe later, when—"

"Theo," Hester said, looking annoyed now. "Do you want to explain what's going on?"

"Seaweed is all I can grow!" he admitted, feeling utterly miserable. "I've tried, but it's the only thing that comes out, tons and tons of it. I don't understand how it can be so easy but I can't produce anything else."

"But your scores are off the charts," she said, flabbergasted. Sprigs of rosemary were growing in her eyebrows. "Your power is so strong – I can feel it."

"I think I just need more practice, Hester," Theo said, with all the conviction of a worm. "I'll get there. Besides, seaweed is really good for the planet," he added desperately. "Seaweed is a carbon sink, pulling the gas out of the atmosphere. It's something really useful we could do with our powers."

Her expression did something strange then – confusion flashed over her features, before she carefully forced them blank.

"You're just trying to keep us working with seaweed because it's easy for you. But you can't use climate change as an excuse to stay in your comfort zone. Not at the detriment of Dalex's real work on biofuels."

"'Real work'? How is saving the planet not *real work*?" he asked.

"You're a hypocrite, Carthew. You pretend to be so righteous and perfect, but your family are *fishermen*. That's just as bad for the planet, isn't it? There's overfishing and bycatch and plastic net waste. You can't accuse *me* of destroying the planet when you're perfectly happy for your own family to benefit from it too."

She was back to calling him Carthew, then. Their truce was clearly over. "You think I don't know that? This whole planet is *screwed*. It's impossible to do anything without hurting someone, somewhere. But you're not even interested in trying to stop that."

She paused. "It's not really my place to get involved in little things like that when I have real skills I can use elsewhere. At least I'm honest about what I can achieve, unlike you."

Coldness leached through him. She was absolutely unbearable. How had he let himself get carried away by her damp hair and red swimsuit? Just because she was good at spinning a story didn't mean that there was anything real behind the performance.

"You have all the resources in the world," Theo snarled, "you just don't want to use them. Bugger off, Daleport."

"Fine, Carthew," she spat back. Her careful armour was flaking away. "Pitch another hissy fit. I hope you know how easily replaceable you are. At least I can actually do *my* job. Maybe come back when you can do yours?"

With that, she swam over to the yacht ladder and pulled herself onto the deck, not looking back.

Well, fine. If she wanted to sulk, that gave him more time to spend teaching the trainees. He could make a whole kelp forest without her permission. Even if it was done out of spite, it still counted.

# All Hail Gabrielle

## Meet the seventeen year old who is spearheading the Climate Rebellion movement

Three months ago, Gabrielle Ventura unknowingly heralded a new era of human possibility. Now firmly entrenched as a household name, Ventura is using her platform to campaign for green energy.

As with most celebrities of her generation, her chosen medium is social media. Her account is a call to arms: the comments call her the "Joan of Arc of the climate struggle", "asexual queen", and claim to "stan her".

In one of her recent uploads, she pulls a pondweed-covered plastic packing crate out of a river using a makeshift net made of reeds. A group of exhausted but beaming teens sits on the riverbank, surrounded by bulging bin bags. She touches palms with another teen and vines tangle their fingers together in the new elite greeting used among <u>Greenfingers</u>. Both girls display tropical flowers in their hair, in an effortless demo of the latest big trend to sweep the streets. Florists have reported a boost in business as non-<u>Greenfingers</u> race to keep up with the fashion.

Ventura represents the intergenerational divide spanning the climate war. She's the perfect person to guide the global army of activists now listening to every word she says.

Climate Rebellion started out as a small school strikes group in the UK, and has grown into a massive international organization with thousands of members. But as the movement grows, their techniques have shifted from passive protests to slightly more radical approaches criticized as eco-terrorism. There are even petitions campaigning for Ventura's conviction. Should the group stick to making reusable coffee cups?

Ventura says, "You would have forgotten my name by now if I wasn't taking these risks. I'm going to do whatever it takes to keep climate change in the news. I was campaigning long before my powers appeared, and I'll keep going even if they disappear."

Whatever the public think of Ventura, her protests continue unimpeded. In an upload from yesterday, Ventura covers a landfill in wildflowers and weeds. She openly admits to breaking into the site to seed-bomb the towering hills of rubbish with clover, vetch and cowpeas – plants that regenerate toxic topsoil.

A hyper-speed bird's-eye view of the landfill site shows patches of bright green appear among the grey-brown dirt. Mustard and sorghum grow among the rubbish, as stray tomato seeds and carrot peelings from household waste burst into violent life everywhere. But beneath the plants, the plastic from food containers and bulging bin bags remains indestructible.

In fact, an intrepid explorer who tried to walk to the summit of the new hill fell almost thirty metres through the collapsing heap, when the rotting matter beneath the turf failed to support his weight. The man had to be airlifted to safety.

Ventura stands firm. "What's the alternative here? Burying this plastic below the ground is still better than burning it in incinerators. That adds more carbon and pollutants to the atmosphere. This way, the plastics are buried underground like the oil they were made from. The only way to actually get rid of landfill sites is by restricting companies who create these materials."

Compostable plastics would turn landfill sites like this into wildlife havens instead of eternal wastelands. Her goal is to draw attention to the real issues at hand – the need for policy changes on an international level. It seems to be working: her updates consistently rack up comments and news articles within seconds of posting.

When asked if she's worried about being arrested, Ventura laughs in my face. "That's the aim. We're trying to make history here. I don't care about whether this goes on my public record. Any employer or university that would hold this against me isn't the place for me. I'd turn around and ask them why their company wasn't doing the same thing."

What's next for Ventura? She's currently in the States, advising on climate activism for off-shoot group Generation <u>Greenfingers</u> (she has offset the carbon from her flight). She will be speaking to the UN next week too. The world is her oyster, it seems.

In a time when every company in the world seems to be recruiting a specialized Greenfingers group for everything from food and plastics manufacture to architecture, her skills will be in high demand. We should all keep an eye on Gabrielle Ventura. She's definitely keeping one on us.

### Related News

<u>TV Show Loch & Ness Introduces Greenfingers Bullying Storyline</u>

<u>Woman Stranded with Baby on Sarasota Apartment Roof Saved from Rising Floods by Greenfingers Vine Ladder</u>

<u>"I'm chuffed to bits!": Water Shortages Cause Stock Prices to Rise, Creates Instant Millionaire Investors</u>

<u>Edgar Warren Posts Cryptic Mechanical Equation Online After Political Debate; Baffles Followers</u>

# Chapter 10

Once, when she was little, Hester had accidentally been left behind when her parents went on a trip. They'd assumed that she was sitting quietly in the back seat of the car. It had taken them an hour to notice she wasn't there. All the while, she had been sitting on the edge of the fountain outside their house, sobbing. That was how she felt now, watching Theo – *Carthew* – and the trainees turn the water green with plants without her.

Their little plant oasis was a wildlife haven in the blue ocean, with feathery clouds of green algae like latte foam. Clumps of seagrass and solid dark-green disks were clustered together like grapes. Deep-toothed fans of purple curled around branching blades and dead man's fingers.

Despite everything, it was a satisfying sight. Since their scheme had been launched, three other energy companies had announced Greenfingers projects too. Hester was trying not to stress about whether they might patent some amazing Greenfingers biomatter processing technique before she had a chance. Their team already worked so well together, surely no one else would catch up. This was the only group being run by an actual Greenfingers, after all.

Hester downed a frozen margarita in three gulps. It had been fun, laughing and swimming around with the trainees. But there was no way she could rejoin them now. Not after they'd watched her fight with Carthew yet again.

He was wrong. She cared about climate change; of course she did. But Hester wanted to change the world in big, permanent ways: build a rocket, not scoop water out of a sinking ship. She could save millions – billions – more lives by working with Dalex than she could by rewilding some water. That was such small beans that it wasn't worth exerting time and energy on. Wasn't it? She didn't know any more.

It felt like she'd been caught up in a wrestling match with herself for the past week. She kept catching herself making assumptions about the climate, but when she tried to work out where she'd got the idea from, there was nothing there. She'd never had the chance to research the science behind Dalex's policies, and that inconvenient gap in her knowledge kept tripping her up.

Well, she had plenty of time now. She would back up her views with evidence and prove Carthew wrong. He'd have to apologize then.

On her phone, she searched furiously for the most recent climate data. She distinctly remembered an article that she quoted in one of her Dalex speeches, which said there was scientific uncertainty in how much the planet's temperature would rise. Another had explained why a temperature rise wouldn't be dangerous. It wasn't as clear-cut as Carthew was trying to make out.

But she couldn't find any of those journal publications now, whatever search terms she used. There were just disputes about old theories on forum sites, and a few blog posts on the official Dalex website. She couldn't exactly hand one of those to Carthew. He'd laugh in her face.

Who did he think he was, anyway? He'd glared at her like she was a monster instead of an innocent eighteen-year-old girl. He was the one who'd been lying to her since the day they'd met; pretending he was so much better than her while hiding his own failure.

The top search results all said that Earth's temperature was rising fast, dangerously fast. But what about the science Hester's speeches were based on? She searched her email inbox, downloading the notes the PR team had sent over before a recent function. She reread them, looking for the bit she remembered.

There.

Scientific uncertainties continue to limit our ability to make objective, quantitative determinations regarding the effects of temperature rises on global climate systems.

There it was in clear English, taken from a real journal publication written by a scientist with a PhD. Carthew could hardly argue with that, could he?

Hester ate a skewer of fresh pineapple, already imagining Carthew's contrite apology. The annoying thing was, they'd *almost* become friends. For one brief, naive moment she'd been convinced that she'd found a partner. Carthew could have been the person she'd been waiting for. Someone to confide in and work alongside, so she wasn't so lonely.

Well, it was his loss. If he was more interested in making a few acres a bit greener, then he could "bugger off" and do that.

She scrolled through the journal article. There was something written under the scientist's name, in a smaller font. *Study funded by Dalex Energy.*

This was a good thing, wasn't it? It meant that the firm was donating money for research. Dad had always been interested in the science.

Still – she couldn't exactly send Carthew a scientific paper that had Dalex's name splashed all over it. It looked a little strange. She'd have to find other studies that were funded by university grants instead of energy companies.

Hester googled the scientist, then nearly dropped her tablet in shock.

**Fraudulent Science Study Climate Science Debunked**

**Energy Company Spreads Misinformation Through Biased Research**

**Misuse of Scientific Data Used by Dalex to Spread Fake News**

What?

Hester wiped goosegrass from her forehead, sticky leaves clinging to her skin. It kept growing as she read, until she was surrounded by weeds.

> Dalex Energy has been accused of intentionally manufacturing three decades of controversy and confusion about climate science through ad campaigns, press releases and fake scientific studies.
>
> Before the millennium, Anthony Daleport gave the President a report signed by "thousands of scientists" objecting to the greenhouse gas theory – but all of these signatures were fake.
>
> "I'm not saying I disagree with the science, but I'm not saying I agree with it either. I need more information to be sure," Daleport has said in many interviews over the years. Since the 1970s, the company has ignored the many peer-reviewed studies that confirm the greenhouse effect.
>
> Dalex has opposed government research into electric cars and forged letters to congress from members of the public, asking for cheaper electricity to be prioritised above green energy. They've even paid dodgy scientists to claim that burning oil might actually be able to stop climate change.

It was like her brain was leaking. How could this be true? Had Dad really hidden the truth on purpose so that Dalex could carry on selling fossil fuels?

Tears dripped onto her tablet. Was everything she thought she knew a lie? Maybe these dodgy scientists had just told Dad what they thought he wanted to hear, because he was paying their bills. Dad would have accepted their expertise.

When she explained the truth, he would be horrified. It

wasn't too late to fix this whole misunderstanding.

How had she let her goals become more important than the entire planet? Becoming CEO felt irrelevant in the face of their future.

The trainees were clambering out of the water. Hester shook herself. She didn't want them to see her upset.

As the yacht headed back to land, the trainees stretched out on the deckchairs, eating freshly cut oranges and drinking iced tea. They were all giggly and excited, playing a game where they sent fronds of fern and pampas grass creeping across the deck to tangle around each other's ankles. Icaro managed to grow an enormous bright sunflower above Daisy's head before she noticed.

Jason was waving their nails at Binh, which had turned into bark during the training session.

"Don't!" Binh screeched, when they tried to tickle him with their nails. "That's gross!"

"Don't body shame me," Jason said.

Hester watched them play from somewhere cold and distant. Everything had changed so quickly. Only an hour before, she'd been one of the group, with friends her own age. Now, there was a chasm separating her from them.

She needed to apologize to Carthew when they were back at the training centre. There was no need to bother him here. They were nearly at the harbour anyway.

Hester jolted. Wait – they were nearly at the port. So why was the water around them still green? The yacht had been anchored in a cove several miles away, but the water here was a deep emerald too.

Summoning her courage, she walked over to Carthew. His frown turned her to ice.

"I know you're mad at me," she forced out. "But look at the water."

He was so shocked that he completely forgot to be angry.

"It's spreading," he said, leaning over the railing to peer into the water. "How is that possible?"

"It must be the ocean currents, right?" she said. "Unless it's doing the same thing that the forest did. Still growing, even after we've stopped using our powers."

"It's not seaweed, though," he said.

She breathed in deeply, trying to identity the vibrations. "It's plankton."

The tiny algae were so small that usually you couldn't even see them. A little bit of Greenfingers power seemed to have made them multiply infinitely. Her chest felt tight.

Carthew's eyes widened. "An algae bloom? That's OK, right?"

Her stomach clenched. The bloom stretched all the way to the horizon. This wasn't the same as turning a few acres of land into woodland. They'd affected miles of ocean.

"Plants feeds off carbon dioxide, don't they? They take it out of the atmosphere. So the more plants, the better it is for the planet."

Relieved, he nodded. "Right! This is great, then!"

A chill ran through her. She kept hoping they'd reach the

edge of the murky bloom, but as they drew up to land, wave after wave of the plankton followed them.

"Yeah," she repeated numbly. "Great."

There was a putrid smell coming off the murky water, as the waves washed green goo onto the pier.

"Oh, god," Carthew said. "I feel sick."

The rest of the group had noticed now. Their laughter fell away as everyone lined up along the railings to watch the flood of algae. A bird caught in the slime wriggled desperately to get free.

As they drew nearer to the dock, a man started waving at them from a small tourist boat. "My propeller is tangled! Can you tow me to shore?"

Carthew climbed down the ladder, unravelling a rope from the rear of the yacht. He threw the end over to him.

"It came out of nowhere," the man said in shock, once he'd tied the rope to his boat. "I've never seen anything like it."

Hester was silent. How could she admit that this was their fault?

They had to climb over a mass of fetid slime to disembark. Hester could feel herself trembling, a deep uncalm to match the ocean's roar.

On the dock, a group of coastguards were engaged in a loud and expletive-laden discussion.

"Excuse me," one said, as Hester veered past them. "Do you teenagers know anything about this?"

He held up a phone, where a Fox News livestream showed

a drone flying over the ocean. There was a green swell spreading through the dark-blue water, almost keeping pace with the footage.

Hester was silent. How could it still be spreading? They'd stopped using their powers an hour ago.

Binh let out a loud sob from the back of the group.

The coastguard folded his arms. "Are you Greenfingers, by any chance?"

"We were trying to help!" Alisha blurted out, then burst into tears.

The coastguards looked disbelievingly at them. "Unlawful use of your powers is a state felony, you do realize that?"

"It's just plants," Carthew said, with an aching shine in his eyes. "It's a good thing, isn't it? We've trying to save the planet by rewilding it."

"Kid, you're not going to save the planet this way. The algae is toxic. It's going to kill all the dolphins because they can't get to the surface to breathe," a woman said furiously. "It'll use up all the oxygen in the water as it rots. The fish will suffocate."

"The plants too," someone else added, subdued. "The bloom will block the sunlight from the sea bed. Over the next few months, everything except the algae is going to die. You've made a dead zone."

Hester covered her mouth. There were florets of purple hyacinths growing between her fingers.

"This kind of shit happens when fertilizers leach into the

water from farmland. The algae goes nuts and kills everything else. And you've done it on a massive scale."

"I'm sorry," Carthew whispered.

Hester's phone rang. "Dad?"

"Hester. Are you still at the harbour? I'm coming back from the ranch. I've sent a car to pick you up."

He already knew. *How?*

Voice quavering, she said, "I had no idea we could grow something like this, Dad."

"I see." Dad already thought her powers were disgusting and unhygienic. Now, she could hear the repulsion in his voice. "You've cost us a lot today, Hester."

"I'm sorry. I'll pay for the fines. I'll sell some of my shares if I have to."

Dad sighed. She could hear him shaking one of his liquid meals. He ate them more than real food. "I don't care about the money. But you posted on social media. The news has already connected the disaster to Dalex. They're calling this the next Deepwater Horizon. The board are furious. You've cost us our reputation. What were you *thinking*?"

# Second Dalex Ocean Spillage in Gulf of Mexico

Today, a team of Greenfingers working for the oil giant Dalex Energy created a toxic algae bloom off the coast of Texas that spread as far as Bayou Vista in twelve hours. The damage will have long-term negative effects on marine wildlife and fisheries – as well as Dalex's stock prices. The company admitted fault after Hester Daleport, daughter of Dalex CEO Anthony Daleport, implicated them in a social media post. [See: <u>Celebrity Meets Business: The Meteoric Rise of the Daleports</u>]

Anthony Daleport has already released their standard statement, in what marks their third public apology in this decade alone.

"We offer our sincerest apologies for the damage caused today. Let there be no mistake – we understand how deeply serious this situation is. This is a tragedy, and the environment and coastal communities will suffer because of our ill-placed good intentions. This is unacceptable.

"We don't yet have answers to all the questions the public are rightly asking: How damaging is this bloom to the environment? Why did we attempt such an activity without further risk analysis? Can we justify such damaging accidents in the search for green energy sources? What regulations should control Greenfingers' powers?

"I hear the concerns, fears, frustrations – and anger – being voiced across the country. However much we apologize, we will be judged only by our actions. We've already made a $50 million donation to Greenpeace, as we work tirelessly to stop the algae spreading.

"But we are unwavering in our environmental commitments. We will ensure that the lessons learned from this incident will make energy exploration and production safer and more reliable for everyone."

Greenpeace said, "With this event, Dalex has claimed a place in history as one of the most harmful companies to have ever existed. Alongside their largest oil spills in 2010, 1997, 1981 and 1959, they have continually released toxic substances such as coal ash into the environment without care or attention.

"No monetary value can be assigned to their long-term impact on the ecology of our planet. A $50 million donation is only the beginning of what needs to be done to correct course over the coming months."

Gabrielle Ventura said in a Notes app screenshot on her social media, "I'm very disappointed that our gifts are being used so cavalierly. Dalex should have been more cautious, for the sake of the teenagers themselves as well as the environment. I am already travelling to Houston, where I will be personally working to limit the spread of this bloom."

This news comes only a week after Dalex rewilded one of their sites without permits, causing damage to a telephone pylon cable and underground water pipe. Local weather researchers have reported wildly variating anomalies in the local pressure and temperature as the new ecosystem settles in place. Lawmakers are still rushing to regulate the Greenfingers power, and Dalex have been quick to take advantage of this temporary loophole.

**Related News**

Australia Provides Greenfingers with Grant for Seed Purchases, Waives Horticultural Course Tuition Fees

Crypto-Witch Uses Greenfingers' Blossoms to Predict Bitcoin Prices

Resurgence of Cholera after Bangladesh Flooding

# Chapter 11

Theo threw himself onto his bed, biting his thumbnail. What an abysmal day. How had they managed to make such a mess of everything?

As soon as they'd reached the coast, Daleport had been whisked away in a black Dalex car. None of the trainees had heard from her since.

Feeling despondent, he rang his mum.

"*Jaan!*" she said, delighted. "What's the latest from across the pond?"

As soon as he heard her voice, a surge of homesickness washed over him. He wanted nothing more than to be back at their old draughty cottage, with the zipwire running from his bedroom window to the barn. It was ridiculous, feeling homesick after only a few weeks away.

"Is Dad there? I have some stuff to catch you up on."

"He's here! Applying for jobs, I think. I was just making him a cuppa. Hang on. OK, you're on loudspeaker."

"Hey, champ," Dad said, in his familiar gravelly voice.

Theo buried his face in his pillow. "Hi. Um … I was on the news."

"Our Theo's turning into a celebrity," Dad said to Mum.

"Not. Um. Not in a good way."

"What happened?" Mum said, more serious. "You sound like you're under the weather."

"I messed up," he admitted. "I've been working for Dalex Energy. We did something really bad."

Without any warning, his face crumpled. He hid his tears in the crook of his elbow, unable to put words to the awful thing he'd done. *A dead zone.* What a horrible description. How could that be something he'd made? He'd been the one who'd kept pushing the trainees to practise with their powers. It had led to this.

"Oh," Mum said softly. "We've found it online. Darling. Why didn't you tell us about this?"

"Because I've sold out. I'm working for the enemy."

"No!" Mum said immediately. "We're never going to blame you for anything you do to help our family."

"Take every penny you can get off the scumbags. Then charge for overtime and expenses too," Dad said. "Don't borrow trouble, Theo. You're our hero."

A weight lifted from his chest. He should have known this was how they'd respond.

"This algae bloom, it's all my fault," he forced out, voice thick. His face felt hot. "I was running the session. I kept pushing them to grow more and more."

"You couldn't have known..." Dad said awkwardly. "No one could have known."

Theo shook his head, even though they couldn't see him. "I should have guessed. We made a forest, too. Of course the same thing would happen in the water."

Hot tears slipped down his cheeks. Theo kicked off his socks, letting seaweed drip between his toes onto the carpet. "I just – I wanted to do something good. To prove my power is useful, even if all I can make is seaweed."

"Still?" Mum asked in surprise.

Theo groaned, burying his head in the pillow again. "*Mum.* Cut me some slack, won't you?"

"Not that there's anything wrong with growing seaweed!" she added. "Not judging!"

"Using your powers is what Dalex is paying you for," Dad said. "You can't blame yourself for doing your job. You can't get anywhere without a few hiccups."

That made Theo feel better, somehow. "I wanted to help the planet, not make it worse. It's made a – a dead zone! It's going to kill everything! And then –" he added, the words coming out fast now, his voice high and wavery – "I got into this stupid fight with Hester too!"

"Who's Hester?" Dad whispered to Mum.

"I'm sure this Hester will forgive you," Mum said, ignoring Dad.

"I don't want her to! I hope I never see her again!"

There was silence, and then Dad said, "This is the CEO's daughter?"

"Are you two going to look up everything I say?" Theo asked. He'd stopped crying, at least.

"Well, you aren't giving us very much to go on here, Theodore," Mum said. "Is she really only eighteen?"

"She's my boss," Theo said miserably. "And she's a bloodsucking monster."

"I bet she is," Dad said.

"Jeff!"

"Well, what else do you expect from the Dalex heir?" he muttered to Mum. "She probably drank crude oil in her baby's bottle."

Theo found himself smiling, listening to them bicker.

"Ooh, I like her dress in that one," Mum said to Dad.

"Stop looking at photos of her," Theo muttered. "She's pure evil." Annoyingly, he knew exactly which picture Mum was talking about. It was a memorable dress.

"Surely not. She looks like a nice girl."

"All she cares about is money," Theo moaned. "I knew that Dalex was awful. But I thought that it was just a massive company full of, like, mildly heartless people. I hadn't realized it's actually a few very powerful people who are *actively horrible*. Hester doesn't care about climate change. Like, at all. I actually think she'd leave the world to burn if she could."

Dad laughed. "No one would do that, Theo. Not even a psychopath. She can't possibly be that bad."

"She is!" Theo said, and then paused. He couldn't exactly

remember any more what she'd said. He'd been hot with fury at the time. "She said she didn't want to use our powers for conservation," he said eventually.

"Well, if she's that evil, we can book you a flight home tomorrow," Mum said. "It's not like we need your salary now. We got the insurance payout."

Theo paused. Oddly, the idea of leaving felt like a cop-out. He'd be missing out on something huge. He wouldn't have a chance to fix his mistakes or make up with Daleport. If he went home, he'd end up sitting in class while knowing he could be on a yacht or private jet or mountain with the other trainees. He'd never find out what other amazing tricks they might discover with their powers.

In the knowing tone that meant she was one step ahead of him, Mum said, "Of course, if you *did* decide to put up with Hester's evil ways and stick around, you could use your powers for whatever you wanted outside of work hours, couldn't you? Why not help fix this algae issue then?"

"Oh," he said, with dawning excitement. "Yeah, I could do that."

His thoughts were veering towards optimism at last. That *firstwithmagic* podcast had been full of ideas for how to help the planet, from rewilding landfills to donating vegetables. There must be something he could do.

"Yeah," he said again. "I can do that. If it's OK with you guys."

"Of course it is," Mum said, oozing smugness.

He sighed. He'd been stitched up like a kipper. "Anyway, have you decided what you're going to do with the insurance money, Dad?"

"I'm not sure yet. I'm still shocked we got the payout at all," Dad said.

Theo had thought that was strange too. Dalex had been determined not to pay for the damage, until he'd mentioned the shipwreck to Daleport.

"Are you going to get another boat?" Theo asked. "Because I've been thinking. Isn't fishing kind of bad for the environment?"

"It is," Dad admitted. "I love the sea, but it's so hard to make money any other way out there. I might have to just move to a different industry."

"Well, you'll have my income until you decide."

"Theo, you know you don't need to take so much responsibility for things, right?" Mum said. "Your caring nature is your best trait, but we are perfectly able to look after ourselves. We're not going to get chucked out on the streets; there are always options."

Dad added, "We are here to take care of *you*, Theo. We want you to focus on your own life and get a good education, so you can get a better job than we ever did. Please don't throw your future away because you're scared that we can't pay the bills."

The words were so articulate and perfect that Theo was certain they'd practised this speech. Were they holding an intervention here?

"I know all that," he said. "I'm not throwing away my future!"

"Theo, you're *delaying school* to pay our bills," Mum said. "That's a lovely thing to do, but this isn't your burden to bear. If you want to stay, do it because it's what *you* want."

"I'm staying," Theo said, feeling determined. He had to see this through.

"That's the spirit. Now, tell us more about this awful Hester," Dad said. "Does she have dreamy eyes?"

"Hmm, what was that?" Theo said. They were the worst.

"He's cocking a deaf 'un," Dad said to Mum.

"Escape while you still can, Theo," Mum replied. "He won't stop teasing any time soon. The hen's got into the kitchen again anyway. We'd best go before it eats the cat food."

"Talk to you tomorrow," Theo said. "Love you."

"And you, *jaan*."

After they hung up, Theo skimmed through the *firstwithmagic* posts. He was so anxious that the letters kept leaping out of order, but he listened to some of the longer blog posts using a text-to-speech extension.

The author – the girl who'd sprouted at a climate protest, Gabrielle Ventura – had just posted a picture of Texas, where she was joining a crisis response team for the plankton bloom. Theo's stomach twisted over in guilt again. That was exactly what he should be doing right now too.

To his surprise, when he messaged Gabrielle's account, there was a reply within minutes.

**theocarth:** Hi. I saw you where in Houston, and I wnated to volunteer to help fix the damage the Dalex algea bloom has done. I was one of the group who made it, and I feel terrible.

**firstwithmagic:** You should.

**theocarth:** Let me help. Ill make up for it in any way I can.

**firstwithmagic:** are you still working with dalex?

**theocarth:** yes.

**firstwithmagic:** then there is something you can help us with. get us on-site at a dalex coal plant.

**theocarth:** what? why?

**firstwithmagic:** do you really think I'm going to tell you that? Lol

**theocarth:** is this actually gabrielle ventura?

**firstwithmagic:** just took this selfie as proof.

↓ **Download attachment [3MB]**

**theocarth:** fair. nice llama.

**firstwithmagic:** I'm staying on an eco farm outside the city.

**firstwithmagic:** will you do it, then?

**theocarth:** I don't know who its possible, but I'll try my best.

**firstwithmagic:** you've got until tomorrow, then you're blocked. make this happen, polluter.

**theocarth:** sorry. OK.

Wow, Gabrielle Ventura didn't mess around with any niceties. Why would she want access to a coal plant, anyway? Was there even a way for him to get inside somewhere like that?

The link in her profile led to the website for Climate Rebellion. On their homepage there was a write-up of a recent rewilding project they'd done at a landfill site, and an auto-play video of Gabrielle speaking to a crowd of protestors.

"This magic is the greatest miracle that humanity has ever received, and it's being used for profit – to save on production and shipping costs by factories! After months of inaction, no one is working to find ways to grow food for the people who are starving, stop natural disasters like fires or hurricanes, or clear the planet of pollution.

"I demand global action on a government level to prioritize the implementation of a Greenfingers power base. We can do good if you'll let us. We need your help, so we can help you."

Gabrielle was a frequent commenter on the website forum too, giving advice to other Greenfingers and brainstorming ideas. One of her posts was called "The Problem with Coal Ash".

## Climate Rebellion Forum

**SECURE COMMUNICATION PLATFORMS – protonmail vs gmail, cryptpad vs docs – PLEASE READ!!** – 16 replies

**Any good march chants? I'm sick of "the oceans are rising and so are we"** – 49 replies

**School strike TOMORROW in DUBLIN – what to bring/safety guidelines** - 6 replies

**Anyone want to arrange a Greenfingers activists meetup? (NJ based/can travel)** – 117 replies

**The Problem with Coal Ash by firstwithmagic** – 628 replies

We all know that burning coal is bad. It makes carbon dioxide, etc etc. But there's another problem with it, which I think GFs might be able to solve.

When coal is burned to make electricity, it leaves behind charcoal and ash. Companies dump this ash in ponds to let the water evaporate off, and then the silt is used to make concrete.

The problem is, the ponds have been used for decades now. And the factories never lined the ground. So all of the coal ash has leached toxic metals into the soil.

The land for kilometres around these factories is now contaminated with arsenic, radium and loads more stuff. Any plants that grow there contain the metals, and the pollutants have got into the rivers, too, so all the fish are mutated.

My question is, if the plants grown there contain the metals, does that mean they're pulling the toxic materials out of the soil? i.e. could a group of us lot go there and grow enough plants to clean the land? We'd be at it for a while, but it could work in theory, right?

- gabrielle

Gabrielle wanted to remove the toxins from the land at a Dalex site as a test, then. Well, that definitely sounded like something Theo could support. It would stop him feeling as guilty about the bloom if he could help repair several acres of polluted land.

He'd have to convince Daleport to take them there for a training activity, then find a way to sneak Gabrielle in. Maybe he could pitch it as a way for Dalex to show that they were atoning for their pollution, by taking press photos of the Greenfingers at work. She wouldn't agree to anything he asked without an apology first, though. Plus he'd have get his power working properly.

After dinner, Theo went outside to practise in the forest. They'd turned branches growing from the trunk of a thick tree into a spiralling staircase. He climbed the steps, shimmied up a ladder, then swung on a vine, propelling himself forward onto the woven reed floor.

The small treehouse he'd made with Jason had developed into an entire network of dens, with bridges and passageways stretching throughout the canopy.

Branches were twisted to form the walls, which were woven with budding sweet peas in an intricate mix of grapefruit pink and maroon, dark cerise and baby blue. A blanket was spread out on the floor of the room, alongside a few empty beer cans. Jason's portable speaker was hanging from a hammock of vines. They mainly listened to synthwave, which wasn't Theo's favourite. He preferred something a bit more folksy.

He slid along a branch until he was sitting over the glade, looking down at a sea of wildflowers. He could do this. He could grow something incredible, and it wasn't going to be seaweed, whatever his body said about the matter.

He would grow a fern between the tree's moss-covered roots. Ferns were similar to seaweed, weren't they? It wasn't that much of a jump.

He imagined every detail on the fern's leaves until it felt so real that he could almost touch it. There was a cluster of silky grey fungi in a crevice between the roots. The fern

145

would poke its way up to the surface right next to it. It was going to work.

Something bubbled inside him. It was coming. He could feel its tender, curled leaf pushing up through the soil.

Before it could appear, there was a crashing noise in the undergrowth, and Hester Daleport stomped into the glade. Her face was damp with tears. Most disturbingly, she was wearing a T-shirt and jeans. Not a Gucci suit, or Chanel swimming costume. Just a T-shirt with *Artemis Fowl* on the front. It didn't look right on her, somehow.

She stopped walking, her gaze fixed on something on the ground where he'd been trying to grow his imaginary fern. Theo cleared his throat, until she noticed him perched in the treetop.

"Evening, Daleport."

Voice sharp, she said, "Do that again!"

Theo leaned over the branch, peering down to see what she was getting so riled up about. A perfect fairy ring of blood-red toadstools had appeared in the damp earth, their white speckled tops glistening in the twilight.

Mushrooms. He'd grown *mushrooms*?

### in the "Greenfingers"

Sc, et al

a sample group of fifteen teenagers
bilities has found that the power draws
resources. When the test subjects were
s in a vacuum, they were unable to do so.

d chamber containing a known volume of
entage of carbon dioxide, nitrogen and water
ped. This reduction correlated with the quantity
wn by the test subjects. This suggests that the
ers" ability uses elements from the air to create plant

latest theory for the emergence of such powers is
aneous endosymbiosis through horizontal gene transfer in
wombs of pregnant women approximately two decades ago,
hen the oldest subjects were in utero.

A bacterium – possibly something similar to the type of
chloroplast found in plant cells – may have fused with human
cells. This could have given the cells new properties that allowed
the production of plant matter.

This mutation is similar to the theory of the origins of
mitochondria, which originated when prokaryotic cells were
engulfed by single-celled organisms millions of years ago. No
evidence to support this theory has yet been found by research
scientists, nor is it clear what could have triggered such
a mutation.

# Chapter 12

After she was whisked away from the harbour, Hester [had] been told to wait outside Dad's office. She held her hand ins[ide] the waste-paper basket to catch a nervous flood of oleand[er]. There was the muffled sound of raised, excited voices fro[m] inside. Dad must be discussing the plankton disaster.

She had to do something about the bloom. The bubble they'd made at sea had been really strong. Perhaps there was a way they could use it to reverse the growth of the algae, like when Theo had suppressed the apple pip in Beatriz's stomach? She'd have to test it – though she doubted they would be able to take the yacht out without being arrested.

When Dad emerged with Edgar Warren himself, Hester quickly shoved the waste basket under her chair. She hadn't realized that he was here.

"Excellent," Dad said. "I'll talk to my people, and we'll be on track to start before the quarter ends."

Dad clasped Edgar's elbow with genuine affection. Hester was surprised – she'd never seen him do that before.

"I have a few contacts in Russia," Edgar said. "I'll try to

grease some cogs there, then we can circle back once the preliminary drafts are written up."

Clearly they'd managed to work something out for that mysterious confidential project Edgar was so interested in.

"Hello, Mr Warren."

Edgar regarded her with a strange expression, like he didn't recognize her. She had thrown a T-shirt on over her swimsuit, and her hair was damp with salt water, tangled into a topknot. She probably looked a lot younger than when he'd last seen her at the launch party.

"Hester!" Edgar said finally, in an upbeat tone that was the opposite of their previous phone conversation. "Great work today."

Hester folded her arms over her chest self-consciously. "On the toxic algae bloom?"

"Of course, that is such a shame," he said, mouth curving into a frown. "But what potential you've all got!"

"We have discovered that we can combine our powers together in a kind of bubble as we work," she offered.

"Well, excellent!" Dad cut in. "Edgar has some ideas for how we can use the team for some exciting projects." He beamed at Edgar like he'd just won the lottery.

"I'm looking forward to hearing all about it," she said politely, to hide her irritation. What could possibly have made them so buddy-buddy? She was the one who'd approached Edgar at that party. This was her deal. But within a few weeks, she'd been cut out of the conversation altogether.

Edgar said, "Let's do breakfast tomorrow, after Anthony's brought you up to speed. I can pop over to your infamous forest."

When he moved past Hester to shake hands with Dad, it felt like he'd reached right through her chest. She might as well not be there at all.

Once they'd waved Edgar off, Dad led her into his office. "Right. We've got a few things to talk about."

He poured them both a drink. She downed a whole glass of iced tea in one long, cool gulp, as he swallowed a bright-green nutrient pill. He was always fixated on some health plan or other, and mainly lived on probiotics and wellness supplements. He'd been in heaven during the Mars trip, when the food had come as pouches of protein shakes.

"I'm so sorry about the bloom, Dad. I promise that I won't rest until Dalex's reputation is restored. I want to delay the training programme for the biofuels so the Greenfingers can rehabilitate some of the damage this algae bloom has done at sea."

Dad frowned. "That would disrupt things with Edgar. It's a nice idea – very PR-friendly – but I don't think we can take the time."

Hester reeled. She hadn't been expecting him to turn her down. "It would only be for a few days. A week at most."

He shook his head. "It's a no, Hester."

She chewed on her lip, hesitating. "Dad – this is really important to me. I feel responsible for what happened. I want to fix my mistake."

"Hester." That was his firm "I'm the boss" voice, the one he rarely used on her. "You know that's not our policy. We have greater things to work towards."

Some of her shock must have shown on her face, because he added in a conciliatory tone, "We'll organize a corporate litter-picking day, how about that?"

Hester nodded mutely. It felt like he'd pulled the rug out from under her. All this time, she'd thought the Greenfingers project was hers. But it was becoming clear that she was just his puppet.

"I had no idea this was so important to you," he said consideringly. "You know, you're going to have to learn to shake off little errors like this. Dealing with difficult situations is a big part of having responsibility. A CEO needs backbone."

"Right." She felt numb. He was right. The more work she did for Dalex, the more she'd be facing these kinds of difficult decisions. Was she ever going to be able to make the unemotional decisions that Dad clearly wanted from her?

"You aren't trained properly for management yet. That's why today happened." A frown furrowed his brow as he ran his thumb over the cut-crystal pattern of his glass. "Anyway, it's in the past now. Bigger things are afoot. Edgar and I have decided that instead of focusing on biofuels, we'd like to see how the Greenfingers' talents might be useful in another context." He held up one hand, as if pushing down his own excitement. "Now, this is all hypothetical, but we have a very exciting idea for northern expansion your team could bring to fruition."

Hester couldn't concentrate on what he was saying. It had abruptly become incredibly important to explain to Dad what she'd found out about Dalex's impact on climate change. It was obvious that he didn't know – that he'd possibly never known. If he had, he'd be trying to help fix things too, like her.

"Do you remember those new tankers we've commissioned?" he was saying. "The ones that can break through surface ice? We think—"

Interrupting, she said, "That sounds great! Hey, Dad, I was wondering – did you know that some of the climate science we're using has been proven wrong?"

Thyme curled around the arms of her chair. She leaned forward, hiding it.

Dad lowered his glass. "How do you mean?"

She traced the grain of the wood on his desk. She remembered being small enough to sit underneath while he worked, drawing with crayons on old blueprints. She'd spent her whole life looking up to her dad.

She tried to break the news gently. "Could be that it's worse than we thought. The temperatures are going to increase a lot faster than those research papers say. We don't have much time to start fixing things."

Dad nodded, solemn and thoughtful. "I see. Well, you don't need to worry about that."

Hester had a moment of relief. He wasn't upset. That would save them some time. It wasn't too late to get back on track.

Then Dad continued, "As soon as Mars is up and running, we'll be moving there. It should only be a few more years."

Hester froze. "What do you mean?"

"Well, that's always been the plan. To keep us safe."

"From *Earth*?"

She had known Dad was excited about Mars, but she hadn't realized it was in such a personal way. Sure, she'd been planning to live there for a few months at some point in her life – but only for a work trip. Everyone going to Mars would want to come home to their families and open air eventually, wouldn't they?

"Of course. The colony can't come a moment too soon, either. I don't think we've got much longer." He grimaced.

"But there must be a way we can still fix things here," she said in disbelief.

Dad shook his head. "It's far too late for that. It's not even worth trying."

So he had already known that climate change wasn't some distant problem. He had no intention of trying to fix it, even.

"What if we got more carbon capture projects going within a few months, wouldn't that be enough?" she asked. "It might cost a few billion, but we'd earn that back by the end of the decade."

Dad had always avoided investing in climate intervention schemes, because he'd lost a lot of money in a failed project in the past. But even if it took them a few attempts to find something that worked, it would still end up being cheaper than going to Mars.

"Oh, that. Carbon capture isn't going to be enough to reverse the temperature change. That's just a line we trot out to reassure the public."

*What?* Her brain was unravelling. A little desperately, she said, "But there must be *some* way to stop it happening."

Dad leaned back in his chair, fingers laced together. "Impossible, I'm afraid. We'd have to stop using oil, coal and natural gas completely. Zero carbon emissions within a year, and Earth might have a chance. But society would collapse if we did that. Think of all the trucks and planes that need our fuel to supply the country with food, for a start." He shot her a glance. "Come on, princess. You know all this."

Did she?

Zero emissions within a year? How could he be planning to keep drilling for more oil, if that was true? They should be building wind farms, not opening this new oilfield in Iran. The idea of tackling such big changes was terrifying – but surely losing Earth was worse?

"So," she said slowly. "We'll keep drilling. Until when?"

What was his endgame, here?

Dad sighed. "Well, at some point it will become too expensive to drill for oil. The climate activists will hassle the government into putting a tax on carbon emissions, and eventually power from renewables will become cheaper. But we've got a few decades before they manage that. There's plenty of reasons to continue expansion until then."

He wasn't even looking at her. Hester's world was being torn apart and he hadn't even noticed.

"Right. And … after that? Once people use renewable energy everywhere instead?" There was something wrong with her hearing. She couldn't focus on what he was saying.

"You'll probably be running the company by then, overseeing things from Mars. But Dalex will be fine – your gramps started developing electric fuel technology when we first found out about the greenhouse effect. We hold all the patents now. Once oil is over, we'll still exert some hold over the energy sector. That's why I bought that silica mine – we supply solar panel manufacturers with their materials."

They'd known about the climate crisis since *her grandad* ran Dalex? Hester was a majority shareholder in denial, but this was appalling even to her. He had this all planned out. Every step of it.

She remembered, then, the meetings they'd had a few years ago about increasing the height of their new ocean oil rigs. Dad had told her that it was to make them more visible to transport ships. But that wasn't true, was it? He'd been anticipating the rising sea levels. Making sure that a minor flood wouldn't stop the oil supply.

"All our friends will be moving to Mars too, if that's what you're worried about," he said. "You won't miss out on anything. Your children and grandchildren will never know anything but

Mars. They won't even miss Earth. And think about how much safer it will be, for all of us! No pollution to make us sick. No smog in our lungs or pesticides and mercury in our food. This planet is ruined, Hester. We have to get away from the toxins."

This made a lot of sense. Of course Mars would be a dream for Dad, who lived on liquid meals and was terrified of bacteria. He could avoid wildlife for the rest of his life. But Hester didn't want to live in a sterile bubble, surviving on nutrient bars and staring out at red dust.

"There will be lots of people left behind, though." Her words came out even and measured, despite the chaotic jumble of brambles growing frantically around her feet. Blackberries leaked juice into the carpet.

Dad waved a hand dismissively. "People who can't afford the ticket price will be able to get a loan and pay off their debt when they arrive."

Hester knew the term for that: indentured servitude. She was quite sure that it wasn't legal. So, they were condemning the poorest people to either slavery or life on a ruined Earth.

"Now," he went on. "As I was saying. Edgar's going to take the lead on the Greenfingers' training for now. It needs someone with more managerial experience anyway. He will—"

Hester stood up so fast that her chair fell over. He was giving her group to Edgar too? On top of everything else?

"Hester!" Dad scolded.

She couldn't look at him. She had spent her whole life trying to emulate her father. But this man in front of her was nothing she ever wanted to be. Not if she wanted to live with herself.

"I'm sorry. I've got a migraine." The words came from somewhere distant. Her head was a chaos of noise and emotions. "Can we talk tomorrow?"

"Edgar's going to—" he started, but Hester held a hand to her forehead. Her mouth felt swollen with the words she wasn't saying.

"Take an aspirin and go to bed, princess," he said gently. "I'll have the housekeeper make you a hot toddy. It must have been a big shock for you today. Your first ocean spill."

*Baby's First Deep Sea Disaster.* Yeah. Sure.

Hester avoided eye contact with any of their numerous employees as she left the executive offices. What was she going to do? Her whole life was collapsing in on itself.

She traced her nails down the lines of her veins, scratching at the endless, irritating eczema. The algae bloom had felt like the worst thing she'd done in her whole life. But her efforts were low-hanging fruit compared to Dad's and her grandad's disasters. They were *destroying the planet*.

Hester had been so interested in learning about the exciting stuff – expanding the company, helping make a settlement on Mars, discovering those tar-black threads of liquid gold under untouched rock – that she'd wilfully ignored the things that were really important.

She was so tempted to pretend she'd never learned any of this, to lock it all inside herself and take the easier route. She could carry on reaping the benefits of life at Dalex – the money, the fame, the control. But it was built on the world's burning corpse. It would taste like ash in her mouth, even from the safety of Mars.

No. Hester couldn't live with herself if she did nothing to stop this. Dad had shown her, in one fell swoop, exactly where her boundaries lay. Just as she'd been about to walk blindly past them.

She cried all the way back to the training centre, filling the car with shrivelled, dying flowers. She couldn't go home tonight. She would sleep in one of the empty trainee rooms until she'd come up with a plan of action. Her brain was too fuzzy to strategize right now.

Hester wanted nothing more than to be alone with an endless supply of rom-coms and chocolate. So, of course, she immediately bumped into Theodore Carthew on her way through the forest to the training centre. He was in a tree, for some reason. And he'd just grown a whole cluster of mushrooms.

"Do that again!" she cried in excitement. Wiping her eyes, she asked, "You can grow fungus? Since when?"

"What?" he asked. "I didn't do that!"

She tilted her head, looking up at him. "Get down here." Before he could get all offended, she added, "Please, Car— Theo."

He nearly tripped climbing down the tree, and then stood in front of her, wiping his trousers.

She eyed him thoughtfully. In her anger at him hiding his issues from her, she'd never actually stopped to think about why his power might be failing.

"Can you grow some seaweed for me?"

Looking reluctant, he grew a stream of seaweed.

She followed the path of his power, paying close attention now. It boiled inside him, waiting to be unleashed.

"Jesus," she said, stunned. "How do you keep this all under wraps? It's desperate to be used."

Theo shivered. "I don't know how to let it out without making seaweed."

He was right. It was seaweed, all the way down.

But seaweed was basic. It was the original plant that everything else had evolved from. Maybe that was why Theo could produce so much of it – because it was the easiest way to use his pent-up energy in one huge burst. Maybe he was struggling to make anything else because his power didn't want to make plants at all. It wanted to make fungi.

All this time, Theo had been going down the wrong path, pushing up against a block that was impossible to break through. The plants he'd tried to make didn't align with what his body wanted to produce.

She took his hand, lowering it to the ground next to the ring of mushrooms. He eyed her strangely, but let her manhandle him.

"Grow."

Theo huffed a sigh, but narrowed his eyes in focus. There was something complex happening inside him that she couldn't interpret.

He made a thoughtful noise, shuffling closer to the ground. He seemed to be listening to the earth. Something appeared on his skin, in the bend of his arm. A curl of grey-yellow fungus grew on his fingernail. Mushrooms were sprouting all over his body, nestled in the dark spaces under his ears and in the creases of his elbows, like clusters of chocolates.

"No way," Theo said, made up with glee. "You're right!"

Hester grinned, feeling victorious.

"*Fungi*, Theo. That's why you can't make plants. You can make fungi instead."

This was perhaps the first time in her entire life that she actually *had* been right about something.

"Huh." He produced a smooth grey stem from his palm, growing a frilled umbrella top from the solid trunk. It was the epitome of a mushroom, delicate and satiny.

"No nosebleed, this time." Hester felt absurdly proud. It wasn't even her mushroom.

"It's so easy," he murmured. "It doesn't hurt or anything."

"I'm going to have to be careful not to make you angry again. You know those are deadly poisonous, right?"

She gestured to the ground where he was kneeling. A ring of white clay tobacco pipes had encircled him.

"Probably," Theo said absently, gazing down at a cluster of bright mould like he was falling in love. At least someone was happy. Hester wished her own problems were so easy to solve. What was she going to do about Dad?

# Use of Petroleum Products in Climate Control

October 1957

Funding and support provided by Dalex Energy

**Abstract**

This study explores various proposals for using oil to modify weather patterns, such as burning oil to blow away smog; coating land in asphalt to change rainfall patterns and avoid drought; and spraying oil from aircraft propellers onto the ocean's surface to divert the paths of tropical storms. Findings to date appear positive.

A new efficient method of capturing carbon emissions directly from vehicle exhausts has been retired from research testing. Exhaust smoke will be released directly into the atmosphere instead, as this is cheaper for production.

# Chapter 13

The next morning, Theo was floating on a cloud of joy. Fungus! He'd never heard of any Greenfingers being able to grow *fungi* before. His power wasn't a dud after all – he just hadn't been listening to it properly.

He'd been treating his seaweed problems in the same way he used to think about his dyslexia, as an embarrassing secret that slowed him down. But he'd forgotten the most important thing: he'd found ways to *manage* his dyslexia. He'd adapted by using voice-to-text convertors, or listening to audiobooks, or changing his screen settings. But he'd been too ashamed to even look for solutions to the problems with his power. And all that time, the fungi had been waiting for him.

He grabbed a bacon butty from the breakfast buffet and took it outside to eat in the wood. He was starting to miss the lush damp greens of the English countryside. The early morning seemed to be the only time of day it was possible to come outside here without boiling, though it was at least cooler in the forest. The woodland was alive with creatures scuffling about in the undergrowth. It had been less than a fortnight since they'd grown the forest, and already the wilderness had been claimed by nature.

A gutsy squirrel was exploring a silver birch when a car pulled into the drive. It was a very cool car – sleek and art deco, glowing in a subtle gold. There was no driver behind the wheel, and the entire roof was see-through. A man was sprawled out on the sofa-sized back seat with a laptop balanced on his stomach. He was ignoring the laptop in favour of playing a game on a handheld console, using a second computer screen embedded in the car seating. There was only one person this could be: Edgar Warren.

The man climbed out, eyeing Theo. "You're the seaweed kid."

"Is this the new Lamborghini?" Theo gaped at the car. "And that Nintendo isn't even out yet!"

Edgar grinned, pushing down a bulky pair of headphones. He disconnected a variety of cables from his laptop, stacking up an iPad, a second laptop, a console, a tablet and three other gadgets that Theo couldn't even identify. "Come on then. Give me the tour and I'll let you play-test it."

He tapped the side of his glasses, which had a reflective interface embedded in the lenses. The car beeped and the entire roof turned into solar panels.

Theo was unexpectedly starstruck. "Are you really sending us to space?" he blurted out.

Edgar shrugged, typing something on his watch. "Sure. Before the Daleport girl appears, let's take a walk around your magical forest. You can tell me what actually happened with that ocean disaster."

Theo balked. "I'm not sure if I should…"

Edgar read something off his watch. "Theodore Carthew, username 'theocarth' on most sites. Inconsistent Greenfingers skills, yet on a higher salary than the other trainees. Graded at the UK equivalent of a B average in your last school exams. Used to work at the docks unloading shipments. Interestingly, quite a lot of the shipments from Junwei Tech reported missing items on days when you were on shift. Usually phones and earbuds."

All of the blood left Theo's face. How had he found out about Theo's side gig at the car boot sale? And – were those scans of Theo's fingerprints on the watch screen? How had Edgar got Theo's *fingerprints*?

"Um – what – I'm not entirely sure you're—"

"Do you want me to continue – because there's plenty more – or do you want to start that tour?"

"This way!" Theo said in a tight, high voice. He could feel sweat forming on the back of his neck. He'd never told anyone about his smuggling at the docks. Not even his friends at school.

"It wasn't my fault," Theo tried to explain. "One of the older guys bullied me into taking them. I didn't even get any money from it."

Edgar stepped over a bluebell patch. "What? Oh, that. I don't care. How did you and Daleport create the plankton bloom?"

Theo paused, recalibrating his attention from potential blackmail. "Er. We were practising growing aquatic plants and it went totally nuts."

"That's it? There was no tech involved?"

Theo caught his shoulder on a bramble, jerking away from the thorns. "There was ... the yacht?"

Edgar looked him over. "Just the teenagers, then." He peered up into the canopy, pressing something on his lenses to turn them into sunglasses. "How long did it take for this forest to appear?"

Theo cleared his throat, doing some quick maths. "Twenty hours. Ish?"

"How wide is it?"

Squinting around him, Theo said, "I guess an acre or two."

"And the bloom was miles wide within minutes, so it travels faster in water. The type of environment makes a difference. Was it the same number of Greenfingers both times?"

"Yeah," Theo answered cautiously. Beatriz hadn't been on their boat trip, but Hester had joined them during the training session.

"We have a direct comparison on scale, then." It didn't seem like Edgar was mad at them for wrecking the ocean, but it was hard to tell. He lifted his watch and said into it, *"Split the individuals up and test the radius of interaction between their growths. Compare initial and current heights for different tree species. Do some varieties grow faster? Potential selection factor for seeds?"*

To Theo, he said, "Where was the epicentre of the inciting event? Is there a radius of decreasing growth around it?"

"Eh?" Theo said, and then, relieved, "Oh, Hester's here!"

She was racing towards them through the thicket, messily tucking in a white silk blouse. She was wearing narrow black braces on top, which did interesting things to her shoulders.

"Edgar!" she said. "Good morning! I see you've met our trainer Theo already."

He tried to send her a silent plea for help. He was in deep over his head.

"Hester." Edgar evaluated her. "I figured I'd come and review my new employees."

Hester bristled. "I'd be happy to introduce you to my team." There was the smallest emphasis on *my*.

"Before you get any of them arrested," Edgar added quickly.

Just as fast, Hester shot back, "The police didn't place any charges for the incident yesterday. It was a misunderstanding."

*Dead zone, dead zone, dead zone,* Theo's mind whispered, like an awful heartbeat. He'd been avoiding checking the news because his phone's BREAKING NEWS notification kept reporting nightmare things like the number of porpoise carcasses on the beach.

"A misunderstanding just like the global news extravaganza you've created, I'm sure." Edgar's voice was bland.

Theo looked between them. His cat sometimes got into fights with the tabby from the farm down the lane. Their snarling exchanges were just like this. Hester and Edgar were batting their paws at each other, claws barely concealed.

"While we're out here, why don't you guys give me a demo?" Edgar suggested. "Let's see those powers in action. Hester, you said you could form a bubble with other Greenfingers?"

Hester nodded. "Since the first time I tried it with Theo, I've got more attuned to it. I can feel other people's powers without touching them now."

Theo was surprised at this. But when he reached out with his power, he actually could sense Hester, even from a few metres away. Were their powers going to keep changing? He had barely come to terms with his fungus yet.

"Let's see how far apart you're able to stay connected," Edgar said. "So we have some idea of what kind of acreage a group could cover, working in unison. Theo, why don't you walk away from us and let us know when you can't feel Hester's power any more?"

Edgar moved his fingers in mid-air and Theo's phone started ringing. He accepted the call without even asking how he'd got his number. Edgar probably knew his school locker pin code too.

He walked away between the trees, feeling slightly relieved to escape from Edgar. Hester's power nudged back against his own in reassurance.

Over the phone, he heard Edgar say to her, "We'll have to make sure we keep track of the data on all our future tests. I wonder if the correlation of growth acceleration with number of people hits a plateau at some point? That could help us determine how many people we'd need to send to – " he coughed – "to Mars."

Theo jumped over a shallow ditch.

"I'd be wary of running any more tests yet," Hester said, voice slightly muffled through the call. "I can't risk a repeat of the damage done yesterday. I'll want to isolate the trainees during tests until the collective strength of the powers is understood."

"That is a bit of a roadblock," Edgar said. "Could we take them out into the desert today? Another forest there wouldn't be the end of the world."

Theo said into his phone, "We could still grow a plague of tumbleweeds that would wipe out the nearest town."

"What? Why?"

"Using our powers seems to trigger growth from seeds already in the ground," Theo said, distracted. He was fifty metres away by now, but he could still feel Hester behind him. How was that possible?

Edgar said thoughtfully, "So you'd expect to see less growth in an area without natural plant life? That's … unfortunate."

"Yes, it will be an issue for Mars," Hester said.

Theo could still feel a link to her, even across this distance. Her power was a low hum, throbbing through the earth.

The soil was positively vibrating with life. He could feel all sorts of fungi in there, quietly existing at that frequency he'd never paid attention to before. He gave the ground a little push. Immediately a crinkled purple growth blossomed, letting off a nutty scent. He'd never had any particular liking for moulds and mushrooms before, but this was the most beautiful thing he'd ever seen.

Theo clawed out a hole in the ground, digging his fingers deep into the soil, searching for – something. Whatever was feeding Hester's distinctive power to him.

There was a white thread webbed through the soil. As soon as Theo touched the filament, electricity shot through him. He could feel Hester as if she were using her power right next to him.

Experimentally, he latched on to the fungus and started thinking *truffle truffle truffle* as hard as he could, pushing the command down the tingling strands.

On the phone, Hester gasped.

"Did something just grow?" he asked, alert. "A black truffle?"

"Oh my god, Theo," she said. "Did you do that?!"

They could transmit their powers? The white strands of fungi spores must be connecting them together. It was a pulsing current like some kind of underground network, stretching through the forest.

"The ground is full of fungi!" he shouted, ecstatic. "It's like it's connecting us together! Touch the ground, Hester, you might be able to feel it too."

There was a moment's pause, and then a tiny stem poked its way out of the soil at Theo's feet, unfolding sharp spikes and a fluffy purple head.

"THISTLE!" he roared.

"NO WAY!" Hester shouted back.

Now he knew where to direct his power, the spores took it up eagerly. Mushrooms started to pop up ten – fifteen – twenty metres away from him. He could feel the network stretching out uninterrupted in a vast expanse beyond that. It went so far that he had to break the connection, feeling dizzy at the immensity.

Theo started dancing around. This whole time, an amazing, invisible world had been waiting for him underground, and he could speak its language.

"Can we use this somehow? Is it useful?" he asked.

"It's not *not* useful." He could hear the grin in Hester's voice.

"Fascinating," Edgar murmured. Theo had forgotten that he was listening in. "Hmm. According to the self-proclaimed Internet's Largest Plant Identification Reference Guide, your fungus is something called the Mycorrhizal network. The fungi grow on plant roots, interconnected throughout the ground."

Theo laughed giddily, running a hand through his hair. "I wonder if there's any limit to distance, then. If this fungus is everywhere, could we grow plants from kilometres away?"

"I'd sure like to find out," Hester said. "And try it with the whole group."

"Can we get them out here now?" Edgar asked.

"I think we'd have to test it somewhere less urbanized,"

Hester said. "There are roots and seeds even underneath the building. We could tear up the concrete foundations."

"I can arrange that," Edgar agreed. "Let's take the trainees somewhere remote in my helicopter."

"Absolutely," Hester said. "I'll choose a location."

Jogging back to them, Theo bit his lip, amused. They were still clawing away at each other, but in the most passive-aggressive way he'd ever seen.

"Yes, you can take your pick. As long as you're not wasting money going off to the rainforest or anything depressing like that. Let's stay focused on our main goals here."

Theo wasn't surprised that Edgar was yet another billionaire with no interest in the environment. He wanted to spend his billions on space travel. Restoring the world wouldn't give him a colony carrying his name. This was a man who wanted to be infamous.

"I have to answer this," Edgar said when his phone rang. He walked back to the building.

"Please never ever leave me alone with that guy, Hester. He would eat me alive. Billionaires are terrifying." Theo held on tight to a branch like he was bracing himself to be flung overboard.

She patted him on the arm. "I've got your back. I totally forgot he was coming today. Everything that happened yesterday distracted me."

Fine grey Spanish moss was curled through her hair, a sure sign that she was stressed.

"Does he want to fire you or something?" Theo asked. "He was acting so weird."

"Dad wants him to lead the group," she said grimly. "I should have stepped back and let him, but I refuse to give up my project. I'm probably getting too cocky."

Theo blinked. That was a lot to gather from one little conversation. But it did make sense of the way Hester had been trying to flex her authority.

"I mean ... you are kind of cocky. In a good way," he said in a teasing tone.

"Yeah," Hester said, sighing. "It's my biggest strength and my greatest weakness. I can handle Edgar, anyway."

She seemed ... different today. More sure of herself, compared to how quiet and sad she'd been the night before.

"That spore thing has blown my mind. I had no idea fungi were so cool." He couldn't stop growing fungi over his fingers. So far, he hadn't made the same type twice. There seemed to be an endless supply of colourful, bizarre fungus.

Hester's eyes lit up. "Come with me. I've got something you'll love."

## From the Chief Superintendent to all officers concerning Operation Greenfingers

All officers should be aware that Climate Rebellion is expected to escalate their protests in the coming weeks. Their recent attempt to blockade a TV news studio with a bamboo forest was safely dealt with by the fire service without harm to the public. However, a manufacturer of petrochemical plastics has now reported sightings of the group – including infamous activist Gabrielle Ventura – outside their factory. They anticipate acts of civil disobedience taking place soon to protest against single-use plastics in consumer packaging.

There has been a rise in occurrences of bullying involving Greenfingers at local schools, some of which have severely endangered life. It's expected that police community support officers will be required to offer a greater presence in schools on an ongoing basis.

The recent rapid increase in drug use can also be linked back to Greenfingers. In particular, there has been a spate of opium-related incidents from the growth of poppies. Often, the manufactured drugs are very low quality, leading to user fatalities.

Activity from Organized Crime Groups has reached a new level of severity, as gangs are no longer restricted by supply. This has led to increased violence between rival factions as they fight over territories. These clashes now present a greater threat to civilians, as gangs implement their Greenfingers powers in personal attacks.

In one case, an entire block of flats collapsed during a clash with a rival cannabis supplier, when attackers grew trees through the stairwell. Another public dispute destroyed a highway, after fighting gang members fired hollow bullets packed with explosive pollen at passing cars.

Other biohazardous weapons being used include grenades filled with acidic sap, as well as the finely ground dust of seeds that have toxic effects when inhaled.

To date, raids on the OCGs have been overwhelmingly unsuccessful, as dealers are able to quickly hide or destroy their supply using their powers. In some cases, they have grown entire tree trunks around the cache, which they then reclaim at a later date. These techniques have also eased distribution to users through botanical drop-off points created by dealers.

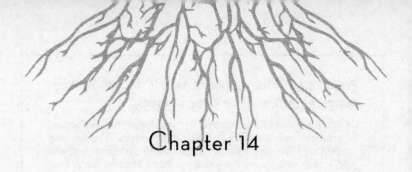

# Chapter 14

Hester led Theo into the training centre's gleaming silver kitchen and started pulling baking supplies out of the giant cooled pantry. They had a bit of time before training started for the day, and she needed to relax after the stress of holding a conversation with Edgar.

"Are we allowed to be in here?" Theo asked.

"It's all mine," she said vaguely. She liked baking. There was something calming about the order and instructions and precision. When she was stressed she made bread or brigadeiro, stirring and stirring as her brain worked through a problem. There was a strategy to moving around the kitchen, conserving energy with efficient choices as she arranged and organized the ingredients. And then she got to eat something delicious afterwards.

"I'm sorry I lied about my power," Theo said, as she poured some dried raising agent into a glass of warm water. He stared down at the murky liquid, swirling the brownish grit in bemusement. "Do you want me to drink this?"

She hid a smirk. "Just wait a sec. And I'm sorry too.

I overreacted. You're clearly very powerful." She gestured at the glass.

Like she'd suspected, it had immediately started frothing up. Beige foam surged up the sides of the glass and dripped over Theo's fingers.

"Ew!" he said, appalled. "What *is* that stuff?"

She grinned. "Yeast. It's a kind of fungi. That usually takes a lot longer than three seconds. You're growing things without even realizing it."

"It actually smells like bread," he said, looking amazed.

When a spurt of bubbles shot straight up into the air and splattered the counter, Hester hastily took the glass off him. "That's probably enough to make a loaf. Or, like, three thousand."

Theo watched her weigh out flour in silence.

"Is it really bad?" he asked. "Are we going to hospital? I mean – jail?" He grimaced, clearly embarrassed to have mixed up the words.

"What?" She twisted to face him. "Oh, the bloom. No, my dad sorted all that. Don't worry about it."

Hester felt guilty, but she'd almost forgotten the algae bloom. Between Edgar's power struggle and the conversation she'd had with Dad yesterday, her brain was full.

Dad had never said no to her like that before. It was clear now that he wasn't planning to let her make any decisions about Dalex's future. Even if he promoted her, he'd probably still try to guide everything she did from his cosy retirement villa.

He had shut her down without even giving her the chance to pitch her idea about how they could fix the algae bloom, and then immediately given the Greenfingers project to Edgar. It had sent a clear message: he would reward her for doing things that would profit the company. And she would be punished if she brought up the moral problems with their work.

Dad didn't want her thinking about pollution and algae blooms. He had taken away all of her power just for thinking for herself. He wasn't proud of her for being independent and self-motivated. He was *annoyed* by it.

Was she willing to work with Dad for the next thirty, forty, fifty years, if their relationship was always going to be that way? She would be butting heads with him for the rest of her life.

"Your dad just waved away the whole algae thing?" Theo asked. "That's not really how the law works, out in the real world. Usually there's an investigation, and these things called court trials, and a judgement…"

Hester was pleased that he was relaxed enough to tease her. "That does sound vaguely familiar. I'll have to let our lawyers know, so they can test it out. They're probably due a challenge." She frowned. "They cost us enough."

"How much…?"

Hester mixed a spoonful of his yeast into flour and milk, kneading it with the palms of her hands. "We donated fifty million dollars to Greenpeace."

Theo blinked at her, mouth half open. "Wow. OK. I mean, it's not like I could ever pay it back, but I'm in your debt, I guess."

He seemed to be re-evaluating the sheer scale of her wealth. She pretended not to notice and focused on slicing chunks of butter into the sticky dough.

"By the way, as it turns out, you were right about climate change. About basically everything, actually. I spoke to my dad and … he told me some things I didn't know. About Dalex."

"Right," he said carefully.

"I was wrong," she said, punching the dough violently. "I didn't think we deserved the blame when everyone on the planet uses our oil. But – we weren't just reacting to demand. Dalex have been actively stopping people using clean energy instead."

"I mean, yeah. You're an *oil company*. Isn't that what you do?"

He wasn't going to make this easy for her. Summoning her courage, she said, "I'm trying to say that I'm sorry I was so awful to you. My dad really got into my head. I think he's been feeding me lies my whole life." She brought her hand up to rub her face, then scowled at her sticky fingers.

She and Dad had an intrinsic difference of opinion about what Dalex's legacy should be. For the first time, she had no idea what her future might look like.

What did she even want?

She knew that she didn't want to be trotted out for public events as a pretty face with no real power. She didn't want to ignore her morals, to focus on profit above all else. She wanted to make a mark on the company, and a positive impact on the world. If Dad was never going to give her that chance, then did she really have a place at Dalex at all?

It was an impossible, awful thing to think. How could she even consider giving up such an important role? She was lucky to have been born into such a powerful family. She should be grateful, shouldn't she?

She'd built her whole future around this company. She didn't even have any *friends*. The closest was Theodore Carthew, who probably thought she was a giant mess.

She watched him attempt to knead the dough, pummelling it with his fists.

"How do you cope with being this afraid *all the time*?" she asked. "It feels like the world is ending."

He nodded. "I've been scared since I was a kid. I didn't think I could do anything except watch the planet fall apart. But now we can actually make a difference. We have a bigger resource than those politicians have ever had, along with teenagers like us across the whole planet. We need to stop fighting each other and do something useful."

Immediately, she said, "What can I do? I want – need – to help."

"The most useful stuff isn't going to be exciting spy missions. It's going to be the dull work of sifting through piles of rubbish. Or cutting plastic rings off birds' legs."

"I'll do anything, Theo. This is something I have to do.

Whatever Dad thinks." He had turned down her request to rehabilitate the algae bloom, but that didn't mean she had to give in. She wasn't his mindless slave. Not any more. This was something she needed. For the first time in days, she didn't feel like she was drowning.

The dough was ballooning around Theo's fingers. She hastily tugged it away before he could grow any more yeast. "That's probably ready to go in now, actually."

Theo forged his way on. "I've been talking to some Greenfingers activists. They gave me a great idea for something we could try with the trainees at one of the Dalex coal plants."

Hester shaped the dough into a ball and slashed it, scattering oats over the top. "Like what?"

"Did you know that the land around your factories is polluted?" he asked.

Hester shrugged, then slid the dough into the oven. "There are some waste pools, yeah. But it's just charcoal. It looks really gross but it's harmless."

"Um, no. Those ponds are super toxic. And they've leaked all the chemicals into the soil. It's caused cancer and stuff in the local kids. I was reading this blog about it, *firstwithmagic.*"

Hester paused, aghast. Was she going to feel this way for the rest of her life? Constantly uncovering ways in which Dad had lied to her? "How is that possible?"

"Whenever it rains, the water pulls the ash out of the ponds and takes it downstream in the river. But there's a theory that the toxins can be drawn out of the ground by growing certain plants there, like pumpkins and fungus. I thought we could try it with the trainees."

Inside the oven, the batter formed a solid mahogany crust. Hester leaned back against the counter.

"I bet Edgar could be convinced to run our training session at one of our coal plants in Dallas," she mused. "I can just say that it's polluted land, so it doesn't matter if it gets a bit messed up."

It might even improve the value of the land, now she thought about it. Those sites really were awful. "You know what, you're right. Sure, we messed up on the yacht. But we can't give up after just one attempt."

When Theo held out a hand to her, she shook it carefully.

"We're on the same side," he said, to be sure that she understood. "No more fighting."

"I dare say I can muster the self-restraint," she said, grinning.

"Save the bickering for Edgar Warren," he added.

Hester snorted. "He winds me up *so much*."

"I can tell. You shouldn't trust him. He's never going to help us fix the environment, because it would actually work *against him* if his technology saved Earth. Right? Then no one would move to his Mars colony, 'cause no sane person would want to live in a bubble unless Earth is uninhabitable."

Hester's eyes widened. It was in Edgar's best interests for

Earth to be destroyed. If Mars became the next New York, he would become the richest man alive. Every government on the planet would be fixing to buy seats on his shuttles to evacuate to Mars. The collapse of civilization was a profitable endeavour.

She whistled through her teeth. "Damn. Whoever his press team is, they're doing a great job. He makes the Mars project sound so futuristic and cool. But it's all just spin."

"The weirdest thing about him is how much he knows about me," Theo said. "I think he uses some kind of high-tech tracking software or something. The minute he met me, he looked me up and found out some very secret stuff that he should have had no way of knowing."

"Like what?"

"Um." He hesitated, looking nervous. "I don't really want to say. I'm just – you should be careful around him. He's the kind of person who wants to know absolutely everything about everyone. He's probably done his weird little search on you too."

Hester waved this off. Dalex had a whole team of online security experts protecting her privacy. And she was curious now. Theo looked so shifty all of a sudden.

"Are you really not going to tell me what he said? You keep a lot of secrets, Theo. We're supposed to be a team, aren't we? But you never even told me about your broken power. If we're going to work together, we have to be able to trust each other."

"I do trust you," he said fervently. "But I think you'll stop trusting *me*, if I tell you the truth."

"No way. I'll try and fix whatever you've messed up. Obviously."

"OK then. Well, he found out that I work at the docks back home."

"Right…" She eyed him, trying to work out if having worked in manual labour was the whole secret.

"I used to, you know, take a few phones or whatever. From the shipments coming from Junwei in China." Theo shuffled, rubbing the back of his neck. "Edgar mentioned it in this weird way, like he was threatening to tell the company about it."

"We—" Hester swallowed, making a strange clicking noise in her throat. "Dalex actually acquired Junwei a few years ago. Did you know that?"

The tips of Theo's ears turned pink. "You what?"

She laughed at him, almost disbelieving. "Are you serious, right now?"

He'd been stealing from *her*, all those years? No wonder Edgar had brought it up. He must have thought it was hilarious.

"Yeeeees?"

"I cannot believe you ever got through the interview process." She made a note on her to-do list app to change her recruitment agency, pronto. "I had better send some emails."

"Don't!" he pleaded. "Hester, *please*. It's not worth anything to you. Just a few phones and accessories now and then. You never even noticed they were missing!"

Hester inspected his face, thinking hard. "This is more of your ethics thing again, isn't it?"

He took a deep breath. "All your decisions have always been made based on how much money you can make. But my family are, like, two bad months away from being homeless. Think about who is going to be hurt by the things you do – real life *people*, out there in the world, not companies. Isn't it worth breaking a few laws to know you're helping someone?"

Hester considered this so hard that her eye twitched. "I'll think about it," she said at last. "I am trying, you know. To be better."

It should have occurred to her to consider the people it would affect. She'd only been thinking of fixing the security weaknesses to prevent interference with their shipments. It was going to take a long time to relearn everything she'd been taught by Dad.

Something flickered across Theo's face at that. "Did you pay for my dad's boat? They got brushed off by Dalex before, but then something made them change their minds."

Hester wrinkled her nose. She had hoped he wouldn't connect it back to her. "I'm sure I don't know what you're talking about."

Theo looked pleased.

"How are your parents doing now, anyway?" she asked. "Will the money be enough to replace the boat?"

"Actually … the crash might be a bit of a relief for them, now they've got over the shock. Dad's been struggling to keep afloat for years. But I don't think he ever thought he could leave the fishing business. It's what we've done for generations.

Maybe now he can move on to something less stressful."

"It was your dad's family business?" she asked.

Theo nodded. "Yeah. My mum's parents are from Bangladesh. They moved to London when my mum was little."

"That's cool," Hester said. "My mom wasn't born here either; she's from Brazil. She met Dad in an investment meeting."

"Mine met at a house party when Dad was visiting his schoolmate at uni. I have no idea how he convinced her to move to a tiny village in the middle of nowhere with him."

Hester regarded Theo thoughtfully. Despite their differences, maybe they could find a way to work together without fighting all the time. It could turn into something wonderful.

When the loaf was done, they sliced it open, still steaming hot, and slathered thick wedges in salted butter and honey. The first thing they'd made together, and it was glorious.

**theocarth:** I got hester daleport to agree to let us fix the coal ash ponds next Monday afternoon. Can you make yourself look like a photographer? Pretend you've been invited there to take press shots.

**firstwithmagic:** Ha. Cute. Coal ash isn't why I want to go there. But nice excuse.

**theocarth:** wait what? what do you mean?? What else are you planning?

**firstwithmagic:** I'll meet you there. Let me know your ETA.

**theocarth:** but what are you going to do there?

**theocarth:** hello??????? Gabrielle???

*carthew fam* **group chat**

**Theo:** flying to dallas write now in a private helicopter!!! Don't bother being jealous, they only have three flavours of san pellegrino :(

**Mum:** THEODORE KALAM CARTHEW, YOU SOD

**Mum:** How's the training going? Have you managed to get your power to play along yet?

**Theo:** ah yes I did! I can grow fungi! Hester hleped me out

**Mum:** Our little mushroom boy <3

**Theo:** please don't call me that.

**Dad:** You're friends with Hester again then, mushroom boy?

**Theo:** HOW DO YOU MANAGE TOO BE THIS EMBARRASSING VIA TEXT

**Theo:** yes. where friends.

**Mum:** Ooooooh. Tell us more!

**Theo:** goodbye.

**Mum:** Send us some pictures!! With your Hester, please!

**Theo:** BYE

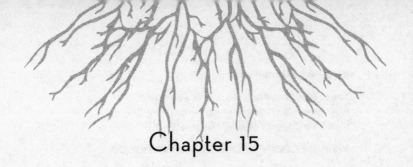

# Chapter 15

Theo had never been in a helicopter before. There was something hypnotizing about being able to watch the odd American landscape, with its jagged hillsides covered in banks of trees, roll out below them as they flew to Dallas in Edgar Warren's airbus.

It had been a week since their plankton disaster. Theo had been using all his free time to study up on fungi and botany, listening to audiobooks and podcasts whenever he wasn't training with the group. They could bubble up their powers across huge distances now, thanks to the underground spores.

Their powers had synchronized as they got to know each other better. Theo was becoming so effortlessly attuned to the others' powers that he could tell exactly where they all were in the training centre, even when he was alone in his bedroom.

If they were standing on bare earth, there was practically no limit to how far away their powers could interact. They'd tested it across the entire city of Houston. The fungus had given them their own private communication system.

He wasn't sure how he'd be able to go back to normal life after this.

However well he worked with the other trainees, nothing had come close to matching his practice sessions with Hester. There was something special about the way they worked together, as if their powers fed off each other in a feedback loop. He could always grow more with her than any other partner – though he wasn't planning to admit that to her any time soon. It was too revealing.

As well as improving his powers, his research had taught him about tidal erosion and coral reefs, about glacier melt and ocean microplastics. But he still didn't know how they were going to fix the algae bloom.

All he could do was focus on other ways they could help make up for the damage, after their trip to the coal plant.

Theo had decided not to mention Gabrielle's involvement to Hester, just in case it scared her off. It was a miracle she'd agreed to help at all.

Hester was sitting in the back of the cabin with Edgar, where he had a bank of computer screens set up on the back wall. He was engaged in what seemed to be an enthusiastic discussion of the *Star Trek* extended universe, while Hester nodded along politely, eyes glazed.

Theo much preferred sitting with the trainees. Icaro had spent the journey orchestrating a corrupt and cut-throat game of Werewolf, to deafening groans and shrieks.

"I had no idea you had it in you," Theo told Alisha in

admiration, after she'd successfully lied her way through murdering half the group.

"I have a deep, unquenchable bloodlust," she said primly.

"I can believe it."

Alisha's skin had recently taken on a green tint. Apparently, she didn't really get hungry any more. The chlorophyll fed on sunlight and kept her full. Theo didn't think he had room to judge. Sometimes it felt like he could lie in the sun and nap for ever.

That morning, he'd woken up rooted to the mattress by white filaments locked around his limbs. There were apparently some downsides to using their powers so much they became instinctive.

Theo eyed Beatriz, who was massaging her stomach. She'd only just been released from the hospital, but she'd insisted on coming along.

"Are you sure you're up to this trip?" he asked her.

Daisy tucked Beatriz under her arm. "I'll keep an eye on her."

"Thanks," Beatriz said to Theo. "I didn't get a chance to say, before. But you saved my life."

"Oh, no problem," Theo said. "I mean, obviously. Any time."

A bit self-conscious, he stared intently outside. They were approaching one of those strangely American hamlets out in the middle of nowhere, one road in and one road out, surrounded by nothing but fields. In the dry brown landscape, there was a single vivid green oasis. A Greenfingers must live there.

He wondered if he would be able to sense them, like they'd done with the person on the cliff from the yacht. The distance to the ground here was a lot shorter.

He extended his power, searching for that familiar vibration he felt with the trainees. To his surprise, he instantly connected with another Greenfingers.

They were in their garden, gently encouraging a clematis to grow along a trellis. When Theo nudged them, it took only a second of hesitation for them to reach back. Out of nowhere, he sensed the entire network of plants below, from the vibration of the wheat in the fields to the slow, deep sleep of an oak tree, and the rustling energy of grasses.

It was all so clear, even from this distance. Through the Greenfingers on the ground, the connection remained strong for a few seconds. Then the helicopter disappeared out of range.

Startled, Theo cast his senses out again, like a radar beam crossing back and forth across the land. There was nothing but bare fields and the dipping heads of oil pumpjacks.

It was only when they passed over a city that Theo realized the full extent of his discovery. There was a whole network of Greenfingers dotted around the urban area, who all nudged him back in greeting.

All at once, the connection amplified. It was like they were linked together in a group, building on each other's strength in the same way that the trainees did when they bubbled up.

The sudden spurt of power was overwhelming. Instinctively, Theo redirected it into a small square of green parkland. Even from high above, he could see the plants explode into colour as they grew.

Theo gaped, trying to process what had happened. Just how far could they project their powers? Could they keep amplifying them over greater and greater distances, until they'd gathered enough Greenfingers to cover the whole of Texas?

By the time he stirred from his thoughts, they were approaching the coal factory – where Gabrielle Ventura would be waiting for them.

## *Taylor Swan Drops a Surprise Greenfingers-themed Single*

The racy lyrics have spurred a spate of rumours, especially after the multi-award-winning singer's Gal Pal (pictured here in Versace sweatpants and a chic topknot bun) reposted the lyrics with a heart emoji.

> *Greenfinger girl, you're my*
> *Greenfinger girl*
> *Leaf me, never leave me*
> *Flush with thorns but sweet as pollen*
> *Every teasing blossom leaves me sodden*
> *Coil your vines tight round my wrists*
> *Keep me rooted in your soil*
> *Greenfinger girl*

If there was any doubt, Taylor has set our minds at rest: green is officially the new black. We're entering a new era of culture, defined by the Greenfingers generation. And we're going to be listening to the latest single on repeat henceforth, obviously.

### *Comments*

**LittleDaemon** you're really going to glorify the GFs without even mentioning the political struggle they're going through right now? There are still no regulations in place to protect GF workers. some kid collapsed in a factory in china last week. they're all gonna be dead within the year if manufacturers are allowed to push their powers to the point of dehydration. but yeah sure nice song I guess t-swan.

> **DoubleXed** they're using GFs to save on production costs so they can lower the price of their products, it helps consumers

> > **LittleDaemon** yeah? that doesn't make it any less inhumane. we have no idea how safely these powers can be used. we need Greenfingers labour laws NOW!

> > > **Dramadiva** like apparently there are loads of GFs getting bone disorders like rickets + osteoporosis. Powers cause deficiencies or something because they use nutrients like phosphorus, calcium and magnesium from their own bodies when growing plants.

> > > > **DoubleXed** No statistics have been released concerning whether the affected patients had the Greenfingers powers.

> > > > > **Dramadiva** Oh yeah? so you think it's just a coincidence that lots of teenagers get rickets after powers appear in teenagers? Sounds legit.

# Chapter 16

Hester eyed the coal factory over her sunglasses. Even she had to admit that it looked like some sort of hellscape. The huge squat chimneys of the factory were surrounded by wide, shallow pits, each filled with watery ash. Smoke drifted in the wind from mountains of black char.

This place was more evidence of her mortifying oversight. She'd visited the factory at least a dozen times over the past few years. Why had she never wondered if anything could be done about the grey slurry pits? Had she assumed that it was a problem beyond fixing, too huge for any company to possibly conquer? Hester hadn't thought about it at all. She had never questioned the way anything was done.

She hadn't seen Dad in over a week. She'd been staying at the training centre so she could avoid him until she'd decided what to do. There had been a lot of restless nights where she'd replayed their conversation over and over in her head, searching for a way to avoid confronting him about climate change.

There was no way out of it. If she was going to have any chance of a future at Dalex, she had to tell him where her boundaries lay. Hester had never stopped working for long enough to appreciate nature before – the natural world had always just been an uncomfortably hot, uncomfortably itchy place with slower internet speeds – but her powers had changed that. It was impossible not to care for the plants around her when she could feel their drowsy, contented vibrations as they soaked up the sunlight and fresh rainwater.

In a best-case scenario, Dad would understand when she explained that she needed to take responsibility for their pollution. He'd agree that they could reconsider their plans, and even if it took a while for them to get back on track, she would be able to stay at Dalex. It seemed unlikely that he'd agree, but she had to try, didn't she? This coal ash experiment would remind him how valuable she could be.

"Crikey," Theo said, looking past the massive piles of coal ash to a sprawling lake of neon azure-blue water.

Hester pinched the bridge of her nose against the acidic smell. "We used to pump the coal ash into the water back in the seventies," she admitted. "The colour comes from the chemicals in the deposits."

Theo dipped his toe into the slurry. In the morning light, dust and sunshine glowed in his hair. "I'm not sure we're going to be able to restore your nightmare factory to good health, but I guess it's worth a try."

Hester wanted to feel indignant, but she mainly agreed with him. She was already exhausted, and there was so much work to be done. How could they ever even make a dent in the endless acres of toxic land?

Her phone buzzed with a message from Edgar, who was watching from above in his helicopter so he could track how far their powers stretched. He didn't know about their plan to remove the toxins from the soil too, and she wasn't planning on telling him unless she had to.

**Edgar:** ready when you are. Make sure they project as far as possible.

Aware that his eyes were on them, Hester quickly arranged the trainees into a loose circle in the middle of the wasteland. "Fill this space with the plants you've been assigned. Try to tap into the fungal network and send the signal as far as you can."

"Take a break if you need one," Theo added. "No nose-bleeds, please!"

A quiet focus spread around the circle. The sun-baked soil quaked and shook as sprouts fought their way into the light. Hester grew a pumpkin plant, letting the tangle of vines spill over her feet. Next to her, Daisy grew red-veined sorrel.

Theo typed something on his phone. Then he started growing fungi, dappled between everything else: bright white spires reaching tall, with pitch-black skin; branching feathery lobes that fused together like antlers; shaggy lichen stains with flaking layers and tufts. He'd been doing some research into fungi that would remove toxins from the soil too, apparently.

He beamed at her, bubbling up his power with hers

effortlessly. Immediately, the sunflower she was growing shot upwards, the tiny hairs on its stem shivering in the wind.

Her power always responded enthusiastically when it combined with his. It was something she tried not to think about too much. If there was one thing she wished she could change, it was how her Greenfingers responded to her emotions. It felt too much like displaying her bleeding heart to the world.

Within minutes, the entire circle was bursting with plants, so thick that Hester was forced to step backwards.

**Edgar:** L I F T  O F F!! Rockin. Keep at it
**Hester:** Yes, my team are doing a great job.

It felt like he was breathing down the back of her neck. Edgar was determined to control their progress, even from above. He'd demanded daily reports on the training activities, even though she was sure he hadn't read a single one of them.

Growing a flat beefsteak fungus that oozed a sticky blood-like sap, Theo asked, "How does your first act of rebellion feel?"

"Pretty great," she admitted. "I think it suits me."

"You should start a rebellion scheme for billionaire offspring. Edgar's sure to have some kids one day who will be very grateful."

She laughed. On the rare occasions when Mom was at home, they played epic seven-hour games of Monopoly. They'd expanded the game with their own economic variables, including a twenty-sided dice that determined how well the stock market was doing on each turn. Talking to Theo felt like indulging in one of these games of strategy with Mom – except the stakes were making Theo laugh, instead of fictional financial stability.

Hester shouted, "Stop there! I want y'all to pull up the plants inside our circle now. I know that feels wrong, but we have to grow more from the same ground."

They began piling up the plants from within the circle. They would be disposed of safely, taking the toxic metal inside their cells with them.

> **Edgar:** What are you doing? Keep growing. You haven't filled the whole plot yet.
>
> **Hester:** I'm testing something, give me a minute.

As they were pulling up the last few layers of weeds, a girl in a baseball cap and sunglasses appeared and started taking photos with a camera. Hester sighed. It was just like Edgar to arrange a press shoot without telling her. It was another way of proving that this was his project, not hers.

"All right, now we need to grow another layer of those same plants!" Hester called out to the rest of the group, who had started a competition to see who could grow the nicest bunch of flowers for their crush. Hester was incredibly glad that she had so far managed to avoid becoming aware of whatever teen sitcom romances the trainees were busy entangling themselves in. Though – Theo wasn't involved in any of that, was he? A pang went through her. She hadn't seen him talking to anyone in particular, but it wasn't like they spent every waking moment together.

This time, the seedlings caught easily on the freshly turned earth. The plants rolled in a wave across the entire scrubland. The silver undersides of willow leaves flashed in the wind between grassy tussocks and heather.

"I need to get my drone up there," Binh said longingly, when they were pausing to catch their breath. "The footage of this would *pop*."

"Absolutely not happening," Hester said, imagining the lawsuits if he somehow damaged Edgar's helicopter.

"Spoilsport," he grumbled.

"You want to go viral so badly, Binh," Jason said. "You should start doing those video requests for bouquets with messages in Victorian flower code."

"Is there a code for 'get back to work'?" Theo asked.

They all laughed, then bent their heads back to pulling up the fresh growth. The next time Hester looked up, Theo had disappeared. The photographer was gone too. She craned her neck to search for them, until her phone buzzed.

> **Edgar:** I think that's enough, excèllenté. We should be able to work with that in the Arctic.

The helicopter veered away, preparing to land on a newly green meadow, where plants had burst into life as the effects of their powers rippled outwards.

Hester stared down at the message. Arctic? What did he

mean? Was it something to do with what Dad had been trying to tell her last week? She'd been too busy freaking out to pay attention. What else had she heard them say? It was something the Greenfingers could do in the Arctic, using Edgar's atmospheric mapping software.

Dawning horror swept over Hester. They couldn't be planning to do something to the *polar ice caps*, could they?

Dad had been emailing her all day, but she'd been ignoring the messages. Now she flicked through them, looking for anything to prove her theory wrong.

> **Dad:** I'm hosting a meeting with the oligarchs about drilling permissions next week. I'd like you to talk about our Greenfingers there.

Dad was negotiating with the Russian state for the rights to build a drilling platform on the Arctic shelf. One of the biggest oil reserves in the world was under the ice, but it was too thick to get a tanker in.

For the rest of the world, the ice caps melting would mean the fight was over – it would signal the collapse of the world as they knew it. But for Dad, it was the dream scenario. There would be no obstacles stopping him from accessing the liquid gold under the ice.

He'd been working on securing the contract for a decade, ensuring they'd be ready if the Arctic ice did begin to melt. If he was rushing to get the deal done now, something had changed. Something with Edgar and the Greenfingers that might help him to access the oilfields a lot sooner.

They must have found a way to speed up the melting. That could explain why Edgar was so keen to see how far the Greenfingers could grow their plants. He wasn't just vying for control of the trainees with silly exercises. He wanted to see if they could do something with the miles of Arctic wilderness.

Hester was willing to bet half her shares on it. Knowing Dad, he'd be planning something wild, like spraying a fresh tundra forest in oil droplets and setting it on fire to melt the permafrost.

Hot fury rose in her chest. If they extracted that oil, then it would be like setting off a carbon bomb. They might as well give up on stopping climate change completely, because they'd have signed Earth's death warrant.

This was it, then. There was no future for her at Dalex, not if Dad was going ahead with something like this. He was never going to give her true responsibility, never let her create a legacy to be proud of.

Dad had chosen his side, and she wasn't going to stand by and watch while he destroyed the world.

Even if it hurt, she had to leave Dalex while there was still a chance she could move on and find somewhere better. She'd have to work her way up from the bottom in a new company, but she had her whole life for that. It seemed a small price to pay to stop this.

Far beyond the trainees, there were red lights flashing at the factory gates. A distant siren was blaring as staff evacuated the building. Something was going on – and Theo was mysteriously absent. This couldn't be good.

# WHAT DOES YOUR PLANT
# PARASITE SAY ABOUT YOU?

do you grow plants out of your skin like the rest of us feral cryptids? find out what that says about your MBTI type/zodiac/ moon sign/whatever by getting slotted into an arbitrary personality category! no logic here, we die like men. if you don't agree w my choices, call your congressman, i don't care

**Do you require water and soil and sunlight for sustenance?**

- ☑ i am thriving. i love dirt and soil and being outside.

- ⭕ i'm a sand fiend, get me a soft mound of the good stuff and I'll be happy for decades.

- ⭕ More water! More! Submerge My Body For One Thousand Years!

- ⭕ Cool and cold, ice and snow, f r e e z e  m e in that sweet sweet frost.

**What is Your Vibe?**

- ☑ I am a threat, a killer, a monstrous being of venom and sap. Stay away. I have sharp spikes and I'm not afraid to use them. Poison? Always.

- ⭕ I crave closeness, soft and gentle, tender touch. Fuzz like velvet. Cradle me. I am safety where others wish only death upon you.

- ⭕ DO YOU WANT FOOD? I'VE GOT FOOD FOR YA.

- ⭕ High fashion femme, catch me out here with the neon accessories and glitter dust, catwalk baby.

You are:

# Ragwort

Asshole. No one likes you. Stop taking quizzes online and go make some friends who aren't INVASIVE.

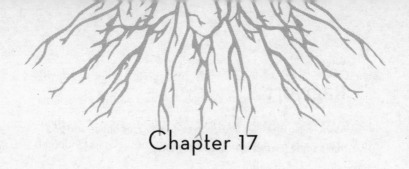

# Chapter 17

Theo wanted to be doing anything other than following a self-declared illegal activist into a heavily secured coal complex right now. Absolutely anything in the world. But he'd lost control of the situation as soon as Gabrielle Ventura had arrived.

"What are you doing?" he hissed, as Gabrielle marched off towards the factory. He cast a helpless look in Hester's direction, but she was thankfully busy with the trainees.

"If we're going to do anything useful today, it will be stopping that factory running even a moment longer," Gabrielle replied. She looked just like she did in all the press videos, with fluffy black hair and a bright round face. Though usually in photos she wasn't glaring like she'd knock out anyone who got in her way.

"What?" Theo asked, startled.

Gabrielle shrugged. "My group is trying to stop carbon emissions in industry."

She pulled some electronic device out of her bag, walking along the perimeter of the fence that separated the factory itself from the wasteland surrounding it. Theo eyed the device warily. He'd seen her videos online, and she was a big fan of morally dubious activism. He'd only brought her here to fix the coal ash pollution. Not make another viral video of some dodgy act of sabotage.

Just because something was illegal didn't mean it was wrong. But there was a difference between acts of desperation, like stealing a few packages to pay the bills, and gleeful criminal acts, like attacking an entire factory. "Aren't you worried about getting arrested?"

Gabrielle grinned, waving the device over the ground as she walked. "Getting arrested is the whole point! We're going to do hunger strikes, like the suffragettes."

Her teeth flashed when she smiled. One of them was dark and strange. It was a wooden tooth, he realized with a vague shock of horror, rooted into her gums.

"Nice," he said, unsettled. "Wouldn't it be a better use of your time to help us remove some of the toxic metals from the soil?"

She scowled. "Dalex are already undoing your hard work by burning more coal." She gestured to a digger that was emptying another lorryload of ash onto the mountain.

Theo frowned. "But you won't stop them this way either. Even if you manage to shut down the factory today, they'll start up again tomorrow."

She shook her head. "This is just a test. We want to find a way to get noticed by the government. I've given speeches and started petitions and campaigns, but nobody listens. If we can do something big, they'll have to pay attention to our demands. I'm mainly interested in the politics of it all."

Theo thought she was "interested in politics" in the same way that Doctor Frankenstein had been "interested in medicine". She wanted to tear it apart and resurrect it into something more exciting.

"What *are* your demands?"

Gabrielle had found another tool in her bag now – what looked to Theo like a long, thin metal spike. "Ban single-use, non-recyclable plastics. Tax carbon emissions at the highest possible level. End government subsidies for fossil fuel companies. Create stricter regulations around corporate pollution. Provide public transportation everywhere, to allow the transition away from cars."

Theo blinked. She'd really thought this through.

"Oh," she added, levering up a clod of turf, "and make these kinds of laws international, so companies can't hide from restrictions overseas."

"But those changes are massive. Is that even possible?" He wiped his forehead. It was cooler in the shadows of the factory, but only slightly.

The damp soil smelled fresh and rich. He tried to ignore the urge to pick up a handful and eat it. Recently, he'd been craving mulch and compost. His power was endlessly hungry.

Gabrielle pushed the metal spike into the ground, using all her weight to press it down through the earth. "I think so.

Definitely. We already know that governments can make rapid changes to how society runs. During the Covid-19 pandemic, the entire world's office workers transitioned to working from home via video calls within weeks. Governments made huge changes to policies super quickly. That needs to happen now, too, just as fast. Climate change is already killing people every day. We need to show the governments that they have to take urgent action."

Theo suddenly felt very silly about what he was doing with Hester. They'd been so proud of their little attempt to take metals out of the land here. But it was nothing compared to what Gabrielle was doing. She wanted the whole world to act.

"I mean, that all sounds great. Totally on board," Theo said. "But how are you ever possibly going to get to the point where they actually do that stuff?"

There was a dull thud as the spike impacted with something below the ground. Gabrielle attached her mysterious device onto the end protruding from the soil. It started clicking.

She grinned at Theo. "We have political leverage already. You messaged me because I've got myself in the news enough that you know my name. That's powerful."

Theo bit his lip. People were hardly going to make all these changes just to shut her up. Gabrielle clearly had good intentions – and a very determined spirit – but she seemed a bit adrift. She knew exactly what she wanted to change politically, but she didn't really have a way to get there yet.

She was like a loaded gun with nothing to shoot at. All she could do was make a lot of noise.

Maybe there was a way they could help each other. Gabrielle needed someone strategic to guide her outbursts of protestation – and Hester needed a way to use her strategic thinking. This might be a match made in heaven.

Gabrielle took his hand and wrapped it around the metal spike. "Now, focus."

"With my power, you mean?" He let his senses sink deep into the rich earth below. He followed the paths of the fungal network to where it stopped at the concrete foundations of the factory building. There was something running perpendicular to the surface. The fungus had to move around it.

"Is that a pipe?" he asked, eyes closed. The metal spike had been pushed all the way down to the top of the pipe. He could see it clearly in his mind, as if the whole network of spores were his eyes underground.

"It's our way in." Gabrielle concentrated her power on the metal. She wasn't as strong as Hester, but when Theo opened his eyes, the top of the metal spike was covered in a thin vine that twisted around its length and disappeared underground.

His mind followed its movement as the plant reached the metal pipe, encircling it. Tendrils curled tightly around the tube.

When Theo realized what Gabrielle was planning, he almost pulled his hand away. He couldn't be involved in this, but … he had to see what happened next.

"What plant is that?" he murmured, eyes closed again as he watched what was happening under the soil. He swatted away a mosquito hovering around his ear.

"Bindweed."

The bindweed was pressing into the metal now, searching for weak spots. When it found one, its pale white roots twisted inside.

Theo felt like he was there with the vines as they crept down the pipe, following the flow of water under the foundations of the factory.

Gabrielle hummed in pleasure as the bindweed curved upwards, bending towards the factory on the surface. When it hit something hard, the stem twisted and flexed. It was stuck in a dead end.

"That's the valve," Gabrielle said. "This is where it gets interesting."

She pushed with all her strength, growing the bindweed until it filled the pipe. The pressure began to build as the plant ran out of space.

Gabrielle paused to rest.

"I've never tried this on my own before," she admitted, panting for breath. "There's always been a few of us during practice tests."

"Can you do it?" Theo asked. He wasn't sure if he wanted her to succeed or fail.

"I don't know," Gabrielle said. "Can I use your power too? I won't tell anyone."

Theo hesitated, but he was too curious to resist. He directed his power down through the spike and into the soil. Immediately, the bindweed doubled and tripled in size, until suddenly he felt the valve burst open. Plants tumbled into the open air in a gush of water. He could feel the light on their leaves, after a long journey underground.

Gabrielle said, "The water will do the rest. It'll flood the basement floor, so they'll evacuate the factory to repair the damage. We need to make sure they can't stop the leak until this place is properly underwater."

Theo could picture the vines investigating the boundaries of the room. "You're searching for the door?" he asked, suddenly wary of what she might be planning next. When she'd seen him growing fungi on the coal ash site, she'd said, "Your mushrooms would make an excellent murder weapon from all the toxins they've absorbed. No one would suspect a thing." He'd kept a close eye on her after that, in case she slipped one into her pocket.

"That's the stairwell. We'll block access to this area."

Plants crept underneath the lip of the door, their network of stems stretching through the basement rooms, jamming up locks and blocking any entrances.

Gabrielle let go of the spike, sighing in satisfaction. "I wish I could see it for real," she said. It was hard to believe that the little vine still twisted around the metal spike was the beginning of such a complex system of plants.

"If you've done this before, why wasn't it on the news?"

Theo asked, licking his dry lips. That had used up his full reserves of energy. He wouldn't have thought it was possible, back in the days of useless seaweed.

Vaguely, he could sense the bindweed being submerged in water as the basement flooded. It was a sense of drowning at the back of his mind, too small to really panic over.

"We haven't done it before," Gabrielle admitted. "This was my first test."

In the distance, they heard the roar of alarms. She grinned. "So we'd better run."

Theo and Gabrielle sprinted back to the group. Hester was boarding Edgar's helicopter with the trainees, peering at the factory evacuation in concern.

"You can give me a lift, right?" Gabrielle asked Theo.

"Oh, bloody hell," he hissed. "All right. Remember, you're the photographer."

How did he always get himself into these nightmare situations? He was not built to deal with this. He pushed Gabrielle in behind Daisy and Beatriz, just as Hester called, "Theo! Where have you been?"

"Toilet – crisis…" he spluttered limply, his mind a writhing sea of panic and bad excuses.

"It doesn't look like it's anything dangerous," Hester was telling Edgar, who spun around to face her. "The manager said it's just a burst pipe or something."

Gabrielle shoved her bag of equipment under her seat,

wiggling her eyebrows at Theo conspiratorially. He bit the inside of his cheek. She seemed to thrive on chaos, which Theo absolutely could not relate to.

"No biggie, that test gave me enough data to work with. You guys covered a lot of ground," Edgar replied vaguely, while manipulating a simulation of what seemed to be the entire Planet Earth. Theo frowned at it. He was interested in *Mars*, wasn't he?

Hester settled in the seat next to Theo, still craning her head to look out of the window. A fire engine was pulling up outside the factory now.

"Good work today, everyone," Theo called as they took off. The words came out as more of a croak, but the trainees didn't seem to notice. Daisy and Beatriz had their arms around each other's shoulders, and Zen and Alisha were playfighting despite their exhaustion – throwing up barriers of nettles and firing cactus bombs across the aisle at each other.

Hester smiled at him. Her gaze caught on Gabrielle, taking pictures of the factory out of the window. Hester's forehead creased into a frown.

Theo's heart stumbled over itself. "What's for dinner tonight?" He sped through the words as if that would stop the dawning recognition from crossing her face. "More deep-fried cheesecake I hope, that was lush! I didn't even know it was possible to fry cheesecake, do you know how it's done?"

There was a burned-coal red shine on Hester's cheeks. "Is that—"

"The photographer!" he said, voice high-pitched. He tilted his head meaningfully towards Edgar, who was moving a joystick erratically in the row behind them. His little head poked up to peer over the seats at them. He looked like a rabbit peering out of its burrow.

Hester glared at Theo. "Right." She looked out of the window again, at the red lights flashing on the roof of the factory, then back at Gabrielle. Every muscle in her body was tense.

Theo had no idea what to say. She had every right to be mad at him. He'd purposefully lied to her about why he wanted to come here today.

When her phone rang, he almost passed out.

"Hi, Dad," she said, eyes fixed on Theo.

He was close enough to hear Mr Daleport over the speaker.

"Princess. Just got an interesting call from a very panicked operations manager out at the Dallas factory. He said their basement flooded – unusual, but nothing to panic about. But all the underground pipes were filled with vines."

"Wow, what?" she asked him, squeezing Theo's wrist like a vice. "Did they have a weed infestation down there?"

Gabrielle was now emailing photos of the shut-down factory to someone, her expression fixed in a rictus of glee.

"Apparently none of it was there yesterday," Mr Daleport said. "Any chance your group was involved?"

Theo tried to sink into his seat.

Hester sighed loudly. "I'm sorry, Dad. I thought we'd got this control issue sorted. Clearly they can project over a much bigger distance than I figured. Though, that's a good thing, right?"

"I bet Edgar's pleased as punch!"

"You could say that, yes." Her voice was dry. "The good news is, we managed to take some of the pollution out of the coal ash ponds during the session today."

"Did you really? However did you come up with that idea?"

As Hester updated Mr Daleport, Theo tapped Gabrielle's shoulder. She was trying to crane backwards over her seat to see what Edgar was doing.

"Be chill!" he begged. Her constant desire to throw herself into any hint of danger was already starting to become a nuisance.

"He's using the new crypto software!" she whispered. "I've read about it online! It isn't released for another three months."

"Please be quiet," he said through a clenched jaw, pressing the heels of his palms to his eyes.

When Hester hung up, her displeasure was almost palpable.

"We are having a long talk when we get back, Theodore Carthew," she said grimly.

Hester had only just agreed to help him, and he'd already messed it up. What reason did she have to ever trust him again?

After a solid twenty minutes of panicking, he remembered his discovery from the helicopter trip on the way over. That might be interesting enough to distract her.

He leaned in and whispered, "I think I found something new we can do with our powers."

Hester was typing furiously on her phone, presumably answering some of the excessive quantity of emails she received on a minute-by-minute basis.

"What is it?" She was refusing to look at him. He watched her casually trade ten grand in stocks.

"Hester. I'm serious. Bubble up with me for a sec?"

Finally, she put her phone down.

He nudged Gabrielle too, until she looked up from her phone, where she was watching someone touring a McMansion 3-D real estate listing like it was a video game.

"Pay attention to my power."

Hester's power wove through his, as easy and natural as breathing now. Theo leaned towards the window again, waiting until a large-ish cluster of streets appeared below them.

He managed to find two people who were willing to respond. When they linked together, there was a noticeable golden surge of energy. Gabrielle's eyes widened.

Theo redirected the energy down to a nearby river, growing trails of seaweed through the water. Hester and Gabrielle looked flabbergasted.

"If we can use our powers from the air, we can rewild miles and miles at a time! Whole counties!" he said, excited.

"Let me try!" Gabrielle said. Theo nudged away Hester's power, connecting with hers instead, so he could show her what to do.

Theo frowned. He could barely feel the Greenfingers on the ground now, whereas his bubble with Hester had reached for several kilometres. "It's not as strong this time."

"You two haven't been practising together," Hester pointed out. "Your powers won't be used to combining."

Theo nodded, but he wasn't convinced. Gabrielle had already used his power when growing the bindweed. There was something else going on here that he couldn't quite work out.

"What did you just do?" The voice came from over Theo's shoulder. Edgar leaned over the headrests, quivering with excitement.

"Edgar!" Hester said. "We were just playing around."

In front of them, Gabrielle pulled her cap down over her eyes, twisting to face the wall.

"Show me that again," Edgar ordered. They'd been dicing with danger. He was too observant to miss something like this.

Hester grew a little row of flowers on the ground below, while Edgar watched on full alert.

"That's so rad. Do you know how it works?"

When Theo opened his mouth to explain that they were connecting with the Greenfingers on the ground, Hester kicked his ankle and said loudly, "I'm the only one who can do it, because my power is really strong. No one else can reach that far. Isn't that right, Theo?"

"Oh, yes, absolutely," he lied in a stiff voice. "Our bog-standard powers could never reach the ground."

Edgar hummed. "It's a shame it's just you. There are so

214

many implications if we could share the skill with the others." His voice was alight with anticipation.

He noticed Gabrielle, then. Her eyes were fixed on one of Edgar's screens on the back wall of the cabin. An astronaut was floating in zero gravity near what looked like a giant, glittering trampoline. It was huge – as big as a house next to the tiny person – and made of a thin sheet of foil stretched over a plastic ring. The whole – sail? wall? solar panel? – sent light refracting into a bright rainbow. The astronaut was giving a big thumbs up to the camera.

Edgar met Gabrielle's gaze. She snapped her head away, staring firmly forward.

"Great work, Hester," he said absently, then returned to his headset and joystick. Gabrielle kept her head lowered for the rest of the flight.

# WOW! STOCK MARKET IN FREEFALL, GET OUT WHILE YOU STILL CAN!!! 📉

I've been warning readers of this blog for <u>many months</u> that oil investments are a no-go. Cheap renewables and online green-trolling has sent public opinion into a nosedive.

If you've failed to heed my warnings and divest your $$$ from Dalex Energy, you may be getting whiplash. Today they rounded off their trifecta of PR disasters with a third Greenfingers incident. Adding to their unauthorized woodland and algal dead zone, they've now transformed land around a coal plant (because why be extra when you could be EXXXXXXTRA?). Their trading prices have been thrown for a loop ever since.

Vocal critics – including Greenpeace – are certain companies like Dalex are causing more damage than good, and not just to the land itself.

The World Health Organization said, "The long-term effects of the so-called 'Greenfingers' power have not yet been studied fully. We're concerned about health risks posed by prolonged use of these powers. Heightened daily use is a considerable strain on an individual's personal resources – mentally, emotionally and physically.

"We don't yet know whether excessive use of the Greenfingers powers could reduce the life span of active users. We advise companies to hold back on employing Greenfingers staff until medical trials are complete, and have sent information packs to companies such as Dalex who have already begun to do so."

Eesh. Their lawyers must currently be sweating buckets. But as we've seen many times, a little legal drama is small beans for a company as big as them. (Citation: every single pollution incident by every energy company in the history of capitalism, pals.)

Hester Daleport – the head honcho's heir and quarter-finalist for this blog's <u>Corporate Hottie of the Year Awards</u> – also recently dropped big news for the TBCU (Texas Billionaires Cinematic Universe): a crossover with Warren Space.

Warren, the noted online sh%tposter and space race nutcase, has been loudly proclaiming the growth of his Mars colony for the last few years. A boost from the Greenfingers power could be just what the settlement needs to ~~actually happen~~ reach true urbanization.

What this means for the stocks -- well, we honestly have no idea. Can Dalex's innovative moves save them from the wind/solar doldrums? Will their competitors copycat their new moves and beat them to the profits? Will Hester Daleport ever corpse in one of her speeches and show a little personality? Who will feral fave Edgar Warren get sued by next?

Only the fates can tell us. And possibly my ex-gf's horoscope Jupiter-rising hocus-pocus. Over and out.

**Related News**

<u>Drugs Discovered Smuggled Inside Unopened Coconuts</u>

<u>President of The Church of Jesus Christ of Latter-day Saints says Greenfingers powers are "a gift from God to His children, rewarding His followers for their kindness and respect, and should be used to fight prejudice"</u>

<u>Teenage Girl Strangles Would-Be Assaulter with Stinging Nettles</u>

# Chapter 18

"I thought you'd be older," Gabrielle said, looking Hester up and down.

Hester tugged her suit jacket closed, feeling a bit self-conscious. "I'm eighteen."

Once they'd got back to the training centre, Edgar had borrowed an empty office for a conference call with Dad. They were discussing the Arctic oilfields, Hester guessed, but she hadn't decided how she was going to tackle that capital-D Disaster yet. She didn't have much leverage to stop them. Their combined resources must add up to a third of the world's wealth. She was nothing in comparison.

"Congrats on shutting down my factory," Hester told Gabrielle.

She made little jazz hands. "Congrats on destroying the planet."

"Simmer down, guys," Theo said, voice tight. "Can we take this somewhere more private?"

Hester led them into her office, away from the trainees lining up for dinner.

"I'm on board with whatever you're planning," she said, jumping in before Theo could launch into the apology soliloquy he was clearly planning. She was still angry he'd attacked the power plant behind her back, but she couldn't waste time arguing about it. Not when Dad was closer to launching his demonic plan with every second that passed.

Theo's pained expression morphed into surprise. "You're not mad?"

"I'm furious, yeah, but mainly at Edgar and my dad." She cast a long look at Gabrielle. She could probably trust her. If anyone should know about the Arctic, it was the public ringleader of Climate Rebellion. "I think they're planning to use the Greenfingers group to melt the polar ice, so they can access the oilfields underneath it."

There was a moment of stunned silence. Hester was suddenly ravenous. She raided her snack drawer, handing out chocolate.

"We need to stop them," she said, just in case that hadn't been clear.

"How can your dad even use us to melt through the ice?" Theo asked.

"The ice reflects sunlight," Gabrielle said. "If they cover the tundra in dark plants instead, more heat will be absorbed by the permafrost."

"Plus, I think he's planning to burn the new growth away," Hester said. "In layers, like we did today to pull out the metals."

"Holy crap."

"That can't be real," Gabrielle said, biting into a peanut butter cup.

"I think it's been coming for a long time." Hester dug her nail into a blood orange, peeling away the pith.

She couldn't wrap her head around the fact that Dad – who cried over dead pets and never killed a spider – was destroying the world. He didn't make sense to her.

"That's why Edgar was so keen on you growing plants from the plane – I mean, helicopter?" Theo asked.

Hester nodded. Once Edgar realized how easily they could grow plants from the sky, the ice caps would be steam within the week.

"What an absolute *creep*."

"How much oil are we talking about here?" Gabrielle asked.

Hester waved her hand. "A few billion dollars' worth, I guess. The market there is huge – you have no idea how much money Russia are going to make from climate change. But I'm ready to do everything I can to stop it. Which means they'll probably fire me, or something." She paused, waiting for a wave of despair to roll over her. Dalex was her whole life. Betraying the firm should feel apocalyptic. Instead, it was freeing.

"If I'm leaving, I might as well go out in a blaze of glory. So tell me what I can do to help your group, and I'll do it. But – I guess I don't really even understand how Greenfingers

"Right," Theo said. "Yeah, I can see how we might be able to help there. Huh."

"We're living through the end of the world, aren't we?" Hester asked, pausing in the process of sculpting her orange seedling into a miniature bonsai tree.

"This isn't the end of anything," Gabrielle said. "You can't think about it like that. We're going to continue living here for ever, however bad Earth gets. Calling this an apocalypse just leads to fear paralysis. It gives people yet another reason to avoid acting. But this is happening; it's real. Set your old 'normal' aside and start working on building a new one."

Theo nodded. "There's no end point where it's suddenly too late to fix the planet. There's always something we can do, however impossible it feels."

"The whole planet is collapsing, though," Hester said, nudging one of the orange stems into an arching, extended branch.

"And even if we can only slow that process, it still means a whole extra generation will get to live in a world where they can go outside, eat good food and breathe the air without getting asthma or cancer," Gabrielle said. "How many times do you think your ancestors felt like they were living through the end of the world? We're not the first people to feel like this, and we won't be the last. People always keep going."

"Well, this is an amazing pep talk, but what do we do about it?" Theo asked. "Between us, we've got a lot of resources right now – our team of Greenfingers, access to helicopters and boats, and Gabrielle's protestors. How can we all work together to stop this happening?"

Gabrielle nodded. "We can't waste any time. Your dad will be planning to work fast, Hester, before the new Greenfingers labour legislation is put into effect."

"Why is Edgar getting involved in this Arctic thing, anyway?" Theo asked. "It seems a bit of a detour from Mars."

"I think he wants cheap fuel for his shuttles," Hester explained. He was going to need to launch thousands of shuttles from Earth's orbit on their way to Mars. If he could get low-cost oil from the Arctic, he would save millions each year.

Edgar must have pitched the idea to Dad, suggesting that they use his atmospheric mapping software to track the temperature changes at the North Pole.

Gabrielle made a small noise. "Wait, no. I think I know why he's helping!"

She pulled out her phone, searching for something. Theo wiggled his eyebrows at Hester. She shrugged.

Gabrielle's forearms were embedded with tiny seeds, like the skin of a strawberry. Hester rubbed her own wrists, where her eczema was peeling away in flakes of bark. The more powerful they became, the harder it was to stop the plants encroaching.

Yesterday, she'd caught herself hypnotized by the sight of a bee collecting pollen from a flower. She'd been utterly mortified when she'd snapped out of it. There was no good reason for pollination to look ... sexy.

"Oh, jeez," Gabrielle said, voice distraught. "OK. Um, this might be a lot worse than we thought."

"What?" Hester said, alarmed.

"When we were on his helicopter, Edgar was looking at photos of a solar sail," she explained.

"Is that what that thing was?" Theo asked. "It looked like a foil trampoline."

"It's like a giant mirror drifting in space. It was designed to sit between the sun and Earth and reflect light away from us. I've never actually seen one before – they're just some crazy geoengineering concept for stopping the global temperature from rising too high."

Hester interrupted, "There is – and I mean this in the least hyperbolic way possible – no fucking way that Edgar is planning to use that sail for anything good."

Gabrielle said, "Agreed. So what if Edgar is planning to focus sunlight on the Arctic ice, instead of away from Earth? That's why he's helping your dad."

"We can't let that happen," Hester said, horrified. "Between that and the Greenfingers' plants absorbing more heat, they could have melted the entire polar ice within a week."

"Is there a way we can stop him? Besides, like, going into orbit to destroy the solar sail?" Gabrielle asked, half joking.

Hester considered it. "You know, he's probably building it on the International Space Station," she mused. The ISS had been expanded a few years ago, with new modules added for Warren Space and a few other private space companies alongside the NASA, ESA, Russian and Japanese sections. She'd spent a few hours on the Warren module before they boarded the shuttle to Mars. It had been full of research labs and testing chambers. It definitely had the capacity to build something like a solar sail. "It's not *that* hard to get up there. They send tourist shuttles up every few days. We could check."

Theo said, "I bet we can get Edgar to send us up if we convince him that our powers would be good for making building materials for this solar sail. Bamboo struts or something. He'd be super keen if he thought it would save him money in materials."

"I think there's a good chance that he's in a rush to take some Greenfingers into space soon anyway," Gabrielle added. "He'll want to test it out before the Greenfingers work permits come into legislation in a few months."

"I'll do a bit of digging through the Dalex files to see if I can find out more about the Arctic plans," Hester said. "But we're going to have to time this all really carefully to make sure we aren't cut off from my resources before we get everything done. This has to stay between the three of us until then."

Gabrielle nodded. "I imagine we'll only be able to organize large-scale Climate Rebellion protests once before we start getting arrested. My group have been doing tests here and there, like the shutdown today, but nothing big yet."

"How many Greenfingers do you have?" Hester asked.

"Enough to cover the major cities." Gabrielle pulled up a world map on her phone, covered in scattered dots. "We're recruiting more people all the time, as word of mouth spreads."

"With that many Greenfingers across the entire planet, we could make a real difference to the ecosystem," Theo said, thinking it through.

Right now, Theo was literally Hester's moral compass. He'd demonstrated more natural talent for the role than she had.

He crammed another row of chocolate into his mouth, mumbling around it, "I wonder if we could grow more forests from the air using that network connection. Gabrielle could get all the Climate Rebellion Greenfingers in an area ready to project their powers, and we could guide the power from the helicopter."

"It'll have to be a simultaneous green rising everywhere," Gabrielle said, grinning. "We can rewild some land, stop the oil drilling in the Arctic and present our political legislation changes all at once."

"You'd really cut yourself off from your family to do this?" Theo asked Hester. "What if Mr Daleport never talks to you again once he realizes you've been lying to him?"

"Theo, if my dad hadn't blocked the science his whole career, then the entire planet would probably have moved away from fossil fuels decades ago. The world is a worse place because he's alive – him, and every businessman like him. Trust me, I don't care if he never speaks to me again. I'm doing this."

Never mind the fact that Dad seemed to be easing her out of the firm anyway. This was the right decision, in so many ways.

Gabrielle clapped her hands together. "Well, I'd better get to work with the Climate Rebellion team, then. Message me when you've got more info out of your dad."

Hester's orange tree jumped in height. The thought of facing Dad again filled her with nervous energy. If this was going to work, she would have to pretend she agreed with everything he was doing until they were ready to act. That felt impossible, but she'd been lying to herself about Dalex for her whole life – what were a few days more?

"I'll try my best," she promised. "If that doesn't work, I'll find another way to fix this."

"You'll have to take it up with the President," Theo joked. "Get him to sort the whole mess out."

The *President*. It would take a lot of leverage to get a meeting, but it wasn't impossible.

At Hester's contemplative look, Theo hissed, "No, Hester, absolutely not! We can't take on the government as well. Enough is enough! You've only been working on fixing the environment for a few days."

"It's going too slowly," she muttered.

Gabrielle giggled. "I'm so glad you guys messaged me. This is going to be *so much fun*."

Something about the gleeful smirk on her face made Hester shiver. What were they getting themselves into?

# Blossoming Buds

## By JASMINE BRONX

OLIVIA FLOUNDERS WHEN SHE'S SEATED NEAR her ghastly ex and his new beau at a floristry conference dinner. To her surprise, a charming stranger surprises her with a fragrant bouquet, grown from the tips of his fingers. Suddenly, Olivia is flung into a fake romance with the gorgeous Greenfingers, whose touchy-feely wooing has her ex glowering at them from across the room.

Their chemistry might be blossoming, but that doesn't always translate to a relationship which can last longer than fresh-cut flowers. When Maxim's Greenfingers power accidentally fills Olivia's carefully tended garden with useless weeds, they both discover that roses can easily show their thorns. If only there was a way Olivia could put Maxim's talents to good use in her floristry...

**PRODUCT DETAILS**
Category: Contemporary Fiction
Paperback $26.00
ISBN 9780593232445
Coming Soon   320 Pages
5½ x 8-¼

# Chapter 19

After sneaking Gabrielle out of the back door, Theo and Hester went to raid the remnants of the dinner buffet. The trainees had pushed the biggest tables together to eat in a group. Beatriz was perched on Daisy's lap, whispering in her ear.

Theo and Hester chose a table on their own, where he systematically worked his way through a plate of fried buttermilk chicken, caramelized onions and rib-eye steak.

"Sorry for being a gannet, I'm starving," Theo said, fighting the desire to eat compost instead. "What do you think of Gabrielle, then?"

He'd been surprised by how well Hester had got on with Gabrielle, considering the whole factory sabotage thing.

"She's fierce," Hester said. "The weird part is doing this in a team – I'm not used to that. My dad works alone, and I've always just copied him. I don't know how to do this with partners. Like, I'm already resisting the urge to ask Gabrielle for updates on recruiting more Greenfingers, and it's only been half an hour."

"We're as invested in this as you are. We're all going to try as hard as we can."

She paused, chewing her lip. "I think I just get too focused on reaching my goal. It doesn't even matter what the goal is, really. Once I'm fixated on doing something, I can't think about anything else until I get there. I just *go go go*. It's like, if I don't put all of my energy into whatever-it-is, then I could never forgive myself if it failed."

Theo considered this. It all made a lot of sense, given what he knew about Hester. She had a one-track mind, and the track didn't stop until it reached world domination station.

Carefully, Theo said, "You know this project probably is going to fail, right? We are never going to fix things completely. It's impossible."

She stared down into her Oreo milkshake. "I know. I should probably reassess my goals. Settle for something like 'improve county air cleanliness' instead. But – it's not failure that scares me, really. I can handle that. What scares me is knowing that I could have tried harder and didn't. Being disappointed in myself."

Theo tried to process this. "So, if you know you've tried your absolute best, you can live with it going wrong?"

She met his gaze. "Yeah. That's it."

He swallowed. "I think I'm the opposite." Now it was his turn to stare down at the table. He mashed the crumbs of his cheesecake into the plate. "Like, I'm too scared to try hard, because if I fail it feels even worse. I can't stand knowing that even my best wasn't good enough, so I hold back. Just so I can feel better about myself when it does go wrong."

Sometimes it felt like all he did was worry. About finding money for his parents, about the future, about the ocean and the crumbling coast they lived on. He had been trapped in a loop of fear.

"But you try *so hard*," Hester said, amazed. "What are you like when you're running at one hundred per cent, if this isn't full power?"

He laughed. "All right. I guess I should have said, that's what I used to be like. It's been different since I got here. I've been trying as hard as I can, since I met you. I've changed."

"*You've* changed?" she repeated incredulously. "Theo, you've turned me into a completely different person!"

He snorted. "I guess it was a big moment for both of us, meeting each other." The words were out of his mouth before he could think them through.

When she stilled, he regretted speaking. It sounded like he'd meant something else by it. Like he was confessing something. But he hadn't meant it that way, not really.

"I think, in hindsight, it was the most important moment of my life," she said, so quietly he almost didn't hear.

Theo went hot all over. His mind was suddenly so empty that he couldn't even remember words, let alone think of something to say.

He pushed his chair back with a scrape, stumbling to his feet. "Refill!" he said, waving his empty Coke glass.

She didn't look up, but there was a tiny borage leaf poking out from behind her ear.

He rested his forehead against the drinks machine as ice rattled into his glass, breathing deeply. Her words were throbbing through his veins like a heartbeat. *Most important moment of my life. Most important moment of my life. Most important moment of my life.* He felt like he'd been gutted.

To his relief, Daisy had come over to talk to Hester at their table. Hester was rubbing at the waxy cuticle of a grey-green desert cactus growing from her shoulder.

"Hey, Daisy," Theo said, leaning into the "distract, deflect, delay" conversational strategy. "How's Beatriz doing? Did she cope OK with the exercise today?"

Daisy nodded. "Yeah, I made her take it slowly." Her skin had changed recently, becoming peach-soft and fuzzy like ripe fruit. It worried Theo a little bit. Would she start bruising like a peach too?

"Beatriz is really nice," Daisy continued. "But actually, I wanted to say thank you for today. It was so nice to do something good after the disaster at sea."

"Oh," Hester said, pleasure and surprise in her voice. "Y'all did a great job."

"We're super proud of you," Theo added, nodding.

"Are we going back tomorrow?" Daisy asked hopefully. "They sent me to ask." She gestured over her shoulder, where the group of trainees were peering over at them intently.

"We're officially banned from using our powers near Dalex

sites after today's attempt," Hester said, grimacing. "So no more coal ash for us."

"We're actually discussing plans for tomorrow's activities right now." After a pause, Theo added, a little optimistically, "Any, er, suggestions?"

Daisy was really good at coming up with training activities, whereas Theo's main plan for the next day involved swindling Edgar into giving him a free trip to space. But since Hester had given him a pay rise for training the trainees, he should probably actually make a token effort towards ... training the trainees.

"Did you hear about Jason's cousin?" Daisy asked. "She got in a car crash last week, and she grew a seed husk around her baby's car seat and saved his life. Maybe we could experiment with something like that."

"That sounds good. We could plan an activity to run together tomorrow, if you like?"

Daisy nodded. "Let's meet over breakfast?"

"You got it."

When Daisy left, Hester was smiling at him. "I'd better watch out. You'll be leading your own department within the month. Clearly you've got a talent for management."

Theo's face contorted. "That is the worst compliment I've ever received. Please never, ever say it again."

She raised her eyebrows. "There's nothing wrong with having a natural corporate synergy for incentivizing your taskforce."

Theo curled over the table, groaning. "Please stop, I can't take it any more. This is awful."

"There's a lot to unpack here, but let's take a deep dive on your core competencies. If we circle back and drill down on the actionable—" That was all she could manage to say before losing her calm. She choked out, "Your wheelhouse—" and then collapsed into laughter again.

"My soul shrivels up every time you speak," he said, earnestly addressing the tabletop. "I'm taking your pudding while you think about what you've done."

"Oh. I'll just sit here and eat my own hubris, then, shall I?" She patted the top of his head.

"I bet you're a riot at the work stand-up comedy nights," he growled. "Clearly you've missed your calling."

Her fingers were still curled in his hair. Theo was absolutely still, not even breathing in case he dislodged them.

"Don't worry," she said fondly. "There's no age restriction on making a LinkedIn account. You don't gotta wait until you're eighteen."

Hester's phone rang and she reached for it to check the caller.

"Your dad again?" Theo asked, sitting up.

"I don't know what I'm going to say to him." Hester was looking at her phone like she was trying to work out how to add "fix relationship with Dad" to her to-do list.

Theo had absolutely no advice to offer. His parents were both so easy-going that he couldn't really imagine it being awkward to talk to them about anything, ever. He should probably check in with them, actually. It had been a few days.

"That's cool," Hester said.

Theo looked up from his phone, where he'd been scrolling through the fam group chat. "What is?"

"On your phone, the colours on the lines. It's pretty."

Theo's neck burned. He'd totally forgotten to hide his screen from her. "It's for my dyslexia, actually. It makes it easier to read when I can follow the colours of each line."

"I didn't even know that was a thing."

Hester didn't seem bothered at all. Theo relaxed. "It helps, unless I'm really stressed out. My teachers are always going on at me for my spelling." He shrugged. "I send a lot of voice memos."

Hester bit her lip. "I have noticed that you sometimes mix words up."

"That's part of it too, yeah."

"I used to have a stutter," she admitted. "Obviously my dad got me a speech therapist when I was like, two, so you can't really tell any more. But sometimes I worry about it during big speeches."

Hester did sometimes stutter when she was nervous, though Theo hadn't realized it was a speech impediment. If he wasn't always paying such close attention, he might never have spotted it at all.

"Do you actually like giving speeches?" he asked. "You're really good at them, but it seems very ... not fun."

She winced. "Dad won't give me anything else to do.

I've been fighting him about it for a while now. It's a work in progress."

Theo thought about his last phone call with his parents. They'd tried so hard to make him see that it wasn't his responsibility to get a good job for them. But even now, it was so hard not to want to pay them back for the work they'd put into raising him. That feeling must be even harder for Hester to ignore, when her dad was pushing her onwards all the time. It must have taken unbelievable nerve to stand up to him at all.

"I think you're doing the right thing. We both are."

She curled her fingers around his wrist, squeezing gently.

After dinner, Theo was making his way up to his room in a pleasantly drowsy food-haze when he passed Edgar in the hallway. He felt deliciously, indulgently happy, in a way he only ever got on Boxing Day after four hours chasing his cousins around and around the fairy-light-filled cottage.

All of Theo's sleepiness snapped out of him in seconds. He hadn't known Edgar was still here. Operation: Space Launch had just got a head start. He could make tracks on getting some Greenfingers up to the ISS to destroy this solar sail.

Without thinking too hard about what he was about to do, Theo called, "Hey, Edgar! Can I help play-test that new Nintendo console you mentioned?"

"One thousand per cent yes," Edgar said, pushing down a pair of VR glasses to peer at Theo.

Ten minutes later, Edgar was yelping, "Behind you! Dive!"

as Theo's character lunged into a cave, shooting sparks at the beast following him.

"Nice, bro!" Edgar crowed, puffing out clouds of menthol-flavoured smoke from a gold vape pen. They'd requisitioned the training centre's meeting room where Theo had first embarrassed himself by giving Hester that mortifying telling-off. That felt like decades ago, now.

"This is amazing," Theo said. "I've never seen an action sequence so crisp without a desktop CPU."

"Right! They must be overclocking the GPU to get graphics that realistic, right?" Edgar said.

Theo cleared his throat as he fought off a banshee. "So, are we really going to get to test out our powers in space one day?"

Edgar leaned back in his chair, propping his fingers together. There was a thick platinum ring on his pinkie finger. "Possibly. If it seems like it'll reap useful results."

"That's cool. What kind of results? Do you want us to, like, grow bamboo walls for the Space Station or something? I bet we could make something just as strong as the stuff you send up there."

"That's certainly an idea. Have you made bamboo structures before?"

Theo shrugged easily, eyes fixed on the screen as if he wasn't pulling this entire conversation straight out of his arse. "Sure. I made my dad a sail mast for his boat before I came here, actually."

Edgar's cheek twitched. "A sail?"

Theo had him. He could practically see the dollar signs in Edgar's eyes as he imagined the solar sails the Greenfingers could build him.

"They're stronger and way cheaper than those lightweight carbon masts you can buy," Theo said lightly, decapitating a vampire. "If you need anything like that, why don't you send a few of us up there to test out if it would work?"

Edgar eyed Theo for a long moment. "Go on then. You can take a few trainees up with you. But I'll expect to see real results if there's a whole group going up. Rocket fuel isn't free, you know."

Theo nodded eagerly. "For sure!"

Edgar made a slight chuffing noise. "We'll send you up on the next shuttle. There's a launch in a few days you can catch a ride on." He was checking some complex software on his phone now, probably a flight plan for shuttles. Almost offhand, he asked, "Who was that new trainee on the helicopter?"

Theo was seconds away from being cornered by a ghoul. He leaped up onto a cliff-face, scrambling for cover. Distracted, he asked, "Who, Gabrielle?" and then froze.

His character died with a screech, dissolving into dust. Damn. Edgar was still doing something with his software, only half paying attention. Had he heard him?

"She was the photographer..." he added weakly.

Edgar chugged the last dregs of a cold espresso. "Huh. Well, I'm off for the night. Keep the game."

"Oh, right, thanks. Night!" Theo sank down in his chair as soon as he was alone, dragging his hands through his hair. He was such a colossal idiot. How had he been so stupid?

Something buzzed on the table. Edgar had left his phone behind. Theo stood up to run after him, then hesitated. What if there was something on it that could help the green rising? He could have a look, just to make sure there wasn't information on the solar sail. For the planet.

Sliding his gaze away from the phone, he started a new round of the game. He would play for a little longer, to see if Edgar came back. If not, he'd return the phone tomorrow. There was no harm in that, was there?

After an hour, it was clear Edgar wasn't coming back. He seemed to have more electronic devices than any one person could use, so it made sense that he hadn't noticed the phone was missing yet.

Theo took it back to his room, trying to hide the bounce of nerves in his walk. This wasn't a big deal. He was just holding on to a friend's phone until he could give it back to him. So what if it was an unreleased iPhone, gold-plated, worth at least a grand? So what if it belonged to one of the world's biggest billionaires?

There was a package waiting on Theo's bed. His parents had sent him a "cheer up" gift – a cushion in the shape of a photo-realistic Danish pastry, which was exactly Mum's sense of humour.

He dropped the phone on his bed, squeezing the pillow to his chest. His knee wouldn't stop jiggling.

Sick of staring at the phone like it was an unexploded bomb, Theo swiped the screen. There was a passcode lock. Of course there was. Relief flooded over him. That dealt with that problem. He'd never be able to guess Edgar's passcode. It could be anything.

He'd seen Hester unlock her phone earlier. When he'd asked if the numbers nine-eight-one-four were her birthday, she'd said it was the highest price the Dalex stocks had ever hit, ninety-eight dollars a share. He had been part appalled, part impressed. His own passcode was his highest score on *Call of Duty*. Her high score was a lot more badass.

Almost idly, he looked up the highest Warren Space share price: $96.55. He was smug on Dalex's behalf. Nine-six-five-five didn't unlock the phone, though. Oh well. It probably would have been a sure-fire route to life imprisonment, anyway. He'd give it back to Edgar tomorrow.

# MEMO

## For: All Security Employees

The United Nations has issued notice of a new terrorist threat – packages containing toxic plant spores that explode and cling to the <u>interior of the lungs</u>. This disrupts respiration, causing long-term damage to health and possibly even **<u>death</u>**. Staff should take ALL POSSIBLE PRECAUTIONS and treat all plants as ***hazardous*** in case of bioterrorist attacks by Greenfingers. Be aware that any apprehended convicts may escape custody through **violent means** using their powers, and extra precautions should be taken. Under no circumstances should they be left alone.

Officers will receive ongoing training to deal with Greenfingers' arrests in collaboration with our new targeted units, who are developing protocols for managing their attack techniques.

# Chapter 20

The morning after the meeting with Gabrielle, Hester started going through Dad's calendar and contacts. She had access to the data as an executive, which included the email addresses of politicians and investors, and addresses of factories and rigs, as well as all of his planned meetings.

Taking screenshots of anything that might be useful, she found an address for a site in Svalbard. It was listed as a Dalex research site. Was that where he was planning to launch the new project?

All she needed was a lead about the Arctic that would help her work out the details of what was going on without having to question him about it directly. Dad was never going to listen if she asked him not to drill there. The only way she could stop him was to turn this into a scandal for Dalex.

If she could find some documents that said in plain language what they were planning, then she could leak it to the press. Maybe she could even give a speech: that was what he always wanted from her, after all. She could give one last speech that would stop Dalex. It wasn't her company any more. Perhaps it never had been.

When her phone vibrated with a new message, she almost jumped. There was no way Dad could have worked out what she was doing already. But it was from Edgar.

**Edgar Warren** decided to see how gfs powers work in zero grav. my jet is picking up the team on fri to bring you to my spaceport in Brownsville for prelim medical testing + training before launch. Will send up 8 trainees. Pack bags for a 2+ week stay – we'll provide accom/food. Will discuss more irl

Hester grinned. Theo had been really proud of his success with Edgar the night before. She wished she'd been there to hear their conversation.

She hesitated before replying. She really wanted to investigate this Svalbard lead, but that would mean finding a way to get there before the trip to the Space Station.

**Hester** will do! But no worries about the jet, we'll take the dalex one to save your pilot the trip ☺

Dad's calendar said he was playing golf right now. He must be taking advantage of the early morning weather before it got too hot. Perfect.

Twenty minutes later, she was waving him down from across the green.

"Hester, good morning!" Dad said, rubbing hand sanitizer into his hands. He was wearing tweed, blond hair tucked under a cap. "I didn't know you were joining me. You've been busy. We haven't checked in for a while."

She winced. She'd been putting off this conversation for days, but she couldn't ignore him for ever. At the very least, it was unprofessional. He was her boss. "Sorry. Edgar's been pushing the group hard. He's even going to send some of the trainees to the International Space Station in a few days."

"Already? Brilliant news, well done." He hummed, choosing a club and polishing the end with a linen handkerchief.

"Is it all right if we borrow the jet for a day or two, to take the trainees over to his spaceport?"

"Sure thing," Dad said. "I'm surprised Edgar didn't offer to send his own, though. I thought he'd jump at the chance to show it off. I hear it's the latest model."

"Oh, I think he's using it for something else," she said vaguely, and bit back a grin. She'd be able to sneak off to Svalbard before they had to fly to Brownsville. By the time Dad saw the flight paths in his end-of-month invoices, it would be too late.

"Well, this moves our timeline up quite a bit. Good luck to Edgar's insurance provider. Let's hope your group doesn't have any more mishaps."

Hester grimaced. "Right."

"You've been spending a lot of time at the training centre. Come home tonight, will you? I know what it's like – when I got my own staff for the first time, I couldn't think about anything but work. I had a camp bed in the corner of my office. It's all well and good, but you can't live for business, princess."

Hester wanted to ask, *What about you? Isn't that what you live for?* but she was afraid of the answer.

"I can't come home tonight. We'll be flying out to Brownsville later," she lied.

Dad's ball spun off across the perfectly manicured fairway to land in a bunker. He shook his head sternly. "The trainees can go, but you're not to join them. I need you to step back and let Edgar deal with the Greenfingers project for now."

Her heart sank. She half-heartedly took her turn, knocking the ball down the course. Annoyingly, it landed near the hole.

"I can handle the responsibility, Dad," she said, voice tight. "I've made a lot of progress with the group already. In fact, I had an idea for how we could use their powers out in the field."

He waved a hand. "Yes, Edgar told me all about the fungus network he found, and his new idea about growing plants from the sky. That does sound promising. He's doing good work there. You should add that to your next shareholder presentation."

She bit her lip. What did it matter now if Edgar took the credit for the ideas she'd found with Theo?

Dad drove the buggy along the path to the hole, leaving Hester to trail after him on foot. She wiped her brow. It was only ten a.m., but she was already so hot that she was sweating.

"Dad, I want to do more than just give speeches. That's been amazing training, but if you let me join the meetings with Edgar, I have a lot more I can contribute. What are you two working on?"

"Oh, you don't need to worry about that," he said, holding a hand up to align the angle of his club. "It's being handled."

He was deflecting again. He'd been doing this for her whole life, feeding her Dalex propaganda as if she was totally incapable of working out the truth on her own. That said everything about his real opinion of her. He thought she was too stupid to notice or understand his manipulations.

Hester grabbed his arm. "Dad, come on. You don't think Edgar's going to stick around once he's got what he wants, do you? He's just after cheap energy for his shuttles! You need me there to make sure he doesn't take all the Greenfingers ideas for himself and cut us out of the deal."

Her father eyed the eczema that still covered her wrists. Disgust flickered over his face. He carefully removed her hand from his arm, pulling out a moist towelette to wipe down his sleeve. "Edgar and I have a mutually beneficial arrangement that doesn't concern you. He's not going to rescind our deal."

It would have been so much easier if he'd just told her everything she needed to know. There was no way to avoid a trip to Svalbard now. What did she have to do to make him trust her? She was his daughter, for god's sake. She'd spent her whole life training at his side!

"I don't understand why you don't trust me!" she cried.

Dad met the eye of a curious businessman passing in a golf cart. "Lower your voice, you sound hysterical," he hissed, flushed pink with mortification.

Hester's rage brimmed over. Before she could stop it, plants were exploding around her. Mint shot through the pristine turf, gouging up the ground in deep claw marks.

Dad jumped back, scraping clods of dirt off his shirt in distress. "I thought I told you to get that thing under control. You're on thin ice here, Hester."

"Y-you aren't listening to me! You th-think I'm just some stupid little girl, but I'm not – I'm g-going to show you just what I can do, you wait—"

She cut herself off. She'd been about to reveal everything they were planning for the green rising.

He clicked his tongue. "Stuttering again? I thought you were over that."

They surveyed each other from across the destroyed fairway.

He sighed. "Look, I didn't want to do this today. But I've been thinking about our last conversation, about the algae bloom. It didn't go quite how I expected."

Hester was filled with relief. He was going to apologize. He was going to give her control of the group back. This had all been a big misunderstanding. "Me too!"

"Princess, you know I've always wanted you to take over my role in the company one day. But it seems like this mutation has changed you. It's making me reconsider whether you're the right fit for an executive role. And with these new prospects with Edgar ... I think it's time to admit that you just aren't suited for management. There's no shame in choosing a more hands-on role that gets you out of the office, where you can vent this excess energy."

Deep down, she'd known this was coming. If she wanted more responsibility, she was never going to get it at Dalex. Not without compromising herself.

"What if I told you that you were right about everything?" she asked, out of curiosity. "That I wanted to help in any way I could?"

His eyebrows lifted. "Well, that might be a different conversation. Is that the case?"

"No," she admitted. "There are some lines I can't cross. Not even for Dalex."

"That's what I thought," he said, but he sounded disappointed anyway. He'd wanted her to be his heir just as much as she had. Clearly they'd both been thinking about this a lot over the last week. He must have been as frustrated with her as she was with him.

"It's about Mars, isn't it? You know the move won't be any different to life here." He gestured at the sky, where the sun was frying the grass already. "It's not like we'll be able to come outside in a few more years anyway."

"I don't want to live in a bubble," she snapped, releasing another wave of plants.

He glared at her.

Hester had always felt ashamed of how much her power responded to her emotions. But now, she wanted him to see that she was upset. She'd spent her whole life training herself to be the perfectly professional heir to his company. Somewhere along the way, she'd got so good at putting on a presentable front that she'd forgotten how to actually express herself. No wonder she'd always found it so hard to talk to people her own age. She really had turned into the business robot that Theo had accused her of being.

The plants made her actually pay attention to all of the feelings she usually suppressed. Well, she wasn't doing that any more. She deserved better than a life of hiding how she really felt, of having a stray flower be the only sign that she was a real person and not a corporation. She wanted to really live. Even if that meant facing up to some hard facts.

"We're done here," Dad said. "Talk to me again when you're ready to behave like an adult. This is embarrassing, Hester."

"Fine. In the meantime, I'm going to the spaceport with the trainees." She left without giving him a chance to respond.

The whole way back to the training centre, she heard nothing but her heartbeat pounding in her ears, a ticking countdown. She had to make that trip to Svalbard now, before he cut her off.

When her car pulled up at the training centre, a rabbit startled, disappearing into the undergrowth. The forest was clearly gaining new inhabitants at a shocking rate. Something big was moving through the bushes. It was Theo, headphones in as he jogged.

Hester rolled down the car window and called out to him, "Good morning!"

He paused, pushing back his headphones. He was wearing a white tank top with dropped armholes, damp with sweat. The sight of him hit Hester in the solar plexus. He was what her grandma would call a "corn-fed country boy".

"Hey," Theo said, and lifted his shirt to wipe his face.

Hester pulled her eyes away from the intriguing shadow of his stomach. "Can you get changed, and meet me out front as soon as possible? I've borrowed my dad's jet; we're going on a trip."

"Have I got time to shower?"

She wrinkled her nose at him, trying very hard to convey how disgusting he looked, all sweaty and damp and breathy and heaving and ... hmm.

"Hester?" Theo eyed her oddly.

She jerked back, banging her head on the top of the window. "What? Oh, yeah. Go ahead."

Wincing, she slumped down in her seat, puffing out her cheeks. The image of Theo was burned on her retinas. Oh. Well. This might be a problem.

# Climate Rebellion Forum

**PINNED: Forum rules (newbies PLEASE read!)**
[12 replies, 1709 views]

**NEW POST: Urgent! Diesel Leak in Russia Needs Local Greenfingers** [58 replies, 119 views]
The melting permafrost has cracked the base of a 20k tonne diesel tank & leaked fuel into a river. The stupid factory owners tried to hide it and it's already spread for 12km!! I live in the nearest city and I have a car – are there any GFs near by who want to come with me to see if we can remove some of the oil with plants? It sounds like they're going to pour chemical reagents in there otherwise :/

**please give us some doodle poll times when you're free next week! (for firstwithmagic's "livestream")**
[42 replies, 235 views]
Gabrielle is trying to finalize the plans for her ~big event~! More details are on the private mattermost server but we wanted to share the poll link here in case anyone is waiting for their account to be approved but is super keen to give us their availability.

**Acid Rain in Peru – what can we do?** [24 replies, 79 views]
I live near to a big metal smelter in peru, and the acid rain is killing all the trees and fish. our government knows about it but they make too much money off the factory. is there anything I can do to stop it with my powers? (sorry for my bad english)

**Solar seeding: yay or nay?** [36 replies, 99 views]
I've been reading about this geoengineering idea to spray chemicals into the atmosphere and block some of the sunlight. Is this a good idea? It sounds kind of dodgy to me. I mean im not sure id be comfortable with breathing in air full of chemicals. Weren't CFCs a really bad idea?

# Chapter 21

"Where are we going again?" Theo asked.

"Svalbard," Hester said tightly, staring out of the window. She was vibrating with barely restrained fury after talking to her dad. She was also wearing a ridiculous golfing outfit, including a baker boy cap and tweed plus fours. Honestly, Theo thought, sometimes Hester dressed like she came from a different universe, not just another social class.

"It should be about nine hours, so you can get some sleep if you want," she added.

He blinked. He wasn't even sure where Svalbard was. Not that he was complaining – the Daleport jet was gorgeous, all butter-soft golden leather armchairs and glass-doored fridges full of food. The flatscreen TV was currently showing an early screening of next year's Marvel movie.

"And we're going because…?"

"We're following a lead."

"Ah, yes," he said sagely. "In our secret mission. Should I have brought my gun and holster with me?"

"That won't be necessary; this is purely corporate

espionage," she said, grinning. "The only weapons we need are two-thousand-page legal documents."

"I'll brace for papercuts and particularly sharp staples, then." Theo selected a bag of Haribo from the snack bar, biting back a grin at the image of Mr Daleport eating them on a business trip. He couldn't get used to having access to so much free stuff. Even the water taps in his town's public bathrooms had been coin-operated since the drought a few years ago.

He curled up in the unbelievably comfy seat, picking at the sweets. He wished he was eating a sod of damp mulch instead, and hated himself for it. "While we've got time, we should practise using our powers to defend ourselves, like they do on TV. Now that we're in the resistance and all."

Something tugged at his wrist. A vine had curled around his arm up to the elbow. When it tightened, Theo was jerked onto the plush carpet.

"Like this?" Hester asked, smirking.

"Um," he managed, trying to wriggle free. The stems tangling around his chest were too strong. It was possible he hadn't thought this through.

Hester propped her chin on her hand, looking down at him. "Hmm," she said contemplatively.

A wave of heat rolled over him. She'd really overpowered him. He'd known that Hester's powers were stronger than his, but he'd never really thought about what that meant before. He could rely on her to protect him, whatever else was happening around them. She had his back.

"You got me," he forced out, when they'd been staring at each other for far too long, neither one of them moving to dislodge the vines. He rolled onto his side. Immediately, the stems loosened around him, slipping away from the thin skin of his wrist.

Theo tried to catch his breath, hiding his fluster. Searching for a distraction, he said, "Have you heard about Beatriz and Daisy, by the way? They finally started dating!"

Hester's face lit up. The girls had been flirting with each other ever since Beatriz had returned from hospital.

"Are they official now? That was unbelievably fast." Hester sat cross-legged, cradling a cup of tea between her hands.

"I don't know how they did it. I act like a pillock around people I fancy."

Teasing, Hester said, "You always act like an idiot, though."

He bit his lip, hiding a smile. "Yeah. Don't think about that too hard."

There was a beat of silence. Hester busied herself sifting through Theo's sweets for a fried egg.

"Tell me everything, then," she said. "How did they get together? I need the second-hand endorphins."

She looked so pretty sitting there – hair curled around her face, with a quiet, relaxed expression that he rarely ever got to see – that Theo found himself feeling brave all of a sudden.

He took a deep breath. "You could have the endorphins first-hand instead, you know."

"What do you mean?" Hester asked, and then, immediately, "OK."

Theo broke into a wide grin. When their eyes locked together, his stomach flipped over. He'd never kissed anyone before. Not properly, anyway – not someone who wasn't an auntie or his nani, or a boy who had kissed him on the dance floor at a social club birthday party once. But not like this, for real.

Definitely not someone like Hester, who he wanted to impress more than anyone he'd ever met in his life. But she was leaning towards him, staring at his lips with a look of terrified anticipation.

Theo shakily touched her cheek. Her skin was hot.

She shuffled closer. Her fingers flexed on his knee, nails scraping at his abruptly sensitive skin. The curve of her chest was pressed against his arm, and she was breathing hard against him.

Was she leaning in? Was he imagining that?

He flattened his hand against her waist, feeling her intake of breath, watching her wet her lip with her tongue.

Their lips were so close that he could almost—

There was a knock at the door to the cabin. Hester twisted away and said, "Yes?" in a high-pitched voice.

Theo couldn't catch his breath.

"We're landing soon," the pilot said, peering at the plants littering the carpet.

Theo found that he was unable to speak.

Hester said, "That's great, thanks!"

After the pilot closed the door, there was a long silence while Theo tried to process what had nearly just happened. Outside, the plane sank down through the cloud layer.

He could hear Hester's breathing, though he couldn't quite bring himself to look at her. There were rose petals scattered around her seat.

"Before we land, we should see if we can use our powers from up here," Theo said, trying to dissolve the awkwardness.

He grew a mushroom on the outer wing of the jet, which immediately blew away into the wind. When Hester extended her power too, it was like he'd been electrocuted. The peaceful calm he usually felt when the trainees all bubbled up had turned into a raging inferno.

It was like their combined powers were drawing on all the pent-up energy from their near-kiss – feeding off their emotional connection, until Theo felt powerful enough to do anything in the world.

Experimentally, he extended the ignited bubble of their powers towards the ground. Immediately he felt a nudge in response.

He leaned back, surprised. "Do you feel that? There are Greenfingers down there."

Hester froze, cupping a handful of freshly popped caramel popcorn to her mouth. "How can we sense them from this high up? It's not possible."

When he thought back to all the times his power had been

strongest, he'd always being working with Hester. Even when they'd tested their powers from the helicopter, he'd been surprised that it was more effective to bubble up with her than it had been with Gabrielle. He'd just assumed it was because they'd had more practice working together. But what if it had worked so well because of how he *felt* about Hester?

It made sense that it would be easier to bubble up with someone you were close with. If that was the case, they were only going to keep getting stronger. He was already closer to Hester now than anyone else in the world, except maybe his parents. Eventually, their bubble might even extend all the way to *space*. If it worked at this altitude, then orbit wasn't really that much further.

They'd have to try it on the ISS. How cool would it be to say they'd grown trees on Earth from space?

"It might be a stupid idea," he said tentatively, "but do you think we could grow a forest from the ISS? We'd be able to connect with a whole country of Greenfingers all at once if our powers work up there."

Hester's eyes widened. "That seems … unlikely. But the more of us there are, the further we can reach, right? If there are eight of us up there, plus a group of Greenfingers on the ground, then … maybe? We can try it, anyway."

From that high up in orbit, the Greenfingers on the ground below would be like mobile phones, bouncing signals off them as if they were a satellite. The ISS looped around Earth every ninety minutes. Could they make a world wide web of Greenfingers across the entire planet, linking them together and amplifying their signal?

"We should have a plan for what we do if we can," he said. "I know it's a long shot but everything to do with our powers has felt crazy. What if this has a chance of happening?"

Hester hesitated. "I guess we could mark up some maps with areas that would be good test sites for rewilding, that sort of thing."

Theo grinned at her. This was going to be awesome.

In Theo's mind, he still imagined the Arctic being the way it looked in films – all deep snow and sharp ice. Even though he knew that was long gone, it was still a shock to see the sparse, damp landscape of Svalbard.

Theo had slept through the drive to Hester's mysterious destination, caught in dreams where Hester tugged him around with vines curled over his wrists. When she shook him awake, they were parked at the end of a narrow track, surrounded by bare fields.

Shivering, he pulled on a thick coat, stomping his feet in his boots. Hester squinted at a map on her phone while her ponytail twisted upwards towards the sky. Recently, her hair had started following the sun, like a sunflower shifting towards the light.

"Do you think we should stop using our powers so much after this is all over?" he asked, tracking its movement. "I don't think it's good for us."

"What do you mean?" Hester replied, as if she wasn't visibly glowing under the sunlight.

He heaved a sigh. It was a problem for another day. "Never mind."

He headed off across the tussocks of thick grass, sliding down a mud-slick slope.

"There's nothing here," Hester called in frustration. "I'm sure this is the right address. There's supposed to be a Dalex office here."

At a raised bank, Theo's feet hit concrete under the slush. A set of steps led down to a metal door in a concrete enclosure. *"Underground bunker!* We've got an underground bunker over here!"

"You're kidding," Hester said, joining him.

"It's locked," he added, wriggling the door handle. "But I think I can get it open, if you don't mind some property damage."

After an audiobook crash course in fungi, Theo now had a wish list of mushrooms that he wanted to grow. One fungus had fruiting spores strong enough to break through concrete. The metal of this lock would be too strong for it, but he hoped it would easily get through the brittle, ice-damaged cement.

"Go wild," Hester said. Her teeth were chattering.

Theo pulled off a thick glove, hissing as he pressed his bare fingertips to the frozen cement. A cluster of grey-capped mushrooms pushed their way out of his skin, pressing their tips against the wall. The tubular caps each exerted a gentle, insistent pressure on the cracks in the cement. Theo focused on nudging the branching structures through the minuscule openings until the shaggy ink-capped fungus had forced them wide.

When Theo winked at Hester, the corner of her mouth lifted. "This was just an excuse for you to make more fungi, admit it."

He shrugged. "Perhaps. What can I say, I'm a *fun-guy*."

She groaned. "Please stop. That was so bad."

Within seconds, the top surface of the cement had flaked away, and the fungus was pushing through to the fixings of the lock. With a well-placed kick, the door flew inwards.

"Ready?" Theo waved away a thick cloud of dust.

"And rarin'."

Theo grinned. He'd hated Hester's southern American accent at first, but it was ... growing on him.

It was obvious no one had been here for many years. They left footprints in the dust as they tiptoed inside, shining their phone lights into the rooms.

"I thought Dad was collecting data for the Arctic expansion from here," Hester said, trailing her fingers across lab benches of science equipment. "I found this address in his contacts. So why's it all shut down?"

Theo shook a metal tray of ash onto the floor. Someone had burned a sheaf of papers. He caught sight of the word "Dalex" before the grey flakes trembled into dust.

"Whatever he was doing, it was ages ago," he said.

The bunker was a warren of tunnels and empty laboratories, many containing more traces of burned documents. Hester found a shred of a letter signed *Anthony Daleport* and held it up to the light to take a photo.

"They were destroying evidence," she said, bemused. "I wonder what made them clear out in such a hurry? We usually auction off the sites we're not using any more. We don't just keep them hanging around empty like this. It's a waste of insurance."

Theo shivered, pulling his scarf tight around him. He was suddenly very aware of the echo of their voices in the dark space. It was like the low ceilings were pressing in around them.

At the end of another corridor, they unlatched a bay door to find an ice-cold, cavernous hangar. It was so huge that Theo was surprised they hadn't been able to see it from above-ground.

He shuffled past a row of skips to tug away a tarpaulin covering a large vehicle. He'd been expecting to find a snowplough, but it was a small Cessna plane.

"Please say we can take this out?" he asked, beaming.

"Absolutely not."

He pouted at her. "Being rich is wasted on you."

Hester ignored him, fiddling with a spray hose attached to the wing of the plane. It had a wide head covered in tiny holes. The tube ran along the fuselage, disappearing into a cannister clipped to the tail.

"What the heck was Dad doing?" she asked, baffled. "Was he trying to melt the ice with this or something?"

Theo shrugged, wandering back to the skips. The bulging bin bags had been there for so long that there was barely any smell at all. He pulled one free, vaguely wondering whether they could work out when the building had been abandoned from the expiry date on a milk bottle. But when he tore open the thin plastic, a stack of torn-up papers fell out.

"They forgot to burn some of these," he said, amused. So much for high security.

Theo kneeled down, ignoring the cold shock of the concrete floor on his knees. He brushed coffee grounds off the scraps of paper, trying to jigsaw-puzzle the pieces back into shape.

"Twenty years ago," Hester said, reading a date over his shoulder. "Hmm. This could be useful, actually."

Theo aligned two shreds of a diagram of the plane's hose attachments, then pressed down a curl of paper to read the title of a memo: SOLAR SEEDING – TEST 2.1.

Hester was peering at it closely. "Solar seeding is a geoengineering thing, it's for—"

A phone alert cut through her words, coming from Theo's pocket.

"It might be Gabrielle, you go ahead and get it," Hester said.

He shook his head, digging through his layers of winter

clothing to find the phone. "That's not my phone, it's Edgar's."

Hester paused, staring at him. "What? Why have you got that?"

"I was going to give it back to him when we got to the spaceport. He left it in the meeting room last night."

"Give it to me?"

"It's locked," he said, handing it over. A notification read: LOW POWER – STOP RECORDING AUDIO TO PRESERVE BATTERY.

Hester flinched back in horror. "No, no, no. Theo, what the hell?"

The words danced across the screen, almost too fast for Theo to pin down. "Stop reading audio?" he asked, bemused.

*"Recording,"* she corrected.

The phone had been recording this whole time? Everything they'd been discussing suddenly flashed through his mind. Had Edgar been listening to it all?

"What do we do?!" Hester hissed, holding the phone like it was radioactive.

What if Edgar hadn't forgotten it at all? What if he'd left it behind intentionally, as some kind of recording device? Theo had even seen him messing around with some software before he left.

"All right, don't panic!" Theo said, panicking. He couldn't believe he'd been helpfully carrying it around in his pocket like a complete numpty.

"I'm not panicking! You're panicking!"

Theo pried the phone out of her hands, turning it off and shoving it deep inside one of his thick gloves. He wrapped it up into a bundle in his scarf.

Almost immediately, Hester's own phone rang. It was Edgar. They both froze in primal fear.

"What did he hear?" she asked, sounding numb. "What did we *say*?"

All he could picture from their journey here was the distracting memory of Hester's vines.

"Nothing," he said quickly. "Right? We didn't talk about the green rising or anything, I don't think."

Hester was shivering when she answered. "Edgar." She seemed to be holding her breath.

Theo was going to be sick.

"Daleport," Edgar said, voice unreadable. "Having a good day?"

"Not too bad."

"I'll get right to it – I have good news and *great* news. First, the weather looks good for a launch on Friday," Edgar said.

"Right," Hester said uncertainly. She shrugged at Theo. "We'll head over to you as soon as possible."

Theo had been expecting a week of training at least before they went up to the Space Station. But this was great – if Edgar was still planning to send them, he must not have found out about their plan for the solar sail. Maybe he hadn't been eavesdropping on them at all. Edgar couldn't stop them from doing anything if they were out of his reach.

Everything was going to be OK.

Then Edgar added brightly, "Even better, I've decided to come up to the Space Station with you."

Ah.

"Oh." Hester seemed unable to add any inflection to the word at all.

Airily, he added, "I have a few things to check up on for the Mars expansion anyway, and I had such fun at our little factory test the other day. I'm fascinated to see your powers in orbit, Hester." Edgar's cheeriness was verging on unhinged.

"Sounds great! We'll be lucky to have you on hand to make suggestions," she replied weakly. "See you soon, then."

"Buh-bye!" Edgar hung up, a note of laughter in his voice.

"He absolutely knows," Theo said in a monotone. "He's totally messing with us. Right?"

"I don't know. He's kind of just … like that." Hester looked shell-shocked.

"So what do we do?" Theo asked. "Just … carry on?!"

"I don't think we have any other choice," she said, resigned. "If Edgar is going to be a problem, we'll deal with it. For now, we have too much to organize." Hester eyed the collage of paperwork, looking thoughtful.

"Jeez, yeah. Let's get going, we don't want to miss the launch."

They grabbed as many bin bags as they could carry, grimacing when one released a dried-up goo. Theo grew a sticky fungus in the broken door lock, sealing it shut as best he could.

It was only when they were settled on the jet, Edgar's phone safely deposited in the hold, that it hit Theo that he was going into space.

**Group chat – *hesterdaleport*, *theocarth* and *firstwithmagic***

**Theo:** Voice Memo ▶ ⏸ ═══○═══════════

[We launch on Friday, can you be ready to go then for the green rising? I know it's soon, but I don't think we're going to get a better chance than this. We've got a minor problem going on at the moment, but we think we can take care of the solar sail. Hester's found some interesting stuff about the Arctic plans which she's working on, so we should be able to stop Dalex in their tracks. We think we might be able to help guide your Greenfingers on the ground from the ISS. If we time the green rising properly, we'll be able to help you rewild your sites. Sorry for the voice memo by the way, I don't write very well.]

**Gabrielle:** Yes, definitely. It's going to be tight, but I think we'll be ready to go when you work out what's going on with the solar sail. We're rushing to pre-record all of our demands/speeches now, so they're ready to go out on the activism social media accounts – "governments have a duty of care to their citizens, they're being negligent by failing to act, putting their citizens at risk and denying their human rights, etc etc."

We have supply caches hidden near all of the sites we're planning to hold hostage, and I've run a workshop on how to use the Mycorrhizal network to connect with other local Greenfingers in bubbles. Everyone has been assigned roles now, and any new members are being given smaller tasks to do in their local areas. The fungi network is really going to maximise activity there.

**Theo:** Voice Memo ▶ ‖ ══════○═══════════

[Wow, that all sounds amazing! Could you ask everyone to try aiming their power at the Space Station when it passes overhead? We think we can use that energy.]

**Gabrielle:** what exactly are you planning to do if this works?

**Hester:** We're researching that right now. We don't want to risk doing anything bad for the ecosystem, so we would focus on encouraging growth of natural plant species in each region rather than adding new stuff. We also want to do a lot of work out in the oceans, where GFs can't normally reach. so: getting rid of plastic pollution, acidity, toxic metals etc.

**Theo:** Voice Memo ▶ ‖ ══════○═══════════
[We think it's best to focus on drawing down carbon out of the atmosphere into plants, then let the temperatures come down naturally as that works. As the carbon levels in the air drop, it will pull carbon out of the ocean too, to make the water less acidic. Coral will have a better chance of surviving then.]

**Gabrielle:** this is all great stuff. Im gonna be so sad if it doesn't work. What's our back-up plan?

**Theo:** Voice Memo ▶ ‖ ══════○═══════════
[I think if it fails we should hold the ISS hostage as an extra bonus encouragement for the governments to actually make policy changes to carbon emissions.]

**Hester:** we are absolutely not doing that

**Gabrielle:** well. I guess I'll leave you two to argue that one out among yourselves?? Lol. You're a cute couple

**Theo:** where not dating

**Gabrielle:** suuuuure. I'm gonna go and update the group on your crazy-ass plans

**Gabrielle:** night, lovebirds ;)

**Hester:** we're not dating

# Chapter 22

Theo said, voice trembling, "Is that it? Our rocket?"

The Warren spaceport was sprawled over a huge site, with a cluster of tall white towers of rocket fuel surrounding the distant launch pad. Theo looked like he could barely believe it was real.

"Don't get too excited. It's mainly bad coffee and peeing in a bag," Hester said, recalling her last space trip. It was a mix of boredom and fear; long waits and quick, explosive movement.

After a day in the air, Hester was ready to hibernate for a month. She had been awake for the whole journey back from Svalbard, reading the documents from the bunker and working out a plan of action. She'd scheduled a call with a lawyer for the earliest morning appointment she could get, to discuss what she'd found. If she was right, this was going to be huge. Both for Climate Rebellion and the Greenfingers.

After that, she'd come up with a few back-up plans for what they could do if things went wrong on the Space Station – all of which had required sending emails to her assistant, stockbroker and solicitors. Hopefully none of it would be necessary, but come hell or high water, Theo and the rest of the trainees would be safe. Whatever Dad and Edgar did.

As soon as they'd landed in Houston, the jet had been loaded up for the trip to Edgar's spaceport. She'd been hoping she could sleep on the flight to the spaceport, but the over-excited trainees had spent the entire journey laughing and joking.

"What do I say if Edgar corners me?" Theo asked in an undertone, as they stepped through a security system that apparently took their temperature and checked for any infections.

"Just … give him back his phone and pretend to be oblivious," she said. "I don't think there's any other way to play this."

They passed by labs full of scientists bent over pieces of motherboard, into a room filled with partially constructed space suits. The trainees were so excited that the sheer energy in the room was a physical shock to Hester's tattered nerves.

"Theo, Hester!" Daisy yelled, tugging them over to a viewing window. "Look!"

There was an enormous swimming pool containing a full-sized spacecraft, submerged under the water. People in bulky space suits were manoeuvring around it as they practised using the equipment.

"Amazing," Theo said, pressing his forehead up against the glass. An astronaut did a backwards flip as he struggled to navigate an underwater doorway.

They were taking six of the trainees up to the ISS with them – Jason, Alisha, Beatriz, Icaro, Daisy and Binh. The others had stayed at the training grounds, ready to welcome a new group of recruits who were arriving in a few days.

Hester had made sure they'd have access to Dalex's helicopter over the weekend, so they could help rewild some areas of Texas during the green rising. Assuming everything went to plan, they'd be able to cover a large area of land, working with Gabrielle's Greenfingers on the ground.

"I sure am glad I've already done the training," Hester said. "I can get some work done."

She turned to Theo, who was already looking at her.

"I have to go and get fitted for a suit," he said regretfully.

Unable to resist goading him a little, she raised her eyebrows. "Why, did you have other plans?"

Laughter lit up his eyes. "I mean, I was kind of hoping to spend some more quality time with Jason, you know…"

She leaned forward and pressed a hand to his chest. He stopped breathing for a moment, until she said, "Later, Carthew. Get to work."

Hester found a seat and plugged her laptop in to charge. There were four emails from Dad which she was too scared to open, one of which Edgar was CC-ed in on. She knew she couldn't avoid them for ever, but hopefully she could put it off until she'd got some advice from her lawyer.

Slipping away from the trainees, she tried to find somewhere private to call the law firm. It was very likely that

Edgar was spying on his staff, too, so she decided to call from a disabled bathroom. Surely even he had to draw the line at hidden microphones in there.

"Miss Daleport, how can I help you?" the lawyer, a viciously professional woman called Alana, asked. "I was a little surprised to get your call. I've never worked with Dalex before. In fact, I'm not sure we'd be the best fit – politically I'm very much against everything your company stands for."

Hester grinned. She'd made the right choice. "That's actually why I called you. I was wondering if you could take a look at some documents I've acquired from Dalex."

Hester emailed Alana photos of the scraps of paper they'd found at the bunker, reassembled into mostly complete documents. It was hard to believe the garbage-smeared remnants could be enough to take down a whole company. "I want to sue my father."

Alana made a shocked noise. "I'm looking now. Is this real?"

Hester sat down on the closed toilet seat, then stood up abruptly. She was wishing she'd chosen a more scenic location. This seemed too life-changing to be happening in a bathroom.

"Yes, it's real," she said. "Dalex tested out a geoengineering technique, where they flew a plane over the Arctic, spraying chemicals into the stratosphere. It was supposed to reflect sunlight away from Earth and stop the temperature of the planet from increasing. But it must not have worked, because they stopped after a few tests and abandoned the research labs."

"It would have been illegal, wouldn't it?" Alana asked. "Is that why they kept it under wraps?"

"I think that if it had worked, my dad was planning to charge governments a fee to operate solar seeding over their airspace. Dad would have been keen on that – Dalex could have sold fossil fuels while also selling the solar seeding service to counteract emissions."

"Can I ask how you came across these documents?"

"I found them while I was working to stop some other activities my father is planning. I think this could be used to file a lawsuit against him. The implications of this trial, it's just – unbelievable. Dalex has always had a history of climate propaganda, but these new documents prove he's maliciously done direct harm to me *personally*, don't they?"

Hester pulled a loose handful of toilet paper from the dispenser, wiping her armpits. She was sweating a river of euphorbia flowers. When she met her gaze in the mirror, her eyes had a startled, panicked look.

"Well, I can certainly see why you'd have a case there. The timing here … twenty years ago. Hmm."

"Will you represent me?" Hester asked, heart in her throat. "I'm on a very tight schedule. I would need to file the lawsuit tomorrow evening. It has to coincide with some other related events I have planned."

"Of course I'll do it," Alana said, surprised. "This is the case I've been waiting my whole career for. To take down

Dalex over climate change … yes. Yes, I'm in. I already know exactly how I'll do it."

Hester fist-pumped. For the first time in days, she didn't feel miserable and overwhelmed. "And – do you think – could there be more than one plaintiff? I was reading about 'class action lawsuits'?"

"Yes. I think that would be a remarkably strong case, if you could get the signatures."

"I'll send over a list of contact details by the end of the day," Hester promised. She would have to ask Gabrielle to spread the message to her contacts through Climate Rebellion. She was sure that Edgar was monitoring her messages by now, so she'd have to be careful not to reveal too much. Hopefully there would be a lot of Greenfingers who would trust her enough to join the lawsuit, even if she couldn't explain what it meant just yet. "I'll pay whatever it takes. Thank you."

When the call was over, Hester spent ten minutes trying to stop her heart from fighting its way out of her chest. This was impossible, impossible, impossible. Was she really going to do this? Sue her *own father*?

If she could use this to expose Dalex's plans in the Arctic, he'd have to give up. It would be an insurmountable scandal. Hopefully.

Hester recorded some videos for Alana to use when the lawsuit was filed, filming herself against the neutral background of grey tile in the bathroom. As long as she didn't pan around, no one would ever know she was sitting on a toilet seat. She was sending them off to Alana when her phone rang. It was Dad.

She let it go to voicemail, unable to face talking to him yet.

> **Dad:** Why is my pilot saying that he flew you to Svalbard yesterday? Call me, Hester. You're on a dangerous path here.

When she deleted the message, she'd never felt so free. Somehow, the bathroom had filled with blossoming lavender.

She headed back to the fitting room, nursing a cup of black coffee, and entered just as Theo said to Jason, "...trade negotiations!"

"You summoned me?" she said dryly.

"We're talking about football." He was wearing the lower half of a space suit. Somehow, it looked good on him.

"Urgh." She pulled a face.

Beatriz and Daisy had zipped themselves into the same oversized jumper and were giggling maniacally. Clearly the long wait before the launch was getting to them.

"Things are going well?" Theo asked.

"All on schedule," she said, trying to be cryptic in case Edgar's ears were listening.

"Budge up," Theo said, and squeezed into the chair next to her, casually draping his arm over the back. His fingertips brushed her shoulder, and a full-body shiver went through her. When she looked back up at his face, his eyes were dark and deep.

Ever since they'd nearly kissed on the plane, things with Theo had been unbearable. She could feel him watching her whenever she turned away, his eyes a hot line on her back. And he kept looking at her *mouth*.

And yet still they hadn't kissed. Hester was going to die.

# Stock Portfolio – Hester Daleport

| Stock | Company | # of shares owned | Current trade value ($) | # of units sold | Transacted value ($) | Notes |
|---|---|---|---|---|---|---|
| DLX | Dalex Energy | 1733.8 | 423,561.92 | 64 | 15,635.00 | Sold for legal fees |
| WRN | Warren Space | 366.5 | 32,618.50 | 0 | n/a | Sell all stock? ☹ |
| HLC | Highland Liquor Co. | 123 | 3,813.01 | 0 | n/a | Bought when drunk. urgh |

| Total Portfolio Value ($) | 459,993.43 |
|---|---|

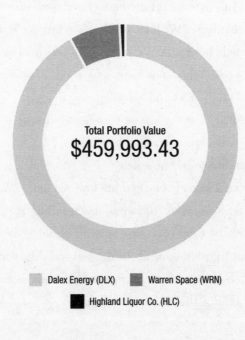

Total Portfolio Value
$459,993.43

Dalex Energy (DLX)　　Warren Space (WRN)
Highland Liquor Co. (HLC)

# Chapter 23

Theo's brain had been turned inside out. The last few hours had been an endless stream of medical tests, practice space launches, fittings for suits and emergency protocol lectures. He should be desperately tired after their trip up north, but he was too jumpy to even think about napping.

"OK, you can leave off the helmet and gloves for now," an engineer told him. "We'll let you know when you're ready to load. It should be around two hours. The weather briefing has said that preliminary conditions look good. There's no wind shear, and no thunder and lightning near by."

Theo headed over to where Hester was already waiting in her bulky white suit, sitting with her laptop.

"Are you nervous?" he asked.

"Nervous I won't get everything finished before we leave," she said, typing quickly. "I have so much still to do."

Theo wasn't sure what she was working on. She'd said she didn't want to risk talking about the solar seeding documents in Edgar's building, which seemed fair enough. But she was up to something, that much was obvious.

He peered over at her screen, where complicated things were happening to a spreadsheet of numbers. "What is that?"

"Water Quality Archive," she mumbled, distracted.

Theo wanted to do something to prepare too, but his brain was already filled to the brim with strategies. He'd spent hours listening to the robotic text-to-speech converter on his phone, reading scientific articles on farming methods, geographical locations, acidification, ocean currents and plant species. He'd wanted to memorize as much as he could in case it was useful during the green rising.

He'd learned that the more regional variety they could provide, the more stable the ecosystem would be. The most important thing was to grow plants that would give nutrients back to the soil. He'd sent everything he'd learned to Gabrielle's Greenfingers and the trainees back at the training centre. Even if they couldn't use their powers from the ISS, everyone else would still be able to rewild the land around them.

"Is there anything I can do to help?" he asked Hester.

"Buy me another twelve hours?"

"Not sure that slowing down time is within my capabilities," he said, "But I can get you a coffee?"

"My hero." Her eyes found his lips and she added, "Actually, I'll come with you."

A buzz of electricity went straight through him. "Yeah! Sure. Er, great!"

They walked to the vending machines together, shoulders

bumping against each other. His heart made a bid for freedom. He needed to kiss her. *Now.*

As if reading his mind, Hester nudged him into an alcove in the hallway, tilting her head up to his. There was a sprig of mistletoe curling out of the back of her suit.

"Don't you want to wait 'til we get to space?" he asked, tangling his fingers in her hair. His emotions were ricocheting. "Seems more cinematic."

"I've already waited long enough, Carthew," she said, lips grazing his. "What am I, a saint?"

"Fair … enough…" Theo managed to say.

They were kissing then, lips catching against each other in a slow, sweet drag. Heat stuttered through him when Hester's mouth opened wider against his.

How could it be so good with someone he'd hated so much? There was no hesitation there, just thirst and desperate longing. Theo had to race to match Hester's intensity, in the same way he always had. He'd been waiting for this for much longer than a day.

When she pulled away, the hallway had gone dark. There was a magnolia tree filling the corridor, pressed right up against the ceiling. It had grown impossibly fast – faster, even, than their training centre forest. Though in retrospect, he wondered how much of that woodland growth had been due to the trainees' high emotions after Beatriz's accident.

Hester shrugged at the tree, unapologetic. "At least you know I was really into it?"

"I wasn't exactly worried about that." He rubbed his fingertips over the rough, feather-fine curls of grey lichen on the tree's branches. He hadn't even noticed he was growing it. Their powers were so strong when they were together.

"I'm starting to like how my power shows my emotions," Hester admitted. "I've been lying to myself for a long time now. This keeps me honest."

"I think you're doing a good job of that all on your own," he said. The tree was flowering as they spoke, unfurling pink, star-shaped flowers.

She pressed their foreheads together. Something sharp jabbed into Theo's temple. One of the magnolia branches was growing from her ear, tugging it back.

When he tried to break it off, Hester cried out. Part of the cartilage of her ear had snapped off too, brittle and wooden.

"Shit. Sorry."

He scrambled for a tissue, but her ear wasn't even bleeding. The raw, exposed edge was rough pith, like the green centre of a twig.

She cupped her ear, staring at him. "It's changing us, isn't it?"

"Sometimes all I want to do is eat mulch," he admitted. "And it doesn't even feel weird any more."

"What if it's permanent? Using our powers on the ISS could push us over the edge."

Theo considered this. How far was he willing to go, to save Earth? Would he risk his whole life? If it worked, then he'd give up everything. He'd go to prison, if it came to that. But what about his body? Would he sacrifice that, too?

Yes. For the sake of the whole planet, for every person alive, and everyone who would be born in the future? He would do this, and more.

"I think it's worth the danger," he said at last. "At least, for me."

Hester looked raw, cut up. "Me too. How terrifying is that?"

"I can barely think about it."

"Well – let's not. We might change our minds. And I have to get back to work anyway," she said regretfully. "Sorry."

"I'll get you that coffee." After a moment, he added, "Daleport."

✿

Just before they entered the shuttle, Theo called his parents on a landline in the loading bay. There was almost zero per cent chance anything would go wrong with the launch – the shuttles went up every few days now, for tourists and engineers working on the Mars settlement – but it still felt more dangerous than getting on a normal flight. He wanted to hear their voices.

"We're watching the livestream!" Mum said. "Good luck, darling! To Hester too!"

"Don't pick your nose on camera," Dad said sagely.

"Thanks for the advice, Dad. I'll be able to message you when I get to the Space Station. Talk later?"

"I dunno," Dad said. "I might be down the social club. I've got other stuff going on, you know."

"Sure," Theo said, laughing.

Dad wheezed down the phone.

"Theo, don't listen to him," Mum said. "He's been bragging about your launch to anyone who will listen all morning. Even the postman is watching you."

Theo swallowed back a wave of nerves. As soon as the news of the green rising got out, everyone in the world would have their eyes on them.

"I'll send you a postcard," he joked, around the lump in his throat. "Listen, guys. Hester and I have been working really hard on this project. It might take you by surprise, when you see what we've been doing. But I know what I'm about, all right?"

"Got it, chief," Dad said. "You're old enough to make your own decisions. If you get a chance, see if Edgar will give you some discount tickets to Mars, won't you? I bet we'd have no problem getting a job out there now we've got a man on the inside!"

"You might not need them by the time this is over." Worried he'd said too much on a monitored phone line, Theo added, "Got to go! Bye! Love you!"

He hung up, looking around guiltily. But no one was listening. Next to him, Hester was saying into the phone, "No problem, Mrs Medan. When she gets out of her meeting, can you tell Mom – just that I said hi, I guess." Hurriedly, she added, "No, no! I don't need to talk to her! Don't interrupt her work, I'm sure she's busy." Hester paused. "Yeah, you too. Have a nice weekend."

Theo pretended not to listen. It must be so lonely, having only the housekeeper to talk to before leaving the planet.

A tide of love for his own parents washed over him. When Hester hung up, Theo reached out a hand inside its bulky glove. "Mum and Dad said good luck to you."

"They did?" she asked, pleasingly surprised.

He squeezed her fingers. "Of course. Are you ready?"

"I think so. I'm so glad I've got you. This would be impossible on my own."

"If you were on your own, you wouldn't be attempting it at all," he said seriously.

"Yeah." She rested her head on his shoulder. "I guess you got me into this mess, huh?"

"And I'll get you out of it."

# FEDERAL BUREAU OF INVESTIGATION
**Dallas, Texas**

**GABRIELLE VENTURA;**

████████████

████████████

**Case #:** ██████████

Ventura's self-proclaimed acts of unlawful "civil disobedience" include the implementation of a new redwood plantation along the planned route of a new oil pipeline in ██████████████. She is identifiable through a hardwood false tooth, which replaces a tooth lost during a boxing match. She is a confidante of ██████████ and is currently under investigation by the FBI concerning allegations of ██████████ ██████████ and suspected involvement in activities undertaken at ██████████.

While still a minor, she has access to significant resources through ██████████ ██████████ (see Document ████). It is thought that her movements in ████████, ██████ indicate a high level of ██████████ ██████████████ taking place through online encrypted platforms such as ██████████████.

Communications have been intercepted that indicate planned action in the ████████ rainforest, which may include an interruption to ██████████████.

Officers are advised to apprehend Ventura on sight at any of the following locations:

████████████████████████

██████████████

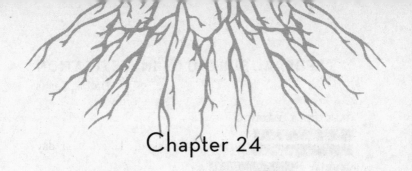

# Chapter 24

Together, Hester and Theo walked through the access corridor to the shuttle. Hester paused at the base of the cabin, raising her voice above the chatter of the trainees as they climbed the stairs to their seats. "Everyone ready to go?"

Daisy looked tense and nervous, but the others grinned back in excitement.

"We've got this, guys," Theo added, punching the air. "Let's go to space!"

"Over here," a voice called. Edgar was waving to them from a row of three seats. He was sitting in the centre, wearing a golden suit that shone against the rest of their plain white ones. Hester was completely unsurprised by his dramatics.

She shot Theo a disappointed look, murmuring, "Nothing for it, then."

Her chest tightened like she was stepping into battle. She hadn't realized how much she was starting to relax around Theo until she had to put her guard up again. Somehow, he'd slipped past her defences and found a way to let her trust him. Unlike Edgar, who was becoming more and more distressing every time they met.

Taking a seat next to him, she asked, "How's your day going so far, Edgar?"

"Wonderful!" he replied, as Theo took the furthest seat.

"My PA passed my phone back to me," Edgar told him, voice pleasantly neutral. "Thanks for hanging on to it."

Theo cleared his throat. "No problem!"

"Very silly of me to leave it lying around like that," Edgar said. He looked hard at Hester as the ground support crew strapped in their feet and buckled the shoulder harnesses.

She tried not to flinch away from his attention. He was clearly testing her, but she wasn't going to give him whatever he was looking for. Not when they had so much to lose.

Something changed in Edgar's expression, like he was satisfied. Voice pitched low in the small space, he said, "Now listen, I'm going to come out with it. I know what you're really doing here."

Right. Here they went, then. She didn't have any other choice but to say, "What do you mean?"

Their seats rotated upwards until they were lying on their backs. Hester resolutely avoided turning her face in Edgar's direction. She wasn't going to give him anything.

"I know about your little green rising."

He was reading their messages. There was no doubt about it.

Theo flung his head around, struggling to make eye contact with Hester. Silently begging him not to speak, she asked, "What?"

"Oh, don't worry. I'm delighted by the idea!" Edgar said.

Every muscle in her body turned to jelly. Could he really be on their side? Maybe he'd decided to get involved once he realized they wanted to help Earth.

"It will be a brilliant test to see if it's possible to rewild a planet before we start terraforming Mars," he added.

A screen started showing the livestream of the launch. As the hatch was sealed and the access corridor removed from the shuttle, a cheer went up through the cabin. Theo and Hester were the only ones who didn't thump their gloves together to clap.

"How would that even work?" Hester asked. "Mars doesn't have the right gases in its atmosphere to grow plants outside."

Edgar nodded. "Sure, right now the carbon dioxide is locked up in the permafrost. But I'm going to melt that by using solar sails to direct more sunlight there. Once the temperature rises, you'll be able to start growing plants outside using the gas released from the ice. The spread of your plants will produce enough oxygen to make Mars habitable in a few centuries."

If Edgar really thought that she was going to waste time growing plants all over Mars when she could be helping Earth, then he was kidding himself. Surely he must know that she would refuse?

"Isn't the sail for the Arctic ice on Earth?" Theo burst out.

Edgar was positively gloating now. "I'm renting out one of the prototype solar sails to Dalex, in exchange for equal shares in the oil. It'll be a great model to determine what the effects might be on Mars. But there will be a whole fleet of solar sails working to warm the climate there. Thousands."

Everything made sense then. Hester had been wondering what could have pushed Edgar to start getting involved in the energy sector, when he was so clearly obsessed with space tech. He needed the Arctic oil for a venture that would cost far more than he could ever drum up from investors: terraforming Mars.

Launching materials from Earth's orbit used a huge amount of fuel – far more than it took to shuttle a few tourists back and forth. Changing the entire atmosphere of Mars would use more energy than any project in human history.

This couldn't be allowed to get any further. They weren't sucking Earth dry of all its resources. Not just to fulfil a billionaire's childhood dream of living on another planet. They had a perfectly good one right here.

"*Pre-launch checks complete,*" the launch director said over the feed. "*Tank depressurized to three bars. Go for launch. Ramp up the engines to full thrust.*"

Hester could see the crown of Theo's helmet as he leaned forward. His hands were clenched in their gloves.

"This all sounds very interesting," Hester said, trying to be polite. There was no use arguing with Edgar. As long as he thought they just wanted to practise growing plants from space, nothing had to change. "If we manage to grow plants from orbit, we can explore doing it on Mars, too."

Edgar laughed. "Oh, no. If you want to use my space station to do this stunt with your little friend Gabrielle Ventura, then I'm going to need something in exchange. You're going to Mars right now, Hester."

"What?" Hester asked, aghast.

On the feed, fuel was being loaded into their rocket. Condensation leaked from the sides of the shuttle, while a series of thumps and rumbles came from below as valves were opened and closed.

"You're the strongest of the Greenfingers, aren't you?" Edgar asked her. "I want you there ready to start terraforming. Theodore can take over the work here. I'll even let him keep the trainees, since the data will be handy for my atmospheric model."

This wasn't happening. They'd worked so hard to get this far. Edgar couldn't just send her off to Mars at the last minute.

*"T minus zero seconds."*

The shuttle began to move upwards, slowly at first. Hester braced herself against the chair, hands fisted in her gloves. Then there was a colossal noise as the shuttle jerked around them. Light flooded into the cabin when the module separated from the launch rocket, uncovering the windows.

Hester had to placate Edgar enough that he'd let her stay on the ISS for just a day longer. She could deal with this ridiculous plan after the green rising.

"If the solar sails aren't even ready for Mars yet, then it will be months before we can start growing plants there," Hester reasoned, over the roar of the engines. "There's plenty of time to run tests on Earth before we start on Mars. We want to make sure the theory works before we commit to anything."

"Do you think I'm stupid?" Edgar snapped. "As soon as your uprising starts, the whole world will be drooling all over you. You'll jump on the first excuse to go back down to Earth again. I want you on Mars, where you can't slip out of this."

"You can't force me," she said, panicked. This couldn't be legal, could it?

"Don't forget that I'm your employer now too, Hester. You work for me. If you want this little project of yours to go ahead, you'll do as I say."

At least she'd filmed those videos in the spaceport bathroom. However far Edgar sent her, he couldn't stop her from revealing Dalex's secrets to the world.

On the screen, the ground crew were cheering. The shuttle was in orbit. Theo rose out of his chair, held in place by only his shoulder harness. She could finally see his horrified expression.

Edgar looked between her and Theo. "Theodore can join you there later, if that's what you're worried about. The more Greenfingers the better."

"I quite like Earth, thanks," Theo snapped. "I'm not interested in fleeing the scene just yet."

"I don't understand how you can do this. The oil you'd need

to terraform Mars like that, it's staggering." Just launching the solar sails from Earth would require the biggest output of energy in human history. She pleaded, "You'd be sacrificing Earth's future if you burn that much carbon. How can you live with that, just for profit?"

Edgar shook his head. "It's not about money. It's never been about money. I want to create a safe home. Just like your father wants, for you. We can give you that on Mars."

"You can give us that – on Earth!" How did he not understand? He knew exactly what they were planning to do with Gabrielle. But even then, he couldn't see Earth as anything except a ruined wasteland. "You're going to kill millions of people if you do this."

Edgar snorted. "The Earth's temperature naturally rises and falls over the millennia. Humans have always adapted before, and they'll be fine now. It's a matter of natural selection and evolution. Things change, Hester. That's progress."

It was chilling, how easily he'd dropped his "harmless cool guy" act, now that he had won.

"Even if you don't believe it'll be d-d-dangerous, you have to admit that all of the things we need to do to stop the crisis are worth doing anyway," she said, pushing back the stems she could feel wriggling beneath her skin. This wasn't the place for an outburst. "More efficient transport, cheaper energy bills, less smog, less garbage, more beautiful forests, no droughts or hurricanes – what part of that sounds like a waste of time to you?"

"It's a waste of *money*," Edgar said, voice flat. "You're a foolish little girl. You're going to bankrupt your family's company if this is how you plan to run it. Anthony has the right idea, sending you away."

Everything slotted into place, then. Edgar wasn't the mastermind here at all. Dad was the one exiling her to Mars, where she wouldn't be able to cause any trouble or embarrass him in public. Somehow Hester wasn't surprised, but it didn't make the pain in her chest any less. The minute she'd suggested they try to fix the damage from the algae bloom, he'd been easing her away from the firm. This had been coming for weeks.

Their shuttle released little bursts of fuel, minutely adjusting its path as it headed towards the orbit of the International Space Station.

"Look, I'm letting you do your little green rising," Edgar went on. "You should be grateful. I could have you all arrested instead."

Hester spluttered like a car ignition turning over.

"Hester..." Theo warned. If Edgar did report them to the police, Hester would be fine. But for Theo and the other trainees, their lives would be ruined.

She couldn't do that to them. She had to stop fighting before she made this situation any worse. The best way she could help them now was to shut up and go to Mars like Edgar wanted.

Hester had done her part setting up the lawsuit. Theo and Gabrielle could handle the rest without her.

Edgar said, "Listen to your boy. You aren't going to talk me out of this. Your father and I have made a decision. You're going to Mars. If you want this game to go ahead – and you don't want your father to disinherit you – then I advise you shut up. Like your wise friend here."

Hester didn't reply. She could almost feel Theo vibrating in his seat. They were at a stand-off.

The three of them drifted in an uneasy silence until the launch director said, *"Alignment for docking complete. We're locking on to the Warren module now."*

There was a jerk as the shuttle tapped against the Space Station module, then with a click and a hiss, it was over. Inside Hester's head, a countdown started. Five minutes, maybe less. And then she would be gone. Once Dad had trapped her on Mars, would he ever even let her come back? He must know that he would lose her for ever if she made it back down to Earth now.

This was it. It was over.

"Welcome to space," Edgar said primly.

She lingered over unclipping her harness while he navigated down the cabin, tugging himself along using the carefully placed handles.

Theo looked stricken.

"He's still planning to melt the Arctic ice," Hester said urgently. "Y-y-you have to destroy that solar sail."

"Come on, Hester!" Edgar called from the hatch. "You don't want to miss your connection!"

Theo shook his head in disbelief. "No, Hester, no. You can't seriously be planning to go with him. We need you!"

"You heard what he said," she managed to force out. "He's going to arrest you all if I don't. Theo, I'm so sorry. But the green rising is more important than me."

He tried to grab her hand, but his bulky glove slipped off her suit. "Hester – please – wait—"

"You can do it without me, I know you can," she pleaded. She forced herself to smile, trying not to feel like her heart was breaking. "Save the Earth for us, won't you?"

She floated through the cabin to the hatch. Theo struggled to unbuckle his harness and follow her, but Edgar pushed her in front of him. As she was propelled down the gangway, Hester couldn't bring herself to look back at Theo. If she did, she would never be able to go through with this.

# Climate Rebellion encrypted server chatlog

**firstwithmagic:** not long to go now, folks! Good luck to everyone who's getting involved in the action irl, as well as our invaluable online helpers. we need all the hands on deck we can get for this. Let's KICK SOME ARSE

**ellawalker:** YESSSS. Heads up tho, I tried to get my older bro involved (he has GFs too) and he got super mad :( he said we're being stupid and we're going to get arrested, and there's no way it will make any difference except to make everyone hate greenfingers even more. I think a group of his friends are planning to come stop us at the docks using their powers

**firstwithmagic:** urgh, I'm sorry ella. we can't win everywhere. the more places we try, the more likely this might work enough to get noticed! anyone else got any concerns or questions?

...several people are typing...

# Chapter 25

Head throbbing, Theo tugged himself down the gangway. The white, modern Warren module was designed to be luxurious for the rich tourists on their way to Mars, so the walls were padded in soft cushioning with handrails at regular intervals. There was nothing for a hapless civilian to break or hurt themselves on.

Theo pulled off his helmet, grimacing when it rubbed against his cheek. His face was swollen and tender. The air smelled musty and old, but he found he didn't mind that. To his surprise, the disconcerting thing was the emptiness. There was a dead void where his power could usually sense plant life. It was so empty that it made him shiver, like something vital was missing. However far he reached out, he couldn't sense anything alive at all.

All of the trainees were gathered in a large circular room, eating sachets of peanut butter as they waited to use the toilet. Theo fought against the lurch in his stomach. His body refused to accept the lack of gravity.

He forced down some food, trying to work out what to say.

Without Hester, he was the closest thing they had to a leader. But he didn't know what to tell them. He'd only been brave enough to do this with her.

"Right," he said to the group, trying to push away his fear. "Well done on getting here intact."

Beatriz, who had been sitting in the nearest row to them during the launch, gave him a sad, private smile. How much had she heard of Hester's sentencing and imprisonment?

"First thing's first: can you all use your powers up here?"

Despite everything, Theo was filled with a giddy, half-hysterical relief when he grew a mushroom between his fingers.

Within minutes, the air was filled with floating leaves. It felt like a surreal dream. Everything was so close and confined, as if they were trapped in high-tech catacombs. From the centre of the room, he could see the modules leading off from one another in every direction, even from the ceiling. Hester could be anywhere.

He closed his eyes, trying to fend off dizziness. This space thing was a lot more stressful than he'd thought it would be.

"Awesome, guys," he forced out. "Right, I want to show you something. This is the important bit."

Daisy and Icaro were already floating over the circular hub in the floor, where a dome of windows gave a perfect 360-degree view of the Earth. Everything was below them now. It was going to take a while for him to reorientate his internal map.

Trails of golden light glowed from cities on the brown mass of land. At the curved horizon, violet bled into the blackness of space above a halo of white. Daylight hitting the ground beyond their orbit across the dark planet.

Theo nudged his face up against the glass, reaching out with his power. Immediately, the speed of the Space Station's orbit rolled over him. They were racing through space, so fast that it just blurred together. He focused on a city in the distance, a sprawling cobweb of lights that followed the twisting line of the coast. Clouds sat over the continent; thick masses of white that seemed impossibly solid.

He tried to stretch out his power to the anonymous Greenfingers below. For a moment, he thought he felt a flicker of recognition. Then nothing. He tried again, imagining himself projecting his power down towards Earth. But he couldn't feel anything.

The trainees were watching him in concern. Theo suddenly felt far too young for this kind of responsibility. He was just a kid. He couldn't be in charge of this. An entire uprising shouldn't hang on whether he could make this happen.

Theo flicked away a mushroom cap that had sprouted on his wrist while he was working. "So, we're not here to grow plants in zero gravity for Warren Space building materials. We've been keeping it a secret, but Hester and I found out that when we're at high altitudes, we can connect our powers with Greenfingers below us on the ground. And we can sort of … guide their power, amplifying it. We wanted to try and use our powers from up here to rewild the planet."

"I knew you two were planning something!" Jason said gleefully. "You were always going off whispering together! Binh, you owe me twenty dollars."

"Yeah, whatever," Binh said. "I'm still convinced they've got a thing."

Theo couldn't bite back his grin. "Well, that too."

Daisy squealed.

"Anyway," he said, trying not to get distracted. "I can't seem to reach the ground on my own. I think we should try bubbling our powers instead."

The surge of power was far greater when they all linked together, but still Theo couldn't feel more than a flicker coming back from Earth. His heart pounded. They'd come all this way, risked everything, and it wasn't working.

Their bubble was nothing like the raging inferno of power he'd felt when he linked up with Hester on the jet. Then, he'd barely been able to keep the energy under control, in the aftermath of their near-kiss. That kind of intensity had helped them reach all the way to the ground, even from a high altitude. Without his connection to her, this wasn't going to work.

He liked the trainees, but he didn't feel about any of them the way he felt about Hester. He *had* to find her if there was any chance they could make this work.

"Keep trying," he told the others. "I'll be right back."

# Climate Rebellion encrypted server chatlog

**oceanofstarsx:** are we going ahead with the plan @firstwithmagic? I get off shift at 6 lol

**firstwithmagic:** I think so! I've been texting them but no reply yet. I know they're in orbit but it might be a while before they can get time alone to test out their powers. be ready to go whenever I give word. It might not be long.

**gremlingrump:** are you still looking for a political representative in puerto rico? I can make the speech here if you want

**firstwithmagic:** thank you so much! The spreadsheet of all the country groups is here, with links to the petitions and press speeches already in place ready to send out when we start. please add your contact details

**firstwithmagic:** we do need to recruit more journalists working for national newspapers who can be clued up in advance so they can prepare balanced articles. ideally freelance people you know irl who can be trusted not to pitch their stories before we kick everything off

**throwawayaccountusername:** ooh I'll ask my cousin! she's been trying to get a byline in ABC here in Australia so this might be her shot

**vulpesvulpes:** did I miss it??? my parents confiscated my phone so I'm sending this from our oven smart screen argh. PLEASE say I didn't miss anything

**knownlibelist:** nothing yet!! stay on standby

Theo dragged himself down a corridor, trying not to throw up. He'd studied maps of the ISS before the launch, but he hadn't realized the Warren module was so closed off. They had clearly made sure there was no way for tourists to get loose in the NASA and Roscosmos research labs.

If he wanted to find Hester and get access to the scientific area where the solar sail was being built, he was going to have to find a way to break out of the consumer zone.

He coated the hatch lock in silvery strands of fungus, keeping an eye out for approaching crew. It released an acid that dissolved the surface minerals in the steel, carving deep channels through the metal and releasing a woody and bitter smell.

When the bolt fell away, Theo yanked open the hatch and slipped through into an empty corridor. He quickly pushed himself off the hatch door and down the central aisle, trying to work out where he was on the map.

Instead of sparse, tourist-friendly white surfaces, the walls here showed the exposed innards of the modules – a mass of wires and devices, all cobbled together in random oddments and pieces. He caught sight of an HP laptop bolted onto the wall, cables coming out of it.

It reminded Theo of his family cottage, with its hodge-podge of mismatched rooms that had been added on over decades. The Space Station had been built up in the same way, expanding outwards from the original structure – except here there wasn't a pet rabbit living in a warren under the scrap heap at the bottom of the garden.

Fighting against the pain in his head, he moved down the maze of gangways, propelling himself faster whenever he caught sight of a scientist working at a computer. Luckily, they all seemed to be wearing headphones.

As he turned a corner, his stomach lurched. Theo couldn't hold it in any longer. He threw up, the liquid forming a ball in the air, droplets of peanut butter spinning off from it.

He panicked, trying to pull the ball towards him before he wallpapered the corridor in vomit. At the same time, he managed to dislodge a tablet, which started beeping loudly.

"What on earth?!" A woman shot around the corner. Theo tried to pretend there wasn't sick in his hair – and on his clothes.

"Help?" he said, feeling blackness wash over him. He couldn't work out which direction was upwards.

"Tourist?" she said, sighing heavily. She used a tissue to herd the vomit into a plastic bag, tying it with a neat knot. Theo got the impression this wasn't the first time she'd done that.

"Come with me," she said, guiding him with a hand on his elbow. "How did you even get out of the Warren module? Don't tell me they left the hatch open again?"

Theo nodded, trying to act confused and bumbling. "I was looking for the viewing cupola. Sorry."

"Don't worry about it. It happens at least once a week. We've tried to talk to the Warren crew about it, but alas. Clearly nothing has changed."

Once she'd deposited him safely back in the module, Theo found a bathroom. He shed the layers of his suit, using wet wipes to clean his hands, the back of his neck and his sweaty armpits.

Cautiously, he manoeuvred into place over the toilet, which had foot straps – and far more tubing than he would usually expect to find in a toilet. Even the simplest things were tricky in space.

He unlatched a compartment set in the rear wall of the bathroom, above the toilet. It revealed an access hatch for the plumbing leading upwards, like a dumbwaiter. Theo squeezed inside, pulling the hatch shut behind him.

It was only just wide enough for him to fit. Using the light of his phone, he wiggled his way upwards until he reached another hatch. He squeezed through and found himself in another narrow tunnel above a gangway.

He almost jumped out of his skin when he caught sight of Edgar tugging Hester down the hallway. Edgar was wearing another gold outfit, made from a high-tech fabric that was presumably designed for space travel. The rest of the crew wore grey tracksuit bottoms and T-shirts, so he stood out like a shiny, underwhelming beacon.

"Frankly, Edgar, I think that in a few decades you're going to regret not taking action," Hester was saying. "And I think, deep down, you know that. Being carbon zero might be enough for most companies, but you have a bigger duty than normal. Your actions need to match that. Your silence is deafening."

"Oh?" Edgar typed something on his phone, not even listening. Hester was still trying to bring him over to their side, even though it was hopeless. Theo wanted desperately to kiss her.

He scrambled along the shaft, following their path until they rounded a corner and disappeared from view. He hesitated, then propelled himself onwards.

Ahead of him, the access shaft hit a dead end. He backed up, then pushed himself off the shaft wall into an empty section of hallway. Through a viewing cupola, he could see the struts where Warren Space's new tourist shuttles were being constructed in zero gravity. Workers in fluorescent-orange jackets were tethered to the module, joining curved sheets of metal together. When he squinted, he could see Edgar's golden suit moving down the gangway.

How was he going to get past the crew to follow them? Theo looked down at his arms, testing out a few brightly coloured fungi on his shirt until he found one that glowed in the same neon orange as the workers' jackets. He covered the exterior of his clothes in a layer of the fungus. Creeping past the crew with his head down, he would look like one of the workers.

He followed an engineer guiding a heavy box down the gangway with one hand. She was taking it to a construction bay filled with something flat and silver and glimmering – the solar sail! It was much larger than Theo had imagined from the pictures. It seemed impossible that he'd be able to destroy it.

Halfway down the length of the bay, he caught sight of Hester near an airlock that led to one of the shuttles, pleading with Edgar. Theo hid behind a crate, straining to hear.

"You're playing around with this technology like you're

a god, but you have no idea what the effects will be. What if you destroy Mars's climate too?" There were foxgloves floating in a halo around Hester's drifting curls: poisonous but beautiful.

Edgar paused for three heartbeats, and Theo almost thought she might have convinced him. He looked like he was teetering on the brink. "What exactly are you asking for, Hester?"

"I want you to think about this, really carefully. You're choosing your side in history, right here and now. If you do this, then you'll be remembered for ever as the man who helped destroy Earth."

Edgar laughed then, a surprisingly hearty chuckle. "Destroy Earth? Hester, your little gang of eco-terrorists are on the Warren Space module. Who do you think is going to get the credit for organizing this green rising? Because it's certainly not going to be you. I'll go down in history as the person who finally fixed climate change – with the help of a few teenagers working for the money, of course."

Theo hated him so much. Edgar had gone fully mad on power. *Of course* he was planning to take the credit.

Hester's voice was taut and furious. "That's not going to happen, because we're not idiots, despite what you might think. In a hundred years, no one will care about your fortune or your cool rockets. All they'll remember is that you abandoned Earth to die. We're offering you the chance to be one of the heroes here. Don't become the villain."

"Goodbye, Hester. See you in a few years, when you've actually done something useful for me."

"I'm sure your cash will be a huge comfort when the world burns," she retorted, as two crew members directed her roughly inside a newly finished shuttle.

Edgar went straight back to texting.

Theo pretended to be rewiring a bit of machinery when Edgar moved back down the gangway to the main module, but he didn't even look up from his phone.

The workers sealed the airlock of the shuttle, which was the size of a minibus. It was fully automated, with all the functions of a self-driving car. It was a pretty easy journey to Mars, which unfortunately meant they'd be able to send Hester straight off on her own. Theo would only have a few minutes to get her out, if it was even possible.

"Get in your seat," one of the workers shouted, miming for her to strap on a harness. Hester bared her teeth at him, pounding on the glass.

The workers started a countdown for ten minutes, then drifted in place chatting about a reality TV show. Theo shifted, frustrated. Were they planning to stand there until the shuttle automatically launched?

Desperately needing to create some sort of a distraction, he pushed himself down the gangway towards them with as much speed as he could gather. As he passed them, he said gruffly, "Warren is looking for you guys."

By the time they turned to look at him, he was twenty

metres down the gangway. He caught himself on a handle, waiting to see if they'd leave. To his relief, they did.

When he made it back to Hester, she burst into a wild grin, pointed down at the hatch and mouthed, "Get me out!"

"How?" he asked, but the glass was too thick to hear her reply.

There were only five minutes left on the countdown. He tried his new favourite trick of growing fungi inside the lock mechanism, but the door to the shuttle was airtight. It was designed to stop any access to the vacuum of space. There was no way through it.

Should he try and break the glass? Surely there was a way to get through without resorting to setting off a dozen alarms.

Theo pulled himself above the hatch, studying the sensors of the locking mechanism. There was a narrow vent in the wall, which was presumably part of the air filtration system, recycling the oxygen around the Space Station. Next to it was a monitor, showing the readings for the shuttle's oxygen, temperature, pressure and fuel levels.

It needed a password, but there must be a safety release for emergencies. Even if the shuttle had been rigged up as a makeshift prison cell for Hester, these systems always had fail-safe alarms. His dad's boat had been the same.

He examined the air vent more closely. Hmm. OK, he might have an idea for how to trigger it. It would be a bit of a botch job, but it should work – and fast.

He propelled himself back down to the hatch, where Hester was waiting for him.

"Grow plants!" he mouthed at her, making gestures with his fingers. He grew mushrooms from his palms, pointing at them and then at her.

Hester blinked, and then immediately started growing algae. It drifted around her head in iridescent clouds, floating in the zero gravity.

"Now what?" she mouthed back, when he gave her a thumbs up.

Theo twirled his finger and mouthed, "Keep going." He pulled himself back up to the air vent. Pressing his finger against the microscopic opening, he filled it with the stickiest, fluffiest fungus he could. The draping threads made a net over the vent.

Hester was still growing algae, and the computer readouts were starting to go haywire. Both the oxygen level and the pressure inside the shuttle were increasing as Hester filled the small space with vegetation. The system had no way of venting the pressure, since Theo had blocked the air filtration piping.

Within seconds, an alarm started flashing on the screen.

ACTION REQUIRED — DEPRESSURIZE SHUTTLE?

Theo clicked the button to take manual control, which suddenly unlocked a huge array of new options. He could launch the entire row of shuttles to Mars if he wanted to.

Instead, he released the airlock. Immediately, Hester

opened the hatch and tumbled out, algae still drifting around her in a cloud.

"You did it!" She dropped kisses all over his face.

Theo bracketed her against the wall and buried his head in her neck, shocked by how much he had missed her. He was almost trembling with relief. Somehow, impossibly, losing Hester had become the worst thing imaginable.

But she was back, and he didn't have to find a way to fix things alone. Somehow, they would have to destroy the solar sail and get their powers working – before Edgar discovered what they'd done.

---

**From:** Alana Richards <alanarichards@dvpandm.com>
**To:** Hester Daleport <hester@dalexenergy.com>
**Subject:** Greenfingers Lawsuit
**Attached:** DaleportHester_Lawsuit.pdf

Hi Miss Daleport,
I'm attaching the final draft of the lawsuit for your approval, ready to file the complaint with the District Court.
As discussed, I will release the documents and the press video when you send word.
Alana

**Attachment:**

---

HESTER DALEPORT; )

THEODORE CARTHEW; )

GABRIELLE VENTURA; )
DAISY MILLS; )
BEATRIZ JULIANA; )
JASON CHESTER; )        **COMPLAINT**
CLIMATE REBELLION, a )
non-profit organization; )
and various collected )
GREENFINGERS minors )
through their guardians )
(see Appendix A) )
Plaintiffs, )

vs.

DALEX ENERGY )
CORPORATION )
Defendant. )
          )

---

INTRODUCTION

Dalex Energy (the "Company") is one of the world's largest fossil fuel companies. For decades, they have systematically misled investors and consumers about climate change to increase short-term capital. They have intentionally sowed public confusion, while in private they have relied on these supposedly "inaccurate" climate models to protect their own drilling infrastructure and obtain intellectual property rights.

The Company has directly impacted the ecological health of the world. The plaintiffs seek, among seven other things, compensatory and punitive damages for this corporate negligence.

Dalex Energy has violated the human rights of the future generations living on this planet, including the plaintiffs. Moreover, the personal health of the plaintiffs has been specifically and directly affected by the Company's actions.

# Chapter 26

Hester had been working herself up into a righteous fury at Edgar, the engineers of the Space Station, herself and all of humanity when Theo had rescued her.

When they finally stopped kissing, her body was pressed against his in a boneless sprawl.

She said desperately, "I hate that tiny little golden man so much, Theo."

"I know. He's like a deranged, despotic emperor."

Hester had to resist the urge to kiss him again, and again, and again. She rubbed his arm, which was covered in a dry orange fungus for some reason. "Did you destroy the solar sail? He's planning to test it on the Arctic ice later today."

Theo shook his head. "I came straight here. We couldn't get our powers to work without you. I think our bubble is stronger because we're, you know, together. We made each other more powerful on the jet. Without our bond, there's just no way we're going to reach Earth."

All of the air left her lungs. "Oh. Well. I suppose we need to hurry up and destroy that sail, then."

She'd been so resigned to going to Mars that it felt almost overwhelming to have another chance at helping the green rising.

"It was crawling with workers when I passed by." Theo grimaced. "We'll have to draw them – and Edgar – away if we want to sneak in."

"We should launch my shuttle before we go," Hester said. "We don't want him to realize I'm still on the Space Station."

Theo's eyes lit up. "Wait – what if we launched them all?" He gestured to the long row of newly constructed shuttles, docked at the port. "They'd freak out."

"What, send them to Mars? Or, wait – let's send them all over the place! Shuttles leaving the Space Station in all directions," Hester said gleefully. "Edgar will be furious."

Theo's smile was so bright she might as well have told him it was Christmas. "It'll take him for ever to sort that mess out. Let's do it! Drastic measures, and all that."

The admin screen he'd managed to access on her shuttle launch pad was still unlocked, so he quickly navigated through the controls until he reached the main access page for the whole gangway.

"Will this really work?" Hester asked doubtfully, peering at it.

"It's just like a video game, look." Theo pointed at the controls. "They made us practise emergency landings using the VR helmet simulator before the launch. This is the same software."

"If you say so." Hester hadn't paid much attention to the simulations, but Theo seemed happy enough. He scheduled a launch for each shuttle, which detached from the airlocks with a barely audible clicking noise. They dropped into the deep blackness of empty space, diverging away from each other in twelve distinct directions.

"Slightly anticlimactic," she said. "What now?"

"Now we get out of here," he said, and grew a layer of the orange fungus over Hester's clothes. "There. Your own fluorescent jacket."

"Thanks," she said dubiously. "It's not going to poison me, is it?"

"I really hope not."

Not reassured, she followed Theo down the gangway. They had only just left the construction bay when a woman swung around the corner, yelling, "Here! The shuttles must have rebooted themselves or something!"

Theo tugged Hester urgently through a doorway to their right. It was an empty sleeping cabin – a narrow, coffin-like space containing a sleeping bag and pillow secured to the wall.

They waited in tense silence, pressed up against each other in the dark. She could happily spend the rest of her life nestled together like this, with his head tucked between her shoulder blades.

There was an exchange of frantic voices in the gangway, as more and more people came to see the missing shuttles.

Finally, they heard Edgar's furious shout: "WHAT DO YOU MEAN THEY LAUNCHED ON PURPOSE? IT'S HESTER FUCKING DALEPORT AGAIN, ISN'T IT?"

Theo stifled a giggle into her shoulder.

"Don't make me laugh!" she hissed, dizzily hysterical.

She could picture Edgar's bright-red face as he shot around the hallways in his golden suit, employees cowering in his wake as he flew past, fists clenched.

"FIND HER! AND THE BOY, TOO!" There was silence as they moved away through the module.

Hester cracked open the door, checking that the coast was clear. They propelled themselves down towards the airlock where the solar sail was being assembled. It looked like a giant trampoline, with thin foil stretched over an enormous framework. It was hard to imagine Edgar building thousands of these in his solo mission to terraform Mars.

"It's so thin," Theo said, amazed. "It's not going to take much to destroy it."

Hester didn't waste time agreeing. She grew shoots of razor grass across the underside of the reflective sheet. Their sharp stems pierced the surface, shredding the material until the bright, shining circle was nothing more than torn scraps.

"ICONIC!" Theo shouted.

They'd saved the Arctic oil beds for at least a few weeks longer – which would buy them enough time to stop Edgar properly. Once her lawsuit was filed, things were going to get a lot harder for him and Dad. She hoped.

They were dragging themselves back out onto the main gangway when gold flashed ahead of them. Edgar turned the corner, simmering with rage.

"What have you done?" he snarled. "Do you know how many millions of dollars you've wasted?"

Hester was moving too fast down the gangway to stop herself. She twisted, barely missing him. Theo knocked right into Edgar, who grabbed his ankle and yanked him back with all his strength.

Theo let out a sharp yelp, banging into the ceiling as Edgar dragged himself in Hester's direction. A thin, white balloon fungus bulged from his gold suit, then spread to the wall next to him, gluing him in place.

Theo dropped his hand, panting.

"I'm going to have you both arrested," Edgar hissed, struggling against the sticky fungus.

"Sir!" An alarmed voice came from the end of the hallway.

Hester quickly pushed herself off and away, with Theo close on her heels. Edgar wouldn't be far behind them. They had to start the green rising now, before they lost their chance for ever.

**From:** Hester Daleport <hester@dalexenergy.com>

**To:** Alana Richards <alanarichards@dvpandm.com>

**Subject:** Greenfingers Lawsuit

Hi Alana,

Can you please release the lawsuit immediately?

Thank you.

Yours sincerely,

Hester Daleport

Executive | Office of Anthony Daleport
(she/her)

---

**From:** Alana Richards <alanarichards@dvpandm.com>

**To:** Hester Daleport <hester@dalexenergy.com>

**Subject:** RE: Greenfingers Lawsuit

Hi Hester,

As requested, I've filed the complaint and sent your video with the press release. I will update you on the response as it comes in.

Best, A

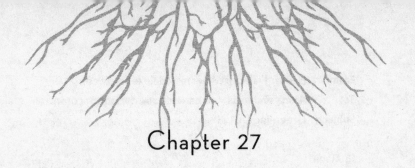

# Chapter 27

The six trainees were all clustered around the dome of windows when they finally reached them. They burst into applause on seeing Hester.

Theo said, "Guys, we've only got a few minutes before Edgar gets here. Long story short, he's a dick and we can't let him back in." With a vicious grin, he added, "Our best play here is to make a barricade."

"YES!" Jason yelled.

"I want you to fill the hallway with the spikiest, thickest, densest plants you can. This entire gangway needs to be filled so he can't get through."

"I'm so glad you're back!" Alisha grew a thistle out of a light fixture with an expression of genuine evil.

Binh was covering the walls in cacti, sharp and dangerous, while Daisy grew barberry into a thorny bush. It bumped up against a gooseberry that Jason was growing from the other side of the gangway, and a holly that Icaro was coaxing down from the ceiling.

Clearly trying to instil some method to the madness,

Hester looped ivy through the branches to form a tight mass of vegetation. Theo couldn't even see through to the corridor when they were finished. They'd blocked themselves off in the tiny dome of the viewing cupola.

"That's enough!" he said hastily. He asked Daisy, "Any luck connecting with the Greenfingers on Earth?"

She shook her head. "We've all tried. We can't seem to make it work like you described."

"Don't worry. I think with Hester here it might be a different story. Can we try again?"

There was a round of determined nods.

"Just to warn you, there's a chance this might get – intense. It could really tip our powers over the edge and transform us somehow," he said, thinking of Hester's wooden ear. "If you're worried about that, we're not going to force you to do this."

Jason rolled their eyes. "We're here, aren't we? We know the risks."

"OK. Well, then…" Stomach in knots, Theo shouted, "Go!"

The planet curved out below them. Right now, they were orbiting the deep navy-blue of the Atlantic Ocean, which was rippled with frosted ice-cream swirls of cloud systems.

It was eight in the morning on the East Coast, so they would have daylight over the Americas, Europe and Africa. They would be able to see everything below them except Australia, parts of Asia and the Pacific Ocean, which was a dark and sleeping void. It would have to be enough.

Theo stretched his hand out to Hester. She tangled her fingers in his, bubbling their powers together. They lit up with hope and joy, as a rush of love surged in his chest. They could do this. Together. He knew it.

This time, the pushback of Greenfingers responding from the ground was so strong that he almost fell backwards. They had been waiting for them. Gabrielle must have been watching the shuttle's arrival on the Space Station on the livestream. There were dozens of smaller bubbles on the ground, as local Greenfingers connected to each other through the Mycorrhizal network underground. Each bubble glowed in his mind as brightly as the city lights.

With Hester at his side, it was easy for Theo to lock into one of the bubbles. Once they'd connected, he reached out to another bubble, a little further away. Using their position above like a satellite, the two bubbles merged together.

He felt Hester bring in another bubble, from further inland – and then a fourth from Daisy, and a fifth from Jason. Hundreds of powers mixed together in one giant web that stretched over the surface of the planet below.

The sheer mass of excited energy coming from the Greenfingers was almost too much for Theo's mind to process. He quickly nudged their attention towards the coastline. From his overhead view, he could guide the group along the shoreline, growing seagrass, mangroves and kelp.

As they drew the green vegetation along the waterfront, more Greenfingers contributed their powers to the pulsing sphere of energy, until there were hundreds of people working as one.

It was a doddle, then, to pull a shelter from the sea bed – a place for fish to hide, for oysters to grow. He imagined the carbon the plants would hold in their leaves; the cleaner waters they would create. A gentle, safe space for coral; a barrier against storms; a forest under the water to keep animals safe from the nitrogen and microplastics being washed away into the ocean from the nearby city.

The bubble's powers were guided along the delicate frills and fronds of the shoreline until they reached a harbour. It became easier to guide the group as they all got used to the sensation. He could feel the local people choosing which plants to grow, guiding the decision-making from the ground. When he finally broke the connection with the other Greenfingers, he was born anew.

It worked. It actually worked. And he barely felt tired. If that was what they could do in a few seconds, over one city, then this—

This could actually work. They could do this everywhere, across the planet. Their plan wasn't foolish, or impractical, or doomed to failure. They were going to save the Earth. Really, actually save it. What a miraculous, wonderful thing they could create together.

Hester was crying, tears of happiness running down her cheeks as she guided the growth.

"Keep going," Theo said, leaning into the joy in his chest.

The trainees were all smiling now, and he could feel the intensity of their emotions making their bubble stronger.

Theo dived back in. He focused on the sea first, helping kelp forests and seagrass meadows to spring up along the coastlines. The outcroppings would lower the water temperature and defend against hurricanes, as well as making the water less acidic. The oceans were absorbing so much carbon from the atmosphere that everything was dying – but these new meadows would give creatures somewhere safe to live until carbon levels began to drop.

There was a growing buzz of excitement in the back of his mind, as the bubble of Greenfingers below understood his plan and began to help.

Out in the deepest waters, where rubbish floated on the surface in a foul mass of plastic, they grew leathery seaweed, using the ribbons to build a net. It guided the waste along the sea currents until it was bundled together.

Theo was jolted out of his dreamy haze by distant shouting coming from behind the barricade. Edgar and his guards were trying to push their way through the gorse bushes.

"Ignore them," he said to the trainees. "Keep going!"

Their seaweed-tangle of plastics was being covered by an enormous mass of plants, compressing down the layers to seal away the rubbish. It was hundreds of kilometres wide, but with the Greenfingers working together, the effort barely made Theo sweat.

Outside, the guards had found something sharp, and were

cutting away at the barricade. Theo redirected some of the energy from the ground towards the bushes, making them sharper and thicker against the attackers. The blood pulsed through his veins like running sap.

Once the rubbish was covered in a thick layer of peat, they began to grow a new forest on the surface of the floating platform. Theo helped seed fungi spores into the root systems of new trees, while an understory of bushes sprang up below the tall canopy.

Behind them, the guards had gone suspiciously quiet. Theo couldn't make out anything through the barricade. When he blinked, brittle grass seeds fell from his eyelashes. He wiped them away, turning back to Earth.

Thick-trunked cypress and beech trees formed a sturdy barrier against the high sea winds on the boundaries of their island, with open glades and thickets inland. Soon, rivers and streams would form as the cool shade of the trees created clouds and rainfall overhead. The platform would be a new island floating on the surface of the Atlantic.

From above, their new country was barely a dot of green in the ocean, but Theo could feel every detail of it. He tasted the orange dust of pollen on his tongue as if he was running through the damp foliage of the undergrowth. He grew mushroom fairy circles in the shadows of tree bark, breathing in the aromatic smell of pine needles and the milky sap of grass stems. It was as real as his own body. He put down roots there, sinking himself into the land.

On the underside of the floating platform, they grew kelp and algae and coral, making a new reef out of humanity's waste.

Already he could feel the inquisitive nudging of fish as they poked around the deep underbelly of the island. It would be a safe space for crustaceans and sea urchins. Maybe even otters, seals and sea birds would come here.

Suddenly Daisy let out a scream. The entire module had gone pitch-black, lit only by a glimmer of light from the Earth below. Someone elbowed him in the face, forcing his teeth to clack painfully together.

A loud voice came from some hidden speaker. Edgar said, "I've cut off the power. You won't have electricity or fresh oxygen until you agree to board a shuttle back to Earth."

"NO!" Theo yelled, livid.

Edgar was only doing this out of spite. He wanted to take the credit for the green rising, but Hester had outwitted him. He would suffocate a whole group of teenagers because they'd damaged his pride. It wasn't even like they'd actually damaged his shuttles – just sent them off on a little diversion.

"We should have at least fifteen minutes of oxygen," Hester said, sounding weary. He reached out towards her dark outline, drifting in the black. She latched on to his fingers. "We can do a bit more, even if it's not as much as we'd hoped."

No!" Theo was furious. He wasn't going to let this megalomaniac tyrant win. Usually Edgar and Hester both operated several moves ahead of Theo, like they were playing three-dimensional chess while he was still struggling with noughts and crosses. Trying to put himself in the mindset of Edgar had always seemed an impossible task. But this time he knew what to do.

Theo propelled himself away from the windows until the barricade pressed sharp and thick against his chest. He grew foxfire fungus from the walls. Immediately, the small confines of the module were lit up with a green glow from the bioluminescence.

It was almost eerie – especially since Alisha had grown a thick blanket of moss over her body as she worked. Their tiny, earthy cave glowed phosphorescent in the darkness of space.

Theo said, "The barricade plants will recycle the oxygen for us, especially if we keep growing them. That should buy us some time. Keep working. I won't let this end here. We can do this!"

"This isn't over," Edgar said over the speaker. He sounded so petulant that it was hard to take him seriously. He was like a child having a giant strop.

"Bugger off!" Theo yelled. When Beatriz started giggling, it quickly became infectious. Their tense panic turned to hysteria. Edgar might have them trapped in a dark tube with no heating or oxygen, but they weren't giving in. Not yet.

Theo pressed his hand against the glass, stretching out his power once more. His entire hand was covered in fungi, with his fingernails growing the fruit caps of mushrooms and warts of lichen. When he tried to peel them away, it sent a sharp stab of pain through his nerves.

The others were transforming too, with alpines and bark and pollen creeping over their skin. They weren't growing plants now – they were becoming them. The green rising was taking what it needed.

Theo went back to work, hoping desperately that they would finish this before it took them over completely. He didn't want to find out how much he was willing to sacrifice to save Earth.

## Climate Rebellion encrypted server chatlog

**lostinature_:** this is SO WEIRD, I can feel what we're doing and control how much of my power I give them? When the ISS passed over my village I actually decided what plants everyone grew. ive never been part of something this big before. Anyone else in the bubble rn?

**ramblingbotanist:** meeeee! Its AMAZING. Super tiring though, I need a nap haha. Were you the one that made us grow some palm trees by a waterfall? That was super pretty.

**melesmeles:** ahhh THAT WAS ME!!! I wonder if I could tell which one you are. everyone's energy feels kinda different?

**ramblingbotanist:** yeah I know what you mean! Like when you make different plants, all vibrating at their own frequencies. But we all synced up so fast, it felt super natural.

**queencuckoo:** yall I wish I was a GF, this sounds cool af. Will have to make do with doing the online stuff instead though.

## BREAKING NEWS: Global Greenfingers Attacks

**1 minute ago: Airports On Lockdown After Suspected Terrorist Attack** – Jet planes were unable to leave the runways of several international airports when unidentified Greenfingers passengers covered the wheels and wings in bittersweet suckers.

> Read More

**5 minutes ago: Shanghai Port Faces Security Threat to Docked Vessels** – Oil tankers, container ships, bulk carriers and cruise liners in the harbour at Shanghai port have been glued to the dock by Greenfingers using seaweed to overwhelm the hulls of the vessels.

> Read More

**9 minutes ago: Police Are Reporting Calls From Service Stations Across Europe** – Trucks transporting petrol to fuel stations across the continent have been covered in ivy so that the lorries can't get back on the motorways.

> Read More

# Chapter 28

As the Space Station left the Atlantic Ocean and began to cross Europe, Hester could think of nothing but the planet below. There were so many Greenfingers pushing their energy up towards space that she hardly had to even think about where she wanted the energy to go. The amount of power at her fingertips sent her into a dreamy, sleepy state of meditation.

Shrubs and sedges, liverwort, lichens and heaths, tussock grasses and reindeer moss filled marshland and tundra. The planet had been waiting for this. It was eager for their attention. Everything felt inevitable to Hester. Nothing so grand as fate, but nothing as random as chance, either. This was the march of life, and they were doing their part to help it progress.

On the dust-bowl farmlands, where the soil was dry and losing nutrients every year, Hester helped the farmers by intercropping the wheat and corn with native trees, woody shrubs and grasses. With the flick of a glance, she seeded alleyways of trees through the fields. The long wildlife corridors would give the crops shade from the sun and wind, and hold the moisture in the soil

As they crossed over the endless red dust of desert plains, Hester grew a green wall along the expanding edges of the desert. She climbed the ecosystem, starting with mosses and then growing more complex plants, until whole trees pushed out of the soil under her command – sand olive, avocado and juniper trees burst into life. The barrier of lush damp shade and coolness would hold down the soil.

Over bare rock where the soil had been blown away, she grew aspen. Soil and leaf mulch would gather in crevices, blocked from the wind, and produce a new layer of earth.

Hester laid down forests in the places where they'd been torn down, as Theo added fungi to the roots of the trees, growing an understory of coffee and cacao, rubber and black pepper, coconut and banana. Crops that could be harvested in the cool shade of the taller overstory of trees.

Rivers snaked across the land like dark branches, breaking off into smaller and smaller fractals. Hester grew peat bogs and mangroves along their banks, filling the mudflats with deep roots to protect the shores from storms.

"Hester!" Theo yelled from somewhere far away. "Help!"

She jerked herself back from the thrumming life of the planet. It took her a moment to work out where she was. She had been immersed in so many living things – a whole world inside her head – that without it she felt small and lost. But a tight pressure on her arm guided her mind back to her body.

The module was shaking around them.

"He's detaching us from the ISS," Theo said, fighting his way through their barricade. "We'll be lost in orbit!"

If their pod drifted away, they wouldn't be able to get back to the ISS before they ran out of oxygen, no matter how many plants they grew. For the millionth time that day, Hester cursed the power of billionaires. Why should they be allowed this kind of influence? Edgar wasn't even afraid of committing murder.

Hester pressed her hand to the glass, growing thick climbing vines from the airlock onto the outside of the ISS. The suckers tried to latch on to the surface, stems tightening and curling inwards. But the delicate tendrils tore away from the smooth metal.

"Theo!" she yelled. "Fungus, now!"

The pod took them further from safety with every second. If they went too far, Hester would never been able to bridge the gap with her vines.

Theo cupped his palm around her hand, adding his power to hers. They coated the outside of the ISS in thick, sticky fungi, clawing a secure grasp onto it. This time, her vines held in place.

"More," she huffed, mentally tugging on the stems until they curled into spirals, pulling the pod back towards the ISS.

"It's moving," Theo said. "Feel that?"

Hester didn't know how much longer she could hold this. It was one thing to grow plants, but to use them like this? It fought against the plants' desire to grow big and strong and stretch tall. And she had already overworked her power today.

Achingly slowly, the pod was pulled back into the ISS. When it banged against the metal helm of the spacecraft, Hester released her control. There was a stabbing ache at her temples.

Edgar glared at her through the windowpane, indignant rage painted over his features. She spat out a mouthful of camomile and waved at him.

"You go back to work," she told Theo. "I'll keep an eye on our little nuisance here."

Theo had a lost, wild look in his eyes – like the forest had taken him in and eaten him up. When he kissed her cheek, his touch was strangely spongy and thick with fungus. "Pull me out if you need me."

He slipped back to the windows. Edgar was still making furious eye contact with her. Certain that he could hear them from some hidden microphone, she said, "Give up, Edgar. It's too late to stop us, but there's still time to reconsider. You can join the right side of history." Hoping desperately that Alana had done what she'd promised, she added, "Check the news."

Edgar frowned at her, then pulled out his phone. Over the speakers, Hester could hear him playing the video she'd recorded in the Warren Space bathroom. The lawsuit was out.

New fear lurched up into her throat. Everything had been so frenetic that it was only just hitting her. Right now, Dad was being told that she was suing him. It was a world away.

*"I'm Hester Daleport,"* she heard herself say. *"My grandfather founded Dalex Energy. My father still runs it today, with controlling majority ownership of the corporation. I'm suing the company on behalf of thousands of international Greenfingers in a class action lawsuit, because Dalex caused the Greenfingers mutation.*

*"Twenty years ago, Dalex Energy ran a secret, illegal experiment in the Arctic. They sprayed a mix of chemicals into the stratosphere, including sulphur dioxide and a disk-shaped nanoparticle. The aerosol particles were made of layers of magnetic materials, designed to stay in the atmosphere using photophoretic levitation and magnetophotophoretic effects."*

"What is this?" Edgar asked, perplexed.

Was Dad watching this in his office, rubbing hand sanitizer into his palms and drinking his little liquid meals, just in case the dirty pollution got into his system?

*"My father hoped that the particles would act as a geoengineering strategy, to stop a proportion of the sun's heat from reaching Earth and counteract the greenhouse effect. However, after a few months it became clear the concept didn't work – it just caused droughts. The scheme was cancelled, and Dalex abandoned their research centre in the north."*

Dad would be furious. She had no idea what he was going to do. Surely he'd known this secret would come out eventually? It was too big to stay hidden. It affected everyone on the planet.

*"The modified nanoparticle discs unintentionally triggered*

a series of reactions with several rare molecules in the atmosphere. These molecules then moved down through the upper layers of the atmosphere until they hit the troposphere."

"Boo!" she heard Theo yell, listening to her speech.

"The molecules reacted with the water in clouds, and the substance fell to the earth in rainwater. I have found evidence from water quality testing data that the modified chemicals entered the water cycle twenty years ago. It didn't take long for the substance to make its way into drinking water – and from there, into the human body."

She held her breath, watching as realization trickled across Edgar's face. It was delicious.

"In pregnant women, the new substance in their systems had the unexpected effect of interacting with the cells of their unborn children. The working theory suggests that the cells merged with foreign organelles, creating babies with latent Greenfingers powers, which emerged in adolescence."

Edgar's eyes were bugging out of his skull.

"To be clear, Dalex Energy are single-handedly responsible for creating the Greenfingers, through an attempt to delay the climate emergency caused by their own oil. They sprayed chemicals into the atmosphere that poisoned an entire generation."

Hester had spent a long time trying to work out how to phrase this. Judging by the shouts from the trainees, it had been worth the effort. And she'd used those lovely public speaking skills Dad had taught her.

"*Dalex needs to take responsibility for what they've done to us. They have stolen our future – and those of endless future generations who will live on this ruined planet. Dalex knew the risks they were taking, but continued in a ceaseless search for more profit. Corporate greed has destroyed the planet. If justice is to be served, changes need to be made to ensure that no one is able to make decisions that affect every human alive on Earth.*"

When the video ended, there was a long silence.

Edgar looked cowed, but soldiered on. "So what? That's a downer, but it's nothing to do with Warren Space."

"My father's reign is over," she told him. "There's still time for you to align with the winning Daleport here. Do you want to be connected to him, or to me? Help us to save the planet, and you can stop Warren Space's reputation from divebombing into the ground alongside Dalex Energy."

Edgar's expression was set in a look of deep resentment. "You win," he said bitterly.

"Win? Edgar, there are no winners or losers here. We're all in the same sinking boat. You might have a life jacket, but that won't stop the water coming."

Edgar wouldn't make eye contact with her, but he unlocked the airlock, letting the module reconnect with the ISS. Fresh oxygen burst through the open door.

"Thank you," she said.

"Whatever." Edgar stormed off down the gangway, somehow managing to convey the effect of a tantrum despite his elegant propulsion.

They were safe.

Hester scrubbed her hands over her face, trying to process what had just happened.

Her phone started ringing. Dad was calling.

**3 minutes ago: Climate Rebellion Issue Statement to Press** – Gabrielle Ventura said, "Today we stand up on behalf of Planet Earth. No longer will we allow the burning of fossil fuels. Kerosene jet planes, diesel shipping vessels and petrol trucks must be retired or converted to electric fuel immediately.

"You are grounded. This is the end. We will not accept the destruction of our planet any more. This is not an act of terrorism, but civil disobedience in the face of government and corporate brutality against the world. To take a stand against the negligence of our peers is not a crime, it's a duty.

"No more fossil fuels will be burned needlessly while we have the powers to stop you. If you try again, you will be prevented peacefully but firmly via the safe immobilization of your vehicles and production facilities. We will block you, and we will keep blocking you.

"We are nature defending itself. We demand change. We will accept nothing less."

> Read More

**4 minutes ago: Clash Between Rival Political Groups in Hull Town Centre** – A Climate Rebellion activist group protesting in Hull have been attacked by a group of alt Greenfingers who disagree with the protest. The nearby streets have been blocked off by police due to the presence of hazardous airborne pollen from exploded handmade grenades. The action is ongoing, with military on the scene. Drone footage shows the rival factions have established trenches behind hedge barricades and appear to be firing acid pellets across the high street.

The activists seem to be communicating through unknown methods. Military phone signal blockers have had no effect on communication between the groups, which act in unison despite being separated by long distances. Satellite footage shows the Greenfingers digging their fingers into the ground before responding to orders from other groups. It is unknown what form this communication takes, whether biological or technology-based.

> Read More

**6 minutes ago: Dalex Energy Responsible for Greenfingers Mutation Through Unlawful Chemical Spraying, CEO's Daughter Leaks Internal Memos; Sues Own Company**

**15 minutes ago: Leading Automobile Manufacturers Pause Assembly Lines at Factories**

**22 minutes ago: Satellite Surveillance Agencies Report Disturbance in the North Atlantic Garbage Patch**

**27 minutes ago: Vegetation Appears in Destroyed Regions of Wilderness**

# Chapter 29

"I can't do any more," Beatriz gasped, pushing away from the window.

Theo dragged himself back from a mountainside, where he was anchoring spruce trees into the steep ground.

"Me neither," Daisy said.

"It's OK," he forced out, as slow as the seasons. It was an effort to speak at all. "Take a break."

When Theo moved his arm, something cracked in his wrist, sharp and sudden. His bone had snapped, brittle where it had become a stem under the skin.

He should take a break too, but he couldn't resist diving back into the pull of energy. It was like being submerged in a pool of cool, fresh water, deep and calm and endless. He could spend his whole life here, working with the planet and all the Greenfingers, and it wouldn't be long enough.

Vaguely he could hear Hester talking to someone, her voice raised.

Theo brushed it away. The Space Station was passing over Bangladesh. He wanted to make sure that the roots of the plants were sunk extra deep there, for his mother's family. He seeded fungi through the roots of farmed crops, where the natural spores had been stripped away by ploughing.

When he blinked, something painful tore at his eye. Everything went dark. His eyes were sealing shut, as lichen pressed down over his face. He swiped it away, hissing as it broke the skin. Back to work. He had to go back to work.

He added mustard, clover, vetch and trefoil to the polluted dead places that humans had ruined – the landfill sites and dust bowls, radiation zones and coal ash slurry pits.

The flesh over his eyes hardened again, as a second layer of lichen grew. He let it spread. It was less painful if he let the plants overwhelm him. Nature needed him.

**1 minute ago: Bitcoin Mining Farms in Georgia, China, USA Under Attack** – All trading of the currency has been suspended temporarily until mining can resume. Edgar Warren, leading bitcoin entrepreneur, was unavailable for comment.

Warren stock prices are dropping rapidly, serving what may be a fatal blow to the man. He is already facing a severe lack of trust from shareholders, after twelve of his Mars shuttles launched simultaneously in an unplanned malfunction earlier this evening. Efforts to retrieve them seem unlikely to succeed.

> Read More

**11 minutes ago: Beef Producers Report Damage to Meat Packing Plants** – Climate Rebellion responds: "Livestock such as cattle take up land and food supplies which must be returned to forest. Cattle breeding must drop significantly immediately, or further action will be taken."

> Read More

**23 minutes ago: Plastic Suppliers for Leading Brands Impacted** – As news continues to flood in on a second-by-second basis, the true extent of Climate Rebellion's interventions is coming to light. Biological methods have been used to halt the production of single-use, non-recyclable plastics used as packaging.

> Read More

**26 minutes ago: US President Issues Statement**

**29 minutes ago: Stocks Disrupted Across All Markets**

**34 minutes ago: Logging Companies Blocked From Gathering Timber**

**42 minutes ago: Coal Mines, Smelting Factories and Oil Rigs Latest Affected**

# Chapter 30

Hester pulled in a huge breath of precious fresh oxygen, then answered Dad's call. Her whole body rebelled against it, but she was suing him in front of the entire world. She could at least give him the courtesy of a conversation.

"I'm here, Dad."

He drew in a quick breath. "Princess. I'm sorry. I had no idea what that silly solar seeding test did to you. I thought it would help save the planet." His voice was thick with stress.

Hester said, "That's a lie, Dad. You might not have known the specifics, but you've always been petrified of every single way you've polluted Earth. It's why you're so scared of getting sick. You don't eat anything grown in the ground in case you consume Dalex chemicals. You know what you've done and it terrifies you."

"I wish you'd let me take you to Mars. You'd be safe there. It might not be too late to fix you." He sounded ancient, as if he'd aged decades in just a few minutes.

Hester laughed. A seed pod rattled somewhere inside her chest. He didn't understand at all. Why would she want him to take away the powers? They were going to save the planet. "You can't imprison me on Mars just because you're angry at me."

"I'm not angry, I'm devastated," he said, sounding surprised. "Hester, I *hurt my daughter*. I've only ever wanted to protect you, but I poisoned you before you were even born. Do you really think I'm a villain? Is that true?"

Before she could answer, he spoke in one quick burst, like the words had been building up inside him for decades. "I'm a good person. I've dedicated my whole life to my work. I've employed thousands of people and given them job security for life. I've built a community. Doesn't that mean anything?"

"You didn't listen to anything I said in my speech," Hester said, dismayed.

"No, I did. It was a very good speech. I believed everything you said. And the rest of the world agrees with you, so ... you must be right. I must have gone wrong somewhere. But – I just don't understand it. I'm not violent. I've never hurt anyone. Is what I did really bad enough to make you destroy Dalex's reputation? We're facing *criminal charges*, Hester. Our stocks have plunged. You didn't need to destroy everything I've worked for. I would have listened, if you'd come to me directly with your concerns."

Hester chewed on her bottom lip. "You wouldn't have."

"I'm sorry I didn't listen to you before. I know I care about profit, but that's always been the safest way to do business.

342

Yes, I've had to muddy the truth occasionally, but that's the way everyone does things. It wasn't an act of evil."

"If you stop now, then we can fix your mistakes," she said, voice gentle even though she wanted to scream. He was in total denial. He must have been lying to himself for decades. "I know it's scary. There's a lot of work to be done, but I can lead Dalex down a better path. You can't recover from a scandal this large. If you want us to build our reputation back up, you need me."

"Is that what you really want? It's a lot of responsibility."

"Yes." Hester ground her teeth together. Even now, he couldn't understand how desperate she was for this. Forging on, she added, "Dalex isn't going to expand into the Northern Fields, not now and not ever. We're transitioning to renewable energy as soon as possible."

It wasn't possible to solve things with fancy tech or chemical manipulation. The Earth was too complex for that. There were always going to be side effects to geoengineering, like the Greenfingers mutation. The Earth couldn't be manipulated like a complicated software simulation.

The only way to stop climate change was to stop burning fossil fuels. However desperate they were to avoid that, it was the only solution.

"Dad, I want to help run the company. I can't wait until you're ready to retire. It will be too late by then. I need to do this now."

Her father was silent. She couldn't tell what he was

thinking. And even if he did agree to her ideas, could she ever trust him? She would always be looking over her shoulder, waiting for the day he'd try to drag her off to Mars again, where he could swaddle her in safety and cleanliness.

"Hester," Daisy said, sounding nervous. "Sorry to interrupt, but I think – there's something wrong with Theo."

Hester spun around, hanging up immediately. Theo had frozen in place, rotating on the spot. His entire body had sprouted fungi. Even his eyes were dark, with mushrooms set into the sockets. He was transformed.

"Theo!" she cried. His skin was too soft beneath her touch, collapsing inwards under the slightest pressure. "Come back."

She had heard of Greenfingers disappearing into the woods and never returning, but she hadn't known it could happen like this – a sudden, abrupt submersion, like nature had decided to claim him.

A cobweb-like filament was covering his lips, wafting with his faint exhales. He was still human enough to breathe, then.

When Hester pushed her power into him, the fungi twisted towards her. It was like diving into a deep pit, rich and earthy and ancient. The mushrooms welcomed her with open arms, engulfing her in calm, sturdy endlessness.

It was tempting to sink into it, to wrap herself up in Theo's arms and let the fungi take them both. They would be together for ever, then. Peaceful, at last.

They'd done what they set out to do. They'd helped Earth. If Dad couldn't bring himself to yield to her, what else was left for them, except being together?

Hester pressed her lips to his, breathing the lace-white filament deep inside her lungs. Yes. Yes. Yes. This was their prize. They'd earned this.

**1 minute ago: Demands From Climate Rebellion Continue** – Activists have gathered in city centres across the world. Many have dyed their hair green, in solidarity with the Greenfingers taking action. Gabrielle Ventura is speaking now to those assembled.

"This is not a rash act. We are holding the economy hostage as a last resort, after decades of pleading with governments to make a change. We're begging you to do something here. But if you're not willing to act, then please get out of our way.

"What are you going to tell your grandchildren when they're starving and thirsty and the water is rising around their ankles? You can't say that you did everything you could. We need you to do everything that's required of you."

Their demands to governments around the world include:
- Ban single-use, non-recyclable plastics
- Tax carbon emissions at the highest possible level
- End government subsidies for oil, coal and natural gas companies
- Improve public transportation to allow the transition away from cars
- End production of new petrol-powered passenger vehicles
- Create stricter regulations around corporate waste disposal and pollution, with active monitoring agencies
- Enforce stricter laws about fixing leaking underground water supplies

> Read More

**34 minutes ago: Warren Space Involved in Climate Rebellion Activities** – Edgar Warren has released a statement on social media, saying that the forest regrowth and garbage islands are the work of his Greenfingers group operating from space.

Warren was quick to emphasize that this collaboration was solely between the young Hester Daleport and himself. He confirmed to press that Anthony Daleport – current CEO of Dalex and subject of a lawsuit regarding the origin of the Greenfingers power – had no involvement in the plan.

He posted, "We're committed to global ecological rejuvenation, as seen from our hard but necessary work here today." He went on to promote his Mars settlement plans.

Anthony Daleport has yet to respond to the allegations.

> Read More

# Chapter 31

Theo was sinking deep into some kind of primal existence, where the only things he needed were soft, rich soil and dark, dank moisture. Anxiety had leached away from him, as his bones and organs abandoned the over-complicated, stress-ridden form of a mammal. He had shed the useless parts and returned to his roots.

Time had lost meaning. The dull, deep thud of his heart slowed. Then there was a sharp burst of heat: something warm and living, pressed against him. A fluttering, lively thing; too quick and frantic to follow. It was almost annoying, in his calm state.

But there was something familiar about the flavour of the magic. The thing kissed him with strangely human lips. Its chest rose against his, forcing his lungs to remember their form.

*Hester?* he asked the figure of warmth, from deep inside his mind.

*Yes.* The words were dreamy and gentle. *Can we stay here?*

*You have to go back.*

*Then come with me.*

With a shock of sound and pressure, he was pulled back into his body. It was all too much: bright and close and hot. Theo writhed against it, trying to pull Hester back into their safe, quiet place.

"No, Theo." She pressed their lips together. "Stay here."

He forced his eyes open, blinking until wafers of organic matter flaked away. Her silhouette shone against the navy-blue oceans of Earth.

Hester had bark in her hair and fronds embedded in her cheeks. But she was smiling at him. Their hands were tightly entwined in a thick mass of ancient roots, withered and brown with maturity. Hester pulled them free, breaking the root ball. It sprouted a perfect, delicate clematis blossom.

There was a sharp pain down the length of his forearm. Something was jutting up towards the surface. He'd pushed himself too far. He had felt the bones weaken as he worked, turning into branches below the skin, but he'd kept going anyway. He hadn't had any other choice.

"Did we do it?" he asked, dragging the words from his throat.

She was holding on to him like she might fall apart if he let go again. He tugged his head above the water. Human. He was human.

They must have been lost inside the plants for hours, because the trainees were floating around them, deep in sleep. Alisha's skin was a bright pea-green, and Daisy's peach-fuzz skin had morphed into real fruit. Jason was almost unrecognizable under the bark covering their face. None of them looked as bad as Theo, though. They must have known to quit while they were ahead.

"We did it," Hester confirmed, pulling him over to the porthole.

Earth's dark waters were turning blue and clear below. Black smog dissolved into pure white clouds as green growth spread over the dusty, dry lands.

"Good," Theo whispered, before fading into unconsciousness.

### firstwithmagic social media video transcript

[Gabrielle is standing on the roof of a skyscraper, harnesses buckled around her torso. Her hair is rippling madly in the high winds.]

**Gabrielle:** Hi, guys! I hope you're all having a nice, chill day. (laughs) Just kidding! I hope you're also undermining a toxic government regime.

[Gabrielle throws herself off the roof, rappelling down the smooth panes of glass. Outside a hundredth-floor window she drills a hole in the glass and eases a narrow stem inside.]

**Gabrielle:** (panting) In today's lesson, we're going to learn how to shut down a bitcoin mining farm.

[The vine wiggles across the floor to a tower of servers, disappearing into a gap. There's a crack of electricity, and the lights on the servers shut down.]

**Gabrielle:** Boom. I think I *aced* that one.

When Theo came round, he was lying in a hospital bed. He groaned, trying to shift upright.

"Stay still. It's OK."

"Hester?" He blinked his eyes open. Flakes of lichen fell from his eyelids onto the bed. Gravity – he was back on Earth, then.

"Do you feel all right?" she asked, helping him take a drink.

"Achy. How long was I out?"

Hester had to actually check the date on her phone. "Three days. I haven't slept much."

She seemed to have set up a makeshift workstation, with three laptops open on his bedside table.

"Has anyone noticed what we've done yet?" he asked.

"Uh, *yeah*, they noticed. Understatement of the century." She giggled and pushed his phone towards him. When he tried to reach for it, he realized that his arm was in a cast. When had that happened?

He took the phone gingerly with his other hand, scrolling through the news. Someone had already made a Wikipedia page about him.

## Theodore Carthew – Climate Activist

This article documents a current event and may change rapidly as the event progresses. Initial news reports may be unreliable. The latest updates to this article may not reflect the latest information.

**Theodore Carthew** (age unknown) is believed to be a student from the UK[1]. He is a **Greenfingers** working under the employ of **Dalex Energy**[2], and a member of **Climate Rebellion**. He is a key plaintiff in the *Daleport v Dalex* negligence lawsuit filed against the company by **Hester Daleport**[3]. He was also a key player in the **"Green Rising"** coup operating from the **International Space Station**[4] in conjunction with **Warren Space**[citation needed].

1. **Activism**
   a. **Greenfingers recruitment**
   b. **Warren Space announcement press conference**
   c. **Dalex Energy algae bloom**
   d. **Coal ash detox**
   e. **Climate Rebellion collaboration**
   f. **Green Rising**
2. **Political Position on Climate Change**
3. **Public Response and Impact**
   a. **Press**
   b. **President**
4. **Personal Life**
5. **In Popular Culture**
6. **References**

The amount of information they'd already gathered about his life was concerning. He clicked onto Hester's page out of morbid curiosity, then quickly back-paged at the sheer quantity of legal terms. His latest social media selfie was splashed over news site homepages, alongside a photo of Hester sunbathing on her yacht.

The photos of Earth were mind-boggling: even though he'd felt it all happening, it was hard to believe the scale of what they'd done. A helicopter filming a new savannah couldn't even fit it all in one shot, it stretched so far into the horizon. Drones flying in the canopy of their new trees were so high that the people standing on the ground below were barely visible.

Theo found an interview with his RE teacher, airing over a livestream on CNN. "This is bizarre."

"Yeah. It's been a weird few days. I don't know how much you remember, but you were basically unconscious for the whole trip back to Earth."

He squinted. He had a vague memory of their shuttle landing at the Warren spaceport. The entire sky had been full of press helicopters, circling at the no-fly limit, with a solid mass of crowds lining the roads.

"Did we – sneak out in a delivery truck?" he asked, confused.

Hester grinned. "Yeah. The press had pretty much surrounded the spaceport. We've been in hospital for days. We had to get treated for nutrient deficiencies. Apparently the barricade against Edgar pulled elements straight out of our own bodies, because there wasn't another source in space. We were all in a bad way."

"Everyone's OK now?" he asked.

"There are a few other broken bones, but no one worse off than you. I think you had to take the brunt of the fungi growth all on your own. It's amazing you're alive."

He nodded. "Any news from Gabrielle?"

"Every time I talk to her, she's in another conference call with what seems like every single president in the world. I think she's having the time of her life." As she caught him up, Hester grew a fresh salad: red amaranth leaves, pea shoots and wild rocket, followed by a lush ripe pear.

Theo's phone buzzed every few seconds while he ate.

He should probably call his parents, but he wasn't sure he had the energy to pretend he didn't feel awful.

"I still can't believe your dad really made us like this," he said.

Hester grimaced. "Yeah. Pretty grim, huh?"

He tilted his head. "I don't know. It's nice to know where it came from – barring the 'dangerous chemicals' aspect. I had been wondering."

"Would you get rid of it, if you could?"

"No," he said, at last. "I wouldn't even swap to plants instead of fungi. It … feels right. Though maybe I'll avoid going so far under again."

"I would appreciate that, yes." Her eyes were twinkling. "I wouldn't change this either. Not for anything in the world."

Theo squeezed her hand. "Maybe don't say that in court, though. It might not help the lawsuit if you're overly grateful."

Despite his pain, he kissed her, palm tight around the back of her head. A shiver trickled down from where their skin touched, all the way to the tips of his toes. They'd done it, and he hadn't lost her in the process. Something, somewhere, had gone very right.

# 45 UNIQUE, ULTRA-MODERN APARTMENTS
## **FOR SALE**
## IN THE MARINA

With **stunning** amenities and design, these new builds **integrate key Greenfingers architectural innovations** to create **breathable, forest-like** suburbs in the heart of a **bustling city**. Where elegant design meets sustainable living, your perfect family home is waiting for you.

Built from award-winning, patent-pending bamboo, willow and hemp technology, all lots include access to the vertical farm co-op on the exterior walls of the skyscraper.

**Reserve your dream home today!**

# Chapter 32

"Get in!" Theo yelled.

Hester yelped, skittering across the sand, waves splashing over her wellies. "It's cold!"

"It's less cold on the bloody boat."

Snarling, she waded through the water, letting Theo hoist her onto the deck.

At the bow, Mum and Dad were having a very robust and strong-minded argument about champagne. Dad wanted to smash it over the hull in a traditional launching; Mum wanted to drink it.

A year after the green rising, Theo finally felt like he could process everything that had happened in space. He could barely remember any of their time there. It was a blur of stress and excitement, despair and hope. But the effects were still rippling outwards, with new changes every day.

After Theo had been discharged from hospital, Hester had quickly transferred them to the local airport before the press realized where they'd gone. The Houston training centre was buried too deep in news vans to get anywhere near, so Hester had asked the helicopter pilot to fly them to a private Daleport lake house.

It had taken the press approximately six hours to track them down, illuminating the house in searchlights and flashing long-range cameras. Months later, they'd finally stopped following their every move. Though Theo was still constantly paranoid that even the sky was watching him – which, knowing Edgar's access to satellites, was probably accurate.

"Ready, kids?" Dad asked cheerfully. His cheeks were flushed red from the brutal winter wind.

Hester looked like she was very much regretting moving to England at all, let alone agreeing to help launch Dad's new boat.

Theo's parents had applied for a grant from the new carbon tax funds to start an aquaculture conservation business, working with local fishermen to improve sustainable practices and care for the kelp forests and oyster beds along the coastline. Dad had finally got his hands on a boat again, even if it was just a small one.

Hester tucked her trembling hands into Theo's pockets as Dad guided the boat out of the bay. "I've changed my mind. I don't want to go swimming after all."

"Gutted," Theo replied, wrapping his arms around her.

The world had shifted in ways he could never have imagined a year ago. At first, Climate Rebellion had been seen as a terrorist group. But as more and more of the good things they'd done had made the news, people's opinions had started to adjust. The media now called the Greenfingers a miracle instead of a security risk.

The protestors were still being investigated by the UN, but their lawyers kept reassuring them that the case would be dismissed as a non-hostile act of civil disobedience. Even if they were convicted, Theo wasn't sure it would make much of a difference. The tide had turned, and there was no going back.

He still wasn't sure if he agreed with the methods Gabrielle had used. He liked to think that their positive actions, like growing sea meadows and forests, would have been enough to change things without the sabotage. But he was probably giving the politicians too much credit. However uncomfortable Theo personally felt about the morality of Climate Rebellion's uprising, he couldn't deny that it had been successful.

Slowly but surely, governments were starting to sign on to environmental policy changes, diverting money towards new renewable energy investments. A few bigger countries were still making a fuss, but even they were giving in, now that the early adopters were starting to see an economic boom from the switch.

Theo caught sight of a flash of white in the water, as Dad steered them towards the new oyster beds near the cliffs.

"Look!" he cried. It was a dark whale breaking the surface, flashing white fins and underbelly as it twisted.

"It's a minke whale," Dad said, awed. "I haven't seen one in decades. I thought they had left the area."

"It's happy that the Dalex rig is gone," Mum said.

Hester made a pleased noise. The tip of her nose was pink.

"Drop the anchor, Theo," Dad said. "This is a good spot."

The whale followed the boat, frolicking like a dancer.

The effects of their uprising on the climate were already being recorded, even after just a year. The sudden growth of plants across the planet had started to pull carbon out of the air straight away. It would take years before the global temperature began to slowly drop again, but there were already fewer wildfires.

"She's got good legs on her, even with the electric motor," Dad said, caressing the rudder of his new boat. "I think she'll do."

"Here's to the *Green Rising*," Mum said. "Try not to sink this one, eh?"

"That wasn't my fault," Dad said, indignant.

"I think she was talking to me," Hester joked.

While Dad cracked open the champagne, Mum handed out *jalebi* fritters, which she had started selling to a local bakery. They were flavoured with rose water made from the flowers that had blossomed during the green rising.

"How's your toxin going, *jaan*?" Mum asked Theo, while they toasted the new boat.

"We're getting close," he replied, around a mouthful of fritter.

Hester and Theo were trying to combine her algae and his fungi to make a symbiotic pairing that would produce a toxin which might help in the research for cancer cures. They'd not managed it yet, but he was sure they just had to make a few adjustments.

"We have to wait between experiments to get the analysis back from the lab," Hester explained. "It's slowing us down a bit."

"Hester hates it," Theo told them. "She wants to fix every issue within a few days. The green rising spoiled her."

"I've got a very long to-do list, that's all," she said with dignity.

Theo and Hester were living together in London while they took a gap year, working with Gabrielle and the British branch of Climate Rebellion on future strategies. Hester's family already owned a house there, which hadn't surprised Theo. The first time he'd visited their Texas mansion, he'd said in disbelief, "So, er, how did you not realize you were one of the bad guys? This is literally a Bond villain lair. There's an *underground bunker.*"

"We should go," Theo said now, as the wind picked up. "We're going to miss Gabby's speech."

Gabrielle was standing as an MP, and her first political event was that evening. Theo was absolutely sure that she would win.

"It's going to rain anyway," Dad said. "Best head in."

"See you both soon?" Mum asked, once they got back to shore. When she hugged each of them goodbye, Hester looked a bit surprised. She was still getting used to the concept of parents actually showing affection, even though Mum was fully ready to adopt her as one of the Carthew brethren.

"That was fun," she said, as they walked across the deliciously rubbish-free shore. "But I'm very glad to go indoors again now."

"Mum and Dad seem happy," Theo said, content.

"You should wear this for the event," Hester said, pulling a floral bomber jacket out of the car boot and smirking at him.

"It's a bit … bright, isn't it?" he asked doubtfully, wondering when she'd managed to sneak it into the car.

For their one-year anniversary, Hester had taken Theo shopping in Paris, travelling by train under the Channel. Theo had felt very awkward in the fancy designer boutiques. He'd panic-bought the neon botanical jacket when the pressure of choosing got to him. Hester had never let him forget it.

"I thought you loved this look?" she asked innocently.

Theo's fashion sense could have been best described as "whatever will best avoid detection by security cameras". He had never given much thought to what kinds of outfits would make him look good, and he'd definitely never bought anything to try and impress a girl before. The attempt had been a horrendous error of judgement, but he absolutely refused to admit that. Which meant he would have to wear the jacket. Over and over again. Possibly for the rest of his life.

"Yeah, it's one of my favourites!" Theo said, forcing lightness into the words.

"Thought so." There was a villainous glint in her eye. "Here, let me take a photo for your mum. She loves florals."

"Can we go now?" Theo asked, once he'd submitted to a fashion shoot. "I don't want to miss Gabby's speech."

"You mean, ours."

"What?" Theo said, alarmed. He still hated public speaking, which was depressing considering all of the press conferences they'd had to do over the last year. "Did I miss an email again?"

He tended to avoid checking his inbox as much as possible. It moved too fast for him – and besides, their PA at Dalex told him about anything really urgent. Theo had never intended to work for a big company, but somehow he'd fallen into it. He wasn't going to say no if Dalex insisted on funding his degree, after all.

"There's no speech, Theo," Hester said, smirking. "Just *winding you up*."

"You'd better watch out – you're starting to get an English accent," he said. They might be spending too much time together, if she'd started saying British things like "winding you up".

"No way," Hester said, horrified. "Do I sound like you? Ew."

"It's hot."

"Not really, that's why you need a coat." She was absently checking her to-do list.

"No," he said, catching her around the waist and pulling her in. "It's *sexy*. That you're stealing my accent."

"Oh!" Hester looped her arms around his neck. *"All right, mate! You 'avin a laugh, babes?* Like that?"

"Hmm. Say 'arse'," he murmured, voice low.

She tilted her head away to consider this, dodging when he tried to kiss her. "Well … if you don't get your *arse* in the car, we'll be late."

He rested his forehead on her shoulder, sighing deeply. Her dinosaur fossil necklace was cold against his cheek. "You're such a pest."

She kissed him then, in the easy way that they had developed after a lot (*a lot*) of practice. Theo still wasn't sure how he'd managed to bag her, but he wasn't complaining. Sometimes she annoyed him as much as when they'd first met – but it was on purpose most of the time.

Their kissing came to an unfortunate end when Daisy rang to tell them to hurry up because Gabrielle's publicist was having a nervous breakdown over her plan for the event. They could hear Beatriz trying to calm her down.

After the green rising, Gabrielle had been wanted by the FBI for a while. She'd dealt with that by making a T-shirt that said "Join the international manhunt" with her mugshot on the front. Theo hoped she wasn't planning to wear it for her speech.

Theo had brought a box of beers for the girls. He'd been experimenting with making craft ales using his yeast. By changing the fungal spores grown in the roots of barley and wheat, he could adjust the flavour profile. He'd become addicted to setting up new batches and waiting to see what the results tasted like.

Now that they weren't all using their powers for twenty hours a day, their odd plant-like characteristics had started to fade away. It was only when Theo pulled an all-nighter working on his home brews that he got the odd craving for mulch.

"Don't forget your dishy jacket," Hester called, when he tried to leave it behind.

Theo winced. Busted.

# AWARD-WINNING
# **GREENFINGERS**
## INNOVATIONS
## OF THE YEAR

**1**

Ocean microplastic-eating fungus

**2**

Algae-based bioplastics for packaging

**3**

New strains of mite- and pest-resistant
crops that don't require fertilizers

# Chapter 33

Hester couldn't think of a single thing that would make her happier than she was right now, sitting in the back of their self-driving car with Theo, her feet in his lap as she closed another acquisition for Dalex.

After the green rising, Hester had spent eight whole days having meetings with Dad and the Dalex board of directors. Somehow, she'd convinced them to stop drilling for oil immediately, and instead invest all of their money into turning the ocean garbage islands into wind farms.

Her lawsuit was still grinding its way through the court, but Hester had been allowed to spearhead the environmental recovery process. Even though Dad had been asked to step down from his position of CEO, the directors thought Hester was "too young" to take over the role. It was ridiculous.

"What do you think of this?" she asked, showing Theo a breakdown of estimated costs for the ocean redevelopment scheme in their algae bloom dead zone.

Theo was still her moral compass most of the time – plus he always had really insightful comments, when he didn't have to read lots of paperwork to understand what was happening. Hester still tended to focus too much on the presentation and statistics and ignore the core ideas.

"What about the porpoises?" he said. He was playing a game on a console as the car drove them to Gabrielle's event, idly rubbing his thumb over her ankle. "And we wanted more of the budget to go to the tidal steam generators, remember."

"Oh, yeah." She chewed her lip. "I forgot about that. OK, I'll get them to revise."

She hadn't heard from Edgar Warren since their conversation through the barricade. He occasionally sub-tweeted about her, though, and he always viewed her uploads on social media. He'd probably get over their fight eventually. He had announced he would be terraforming Mars using only renewable energy, which would take decades longer – something she was sure made him livid.

Gabrielle had been persuaded – after much convincing – to let Hester be her campaign manager. Hester had run the numbers in her spare time, and she was eighty per cent sure that she could get Gabrielle elected as prime minister within the next four years. Politics was just a matter of spin, and Hester could do spin. She needed the challenge.

"Shall I make fish curry tonight?" Theo asked. "Mum sent me a recipe, and we've got some pollock in the freezer. You'll have to grow me some limes, though."

She wriggled her toes. "All right. I'll grow enough to make caipirinha cocktails, too."

"Nice," he said in satisfaction. "It'll be *dha*licious." He sniggered at his own joke.

Hester finished her email to the Secretary-General of the UN, then closed her phone, watching Theo play his game. He was chewing on the corner of his lip, and there was a delicate green mushroom sticking out of his collar. It was almost definitely highly poisonous.

His dark hair was flopping down over his forehead, and his power nudged against hers, as unconscious and natural as breathing. When they were asleep, he always buried his face between her shoulder blades. He was still wearing that stupid floral bomber jacket, which made her choke back a laugh every time she saw him in it.

"I love you, Carthew," she said, all of a sudden. The car was pulling up outside the venue, but the words couldn't wait, not now that she'd thought of them.

Theo dropped his remote. "Um. Me?" Shaking himself, he said, "I mean, me too! I love you too!"

She grinned and climbed into his lap, snaking out a vine to wrap around his wrist. "I know. Do you think Gabby will miss us if we stay here and make out until her speech starts?"

He tangled his fingers in the hair at the back of her neck. "She's forgiven us before. I'm willing to risk it."

Gabrielle was, of course, a smash hit at the event. She was the face of the Greenfingers – the one who had led the world to salvation. Hester thought that even if she barely tried, the country would vote for her – especially now that scientists seemed confident the Greenfingers power would be staying for good. Despite her sabotage and rebellion, she had made a difference where no one else had managed it.

"There is still work to be done. Whenever I feel like the fight is over and we've saved the world, a company tries to sneak emissions past the regulations," Gabrielle was saying.

The first time Hester had seen Gabrielle in person after the green rising, she'd been missing half of her little finger. All she'd been willing to say about it was, cryptically, that there had been "an incident on a mission". It only seemed to add to her mystique.

Gabrielle continued, "Some of them are even worse now that they know Greenfingers can reverse the damage they do. This is only the beginning of the fight for Earth. We have to stay vigilant, watching everything from government policies to factories to make sure that industry doesn't pollute the planet all over again. There are always going to be people willing to destroy the world for money, then flee to Mars."

Theo let out a wolf-whistle.

Luckily, most companies were caught quickly if they diverged from the new green laws. A satellite in space used spectrometers to detect areas of high emissions of carbon dioxide and sulphur dioxide in the atmosphere. The factories in that region could be tracked down and fined for the pollution. Sometimes, a few Greenfingers would stick around to keep an eye on things, but often they weren't needed at all.

Gabrielle went on, "If I'm elected, I'll campaign for the funding from the carbon tax on fossil fuels to be used to build renewable power stations in underdeveloped countries. I would also support funding to pay indigenous people to protect their native wildernesses."

Hester clapped loudly.

As time went on, it was becoming clear how close they'd been to disaster. The worse things got, the faster the terrible onslaught of changes would have come. They had acted just in time. If they hadn't cut down their emissions, who knew what would have happened. Hester could barely stand to think about it.

"There is more change to come," Gabrielle said to the roaring crowd. "This is only the beginning. But I'm ready to fight for you all, if you'll let me. So who's with me? Shall we change the world?"

Hester roared so loudly that her throat hurt. She ducked under the waves of candyfloss-coloured blossoms that Greenfingers were shooting up into the air.

Together. That was how they were going to build a better world.

# Author's Note

The situations and effects outlined in this book are not accurate. We can only guess at the possible outcomes of further manipulating our planet's natural systems. The concepts I've outlined shouldn't be taken as fact, but rather inspirational ideas of what might be achievable if we start working together.

We don't know what would happen if we started changing the environment, just like Hester and Theo don't know the results of their experiments here. What we do know is that the planet is changing because of our actions already, and that needs to be addressed. Some of our attempts might not work, but we cannot in good conscience stay apathetic. It's better to fail than to watch the Earth die, knowing we didn't even try to save it.

While magic is fantastical, the ability of humans to fix the climate emergency is not. It will take money, sacrifice and time, but we can create a better world, just like Theo and Hester wish to do. This has to start with policy changes, immediately.

The carbon emissions responsible for climate change are largely caused by industry, and can only be reduced through government action. However, if you'd like to make lifestyle changes to help limit your individual emissions, here are the most effective changes you can make. Some of these will take many decades to achieve, but long-term societal changes are the only way we can tackle this problem.

- Vote in all political elections you are able to, and make sure your representatives are aware that your vote is based on their climate policy views
- Replace garden lawns with wildflower meadows
- Switch to LED lightbulbs
- Don't fly – and pay for carbon offsetting for any flights you are required to take
- Make sure your savings and pension schemes are not invested in companies contributing to climate change. Ask your company to divest from their harmful default options
- Avoid eating beef, and transition to dairy alternatives
- Buy in-season food, grown locally (avoiding hothouse produce grown out of season)
- Change to a renewable energy utility supplier
- Buy electric cars – but only once your current car is absolutely unable to be fixed. Keep current cars on the road for as long as possible, to keep manufacturing emissions low

- Install solar panels or solar roof tiles
- Air dry clothing instead of tumble drying
- Avoid disposable, cheap fashion and invest in long-term, quality pieces that can be worn for many years

And, of course, plant trees wherever you can. They truly are the lungs of our planet. Depleted forests, savannahs, peatlands, mangroves and wetlands have the ability to grow back quickly, but we need to give them the opportunity to do that.

In a 2008 paper "On the regulation of geoengineering" by David G. Victor, the name "Greenfinger" is given to a lone geoengineer who decides to change the climate, named after the Bond villain "Goldfinger". I found this out a long time after naming my green-fingered magicians, but I thought Victor deserved to be mentioned here anyway.

The following books were helpful when writing this novel:
*Drawdown: The Most Comprehensive Plan Ever Proposed to Reverse Global Warming* by Paul Hawken
*The Uninhabitable Earth: Life After Warming* by David Wallace-Wells
*SOS: What you can do to reduce climate change* by Seth Wynes
*Wilding* by Isabella Tree
*Given Half a Chance: Ten Ways to Save the World* by Edward Davey
*No One Is Too Small to Make a Difference* by Greta Thunberg

*The Secret World of Oil* by Ken Silverstein

*The Ministry of the Future* by Kim Stanley Robinson

*Feral: Rewilding the Land, Sea and Human Life*
    by George Monbiot

*The Garden Jungle: or Gardening to Save the Planet*
    by Dave Goulson

*The Future We Choose* by Christiana Figueres

*What We Need to Do Now* by Chris Goodall

*There is No Planet B* by Mike Berners-Lee

*How Plants Work* by Stephen Blackmore

*Beyond Business* by John Browne

*Private Empire: ExxonMobil and American Power* by Steve Coll

*Sustainable Energy – without the hot air* by David JC MacKay

*How Are We Going to Explain This? Our Future on a Hot
    Earth* by Jelmer Mommers

*The Planet Remade: How Geoengineering Could Change the
    World* by Oliver Morton

*Entangled Life: How Fungi Make Our Worlds, Change Our
    Minds and Shape Our Futures* by Merlin Sheldrake

Center for International Environmental Law's Smoke and
    Fumes database

*Hope in Hell* by Jonathon Porritt

*This Changes Everything: Capitalism vs. The Climate* by
    Naomi Klein

*Houston, We Have A Problem* (2009)

*Doughnut Economics: Seven Ways to Think Like
    a 21st-Century Economist* by Kate Raworth

*How to Talk About Climate Change in a Way That Makes a Difference* by Rebecca Huntley

*1001 Ways You Can Save the Planet: Practical Ideas to Heal and Change the World* by Joanna Yarrow

*After Geoengineering: Climate Tragedy, Repair, and Restoration* by Holly Jean Black

*A Better Planet: Forty Big Ideas for a Sustainable Future* by Daniel C. Esty

Case Juliana V. United States

*All We Can Save: Truth, Courage, and Solutions for the Climate Crisis* edited by Ayana Elizabeth Johnson and Katharine Keeble Wilkinson

*Photophoretic levitation of engineered aerosols for geoengineering* by David W. Keith

*Global priority areas for ecosystem restoration* by B B N Strassburg et al.

*Technological Requirements for Terraforming Mars* by Robert M. Zubrin and Christopher P. McKay

# Acknowledgements

Thank you to my editors, Annalie Grainger and Emily McDonnell, and my agent, Claire Wilson. When I was staring down the huge stack of research reading required to write this book, it felt impossible to pull off. Their encouragement kept me going, and they were suitably enthusiastic even when the story was weighed down with science. It's hard to write about an emotional topic like climate change without getting intense, but their clear vision helped guide me in the right direction.

The team behind the scenes – thank you to Pete Knapp, Michelle Kroes, Emily Hayward-Whitlock, Seldy Gray, Stuart White, Kirsten Cozens, Non Pratt, Frances Taffinder, Rosi Crawley, Ellen Abernethy, John Moore, Bethany Nevile, Anna Robinette, Louise Millar, Jenny Glencross and Lara Armstrong. Plus Beci Kelly and Chloé Tartinville for the gorgeous cover.

Shout out to The Amazing Devil, whose music was mainlined on repeat the entire time I wrote this book.

For the inspiring writing chat, thanks to Alice Oseman, Emma Mills (I'm having so much fun writing with you!),

Sara Barnard, Beth Reeks, Laura Wood, Lucy Powrie, Charlie Morris, Lucy Aldridge, Laura Lam, Krystal Sutherland, Alice Hildreth and Stephanie Herbert.

To Sarah Barnard, Clare Samson, Madison Crawford, Kat Lupin, Rosie Hans, Heather Kincaid and all the other members of the Full Moon Fanclub – you kept me sane throughout lockdown with werewolf game shenanigans! You can't spell suspicious without us.

This book was supported by Arts Council England's COVID-19 Emergency Response Grant and a grant from the Coventry City of Culture 2021 Coronavirus Impact Resilience Fund.

Thank you to my Patreon supporters – Ria, Jamie, Lydia, Joanna, Chrissie, Emily, Marina, Alex, Carolina, Charlotte, Ember, Lizzie, Chelsey, Shannon, Victoria, Benno, Jemma, Eloise and Emma. Special thanks to Ellie and Kate for their hard work moderating my fan Discord server.

Mum, Dad, Chris, Charlie – my favourite people, thank you for everything.

**LAUREN JAMES** is the twice Carnegie-nominated British author of many young adult novels, including *The Reckless Afterlife of Harriet Stoker*, *The Loneliest Girl in the Universe* and *The Quiet at the End of the World*. She is also a Creative Writing lecturer, freelance editor, screenwriter and the founder of the Climate Fiction Writers League (climate-fiction.org).

Her books have sold over a hundred thousand copies worldwide, been translated into six languages and been shortlisted for the YA Book Prize, STEAM Children's Book Award and CrimeFest Award.

Her other novels include the Next Together series, the dyslexia-friendly novella series The Watchmaker and the Duke and serialised online novel *An Unauthorised Fan Treatise*.

She was born in 1992, and has a Masters degree from the University of Nottingham, UK, where she studied Chemistry and Physics. Lauren is a passionate advocate of STEM further education, and many of her books feature female scientists in prominent roles. She sold the rights to her first novel when she was twenty-one, while she was still at university.

Find out more on her website, laurenejames.co.uk, where you can subscribe to her newsletter to be kept up to date with her new releases and receive bonus content.

#GreenRising

🐦 @Lauren_E_James  📷 @laurenelizjames
🐦📷 @WalkerBooksUK  @WalkerBooksYA

THE
LONELIEST
GIRL
IN THE
UNIVERSE

·LAUREN JAMES

**"A TENSE PSYCHOLOGICAL THRILLER THAT
WILL LEAVE YOU GASPING FOR AIR."**

**SCOTSMAN**

Can you fall in love with someone you've never met, never
even spoken to – someone who is light years away?

Romy Silvers is the only surviving crew member of
a spaceship bound for a new planet. She is the loneliest girl
in the universe, until she hears that a second spaceship has
launched from Earth, with a single passenger on board:
a boy called J. Their only communication is via email, and the
messages take months to transmit, yet Romy finds herself
falling in love. But what does she really know about J?
And what do the strange new messages from Earth mean?
Sometimes, there's something worse than being alone...

## "A HUGELY REWARDING READ."

### SFX MAGAZINE

How far would you go to save those you love?

Lowrie and Shen are the youngest people on the planet
after a virus caused global infertility. Closeted in a pocket
of London and doted upon by a small, ageing community,
the pair spend their days mudlarking and looking for
treasure – until a secret is uncovered that threatens their
entire existence. Now Lowrie and Shen face an impossible
choice: in the quiet at the end of the world, they must
decide what to sacrifice to save the whole human race...

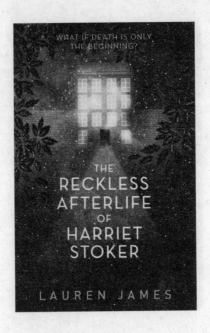

## "I WAS HOOKED FROM THE VERY FIRST CHAPTER."

### ALICE OSEMAN

What if death is only the beginning?

When Harriet Stoker dies after falling from a balcony in a long-abandoned building, she discovers a group of ghosts, each with a special power. Felix, Kasper, Rima and Leah welcome Harriet into their world, eager to make friends with the new arrival after decades alone. Yet Harriet is more interested in unleashing her own power, even if it means destroying everyone around her. But when all of eternity is at stake, the afterlife can be a dangerous place to make an enemy.